Deep

A M

"4½ stars! Lane's ou███████████████████ r-
ing knack for creatin█████████████████nt
settings are on full dis█████ans of this series will love
[it], but new readers won't have much trouble feeling right
at home in this terrific town."

—*RT Book Reviews*

"A funny and quirky romance...full of very memorable
characters."

—HarlequinJunkie.com

FLIRTING WITH TEXAS

"4½ stars! [A] complete success, blending humor, inno-
vative characters and a wonderfully quirky town with
an unlikely and touching love story. [Lane's] insight and
humor are pitch-perfect, making the sizzling chemis-
try between her leading couple a constant surprise and a
delight." —*RT Book Reviews*

"Extremely entertaining and amusing...Every turn of
the page is an unexpected journey full of humor as well
as emotion...[Katie Lane's] writing is stimulating and
doesn't allow the reader to put the book down."

—FreshFiction.com

TROUBLE IN TEXAS

"Sizzles with raunchy fun...[Elizabeth and Brant's] dynamic provides the drama to complete this fast-paced novel's neatly assembled package of sex, humor, and mystery."

—*Publishers Weekly*

"Romance, heart-warming affection and some mighty intriguing characters. Readers are in store for some fine surprises and a glimpse at stories yet to be told."

—*RT Book Reviews*

"I really enjoyed reading *Trouble in Texas*. The small-town feeling with its grudges, history, and eccentric residents was a blast. I spent a lot of my time giggling and wondering what the henhouse ladies were going to do next."

—TheBookPushers.com

"Lots of fun and games, enticing intrigues with tidbits of wisdom here and there make *Trouble in Texas* a tantalizing tale...Katie Lane's writing style keeps the reader turning pages."

—LongandShortReviews.com

CATCH ME A COWBOY

"4½ stars! This is an emotional story that will bring the reader to laughter as well as tears and spark a desire to see more of the characters, both new and old, who live here."

—*RT Book Reviews*

"Lane gives readers a rip-roaring good time while making what could feel like a farce insightful and real, just like the characters themselves."

—*Booklist*

"Nosy townsfolk, Texas twangs, and an electric romantic attraction will leave readers smiling."

—*BookPage*

"Katie Lane is quickly becoming a must-buy author if one is looking for humorous, country romance! This story is an absolute hoot to read! The characters are real and endearing...the situations are believable (especially if one has ever lived in a small town) and sometimes hilarious, and the romance is hot as a June bug in July!"

—*Affaire de Coeur*

MAKE MINE A BAD BOY

"A delightful continuation of *Going Cowboy Crazy*. There's plenty of humor to entertain the reader, and the people of the town will seem like old friends by the end of this entertaining story."　　　—*RT Book Reviews*

"Funny, entertaining, and a sit-back-and-enjoy-yourself kind of tale."

—*RomRevToday.com*

"If you're looking for a romance true to its Texas setting, this is the one for you. I simply couldn't put it down."

—*TheSeasonforRomance.com*

"I absolutely loved Colt! I mean, who doesn't like a bad boy? Katie Lane is truly a breath of fresh air. Her stories are unique and wonderfully written...Lane, you have me hooked."

—LushBookReviews.blogspot.com

"Another fun read and just as good as [*Going Cowboy Crazy*]...a perfect example of small town living and the strange charm it has. I really enjoyed reading this one and hope that Katie Lane is writing a third."

—SaveySpender.com

"It will make you laugh, and then make you sigh contentedly. *Make Mine a Bad Boy* is a highly entertaining ride."

—RomanceNovelNews.com

GOING COWBOY CRAZY

"Romance, heated exchanges, and misunderstandings, combined with the secondary characters (the whole town of Bramble), who are hilarious...This is the perfect summer read. Katie Lane has a winner on her hands; she is now my new favorite author!"

—TheRomanceReadersConnection.com

"Entertaining...[with] a likable and strong heroine."

—*RT Book Reviews*

The Last Cowboy in Texas

Also by Katie Lane

Deep in the Heart of Texas Series

Going Cowboy Crazy
Make Mine a Bad Boy
Small Town Christmas (anthology)
Catch Me a Cowboy
Trouble in Texas
Flirting with Texas
A Match Made in Texas

Other novels

Hunk for the Holidays
Ring in the Holidays

The Last Cowboy in Texas

KATIE LANE

FOREVER

NEW YORK   BOSTON

Copyright © 2014 by Cathleen Smith
Excerpt from *Ring in the Holidays* copyright © 2014 by Cathleen Smith

Forever
Hachette Book Group
1290 Avenue of the Americas
New York, NY 10104

www.HachetteBookGroup.com

Printed in the United States of America

First Edition: December 2014
10 9 8 7 6 5 4 3 2 1

OPM

Forever is an imprint of Grand Central Publishing.
The Forever name and logo are trademarks of Hachette Book Group, Inc.

The Hachette Speakers Bureau provides a wide range of authors for speaking events. To find out more, go to www.hachettespeakersbureau.com or call (866) 376-6591.

The publisher is not responsible for websites (or their content) that are not owned by the publisher.

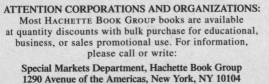

*To John Sedberry and Donny Sevieri,
for being the kind of heroes I always
wanted for my daughters*

Acknowledgments

When I started writing *Going Cowboy Crazy*, the first book in my Deep in the Heart of Texas series, I never dreamed I would end up with seven books and a novella about the lovable and zany townsfolk of Bramble, Texas. Now here I am at the end of this amazing journey with so many people to thank for making it possible:

God for his guidance and love.

My agent, Laura Bradford, for believing in me.

My editor, Alex Logan, for loving Bramble and wanting my series to be the best it could be.

All the wonderful folks at Grand Central Publishing for being so good at what they do.

Marine Sergeant Joe Siebenthal for his service to our country and for taking the time to answer my many questions. You are a sweetheart, Joe, and please forgive me for tweaking some things for the story's sake.

The bloggers and reviewers for taking the time to read my stories and let people know what they think.

My husband for loving a crazy writer who sometimes has trouble separating her two worlds.

Acknowledgments

My daughters for being willing to chat about characters and plot—over and over again.

My granddaughters for keeping my feet grounded and my heart full.

My family and friends for keeping my life balanced.

And you, the readers, for graciously opening your hearts to Bramble—and to me. Thank you! Thank you! I feel so very blessed and hope you like my next series as much as you did this one :o)

The Last Cowboy in Texas

Chapter One

STARLET BRUBAKER HAD DISAPPEARED.

The only evidence of her existence was the tiny mole just above the right corner of Star Bentley's glossy, pink-painted lips. Everything else was completely different. The green eyes. The blond hair. The skinny body. And the simple, loose-fitting, flowered dress. Nothing but the mole remained of the awkward, fat girl from southeast Texas.

Starlet pulled her gaze away from the mirror and looked down at the half-eaten banana MoonPie in her hand.

Well, maybe there were a few other things that remained.

A tap on the bathroom door had her cramming the rest of the pie in her mouth.

"Star?" Kari Jennings, her manager, trainer, and general ballbuster, called through the door. "You okay? Did you need something? Because we can't have the sweetheart of country music going without."

Food. The sweetheart of country music needs food. But instead of saying it, Starlet chewed faster and swallowed hard. "No. I'm good. I'm just touching up my lip gloss."

There was a pause. "But your lip gloss is out here in the dressing room, sugar."

Starlet rolled her eyes at her own stupidity and quickly wiped the crumbs off her mouth. One slipped beneath the neckline of her dress and into her bra, but she ignored it and opened the door, giving her manager a bright, Star Bentley smile. "Silly me. I guess I'm just nervous about the concert tonight."

Even in her power heels, Kari barely came to Starlet's chin. With her petite body, short blond hair, and big blue eyes, she looked just like Tinker Bell. Which was exactly why Starlet had hired her. Unfortunately, at the time, Starlet hadn't realized how vicious and manipulative pixies could be.

"No need to worry." Kari tugged up the neckline of Starlet's dress. "You've played much bigger venues than this." Her brow knotted as she stared at Starlet's boobs. "Speaking of bigger, I still think you should consider breast reduction. These just don't go with the new persona I've created."

"They look like they go pretty good to me."

Cousin Jed appeared in the dressing room doorway. Or more like filled it with his hulking frame, which had won him the title of "the Crusher" on the amateur wrestling tour and "the Asshole" at more than a few Texas nightclubs. While Starlet had never officially hired him, Jed had assumed the role of her personal bodyguard—something he excelled at, given that he was always getting too personal with her body.

He shifted the toothpick to one corner of his bulldog-drooping mouth as his gaze wandered over her breasts. "There's some rodeo cowboy out there that claims you invited him backstage. Says you owe him money. You havin' to pay for your nooky, cuz?"

Since her manager disapproved of rodeo cowboys more than MoonPies, Starlet played dumb. "Now, that's strange. When would I have had a chance to talk with a rodeo cowboy?" She fanned a hand in front of her flushed face. "Is the air conditioner on in here?"

"Check the air conditioner!" Kari bellowed at her assistant before turning to Jed. "Tell the cowboy he's out of luck for a backstage pass, but give him a couple tickets—not front row."

"We don't have front row, anyhow. They're filled with a bunch of hotshot military dudes. And I'm not Ticketmaster. I'm the head of security, and *some* people need to show a little respect."

Kari barely gave him a glance as she fluffed Starlet's hair extensions. "You'll get respect when you've earned it. So far, all I've seen you do is stand around chatting with the T-shirt vendors."

"Nothin' wrong with being friendly." Uncle Bernard pushed his way past Jed. Back in Texas, Starlet's uncle had always worn overalls and a white T-shirt with ketchup stains. But since following his niece on tour, he'd taken to wearing western suits and matching Stetsons, which, with his small frame and pointy features, made him look like a Keebler Elf gone country. "Just a few quick signatures, Star Baby." He held out a stack of ball caps with a hideous picture of her on the front. While she gaped at the picture, he pointed a black Sharpie at her mouth. "MoonPie?"

Starlet quickly brushed at her lips, but it was too late. Kari had zeroed in.

"MoonPie?" Her voice hit a high note that had chills

tiptoeing down Starlet's spine. "You know you have to watch your sugar intake, Star, especially with your metabolism. This means that you'll have to work extra hard with the ThighMaster tomorrow." She turned her evil eye on Uncle Bernie. "And didn't I talk to you about nonauthorized merchandise?"

"I don't know how much more authorized you can get than family." Uncle Bernie polished the top of one cream-colored, lizard-skin boot on the back of his pant leg. "Especially when I raised Star like one of my own. It seems only right that she would want to repay me with a few autographs."

"You are so full of shit, Bernie." Starlet's mother finally roused from her preconcert catnap and sat up on the couch, her hair wild and her eyes bloodshot. Starlet had poured out the bottle of vodka she'd found on the tour bus, but obviously, her mother had found another one. "You and that bitchy wife of yours—God rest her soul—treated my kid like crap."

Uncle Bernie retained his smile. In fact, Starlet couldn't remember a time when her uncle wasn't happy and smiling. Maybe that was why it was so easy to forgive his shortcomings.

"Now, Jaydeen," Uncle Bernie said, "let's not go down that road again. I believe it was Shakespeare who said 'Thee proof is in thee puddin'.'" He reached out and pinched Starlet's cheek. "And there's no better puddin' than our little Star Baby."

Her mother groaned and flopped back on the couch. "Anyone have a hit of cocaine?"

Jed's gaze remained on Starlet. "I know what I'd like a hit of."

For being more trouble than they were worth, there was one thing Starlet had to give her family: They kept her from getting stage fright. Being stuck with them in a dressing room was much scarier than being responsible for entertaining thousands of fans.

She turned to Kari. "I'm ready."

"She's ready!" Kari called out, prompting Jed to unclip the radio from his shirt collar and speak into it.

"The Star is walkin'."

En masse, Starlet's entire misfit posse headed for the door, even her mama, who, regardless of her hungover state, looked skinny and beautiful in her tight jeans and low-cut top. When they reached the stairs to the stage, Kari did more clothes adjusting, Jed did more gawking, her mama flirted with a security guy, and Uncle Bernie leaned in and whispered, "Don't worry about the hats, Star Baby. I'll take care of them."

Starlet sent him a weak smile before climbing the stairs. As soon as she stepped onstage, a spotlight hit her, and the entire coliseum released a deafening roar of applause and whistles. She might've panicked if a stage-hand hadn't slipped her guitar over her head. The feel of the lacquered wood calmed her, and she walked to center stage and leaned in to the microphone.

"Hi, y'all. You ready for a little music?"

The answering applause had barely fizzled when her band kicked in. Then there was nothing but the music. It washed over Starlet like Texas sunshine, transforming her from an awkward, insecure woman to a graceful, confident entertainer. An entertainer who could tease the crowd, flirt with her band members, and be completely comfortable sharing all the emotions she normally kept well hidden.

As usual, while performing, time flew by much too quickly. Before Starlet knew it, she had finished her last song and was headed offstage to wait for her encore.

Kari met her on the stairs. "You didn't give enough attention to the marines in the front row."

"I thanked them for coming and dedicated 'The Price of Freedom' to them. What more did you want me to do?" Starlet took the bottle of water handed to her by a security guy and nodded her thanks before taking a deep drink.

"Something for a picture op," her manager said. "Call one of them up and sing to him for your encore."

Starlet shook her head. "I always do 'Good-bye Kiss' for the encore. And I'm not singing that to anyone but—" She caught herself. "I'm not singing that to some marine."

Kari smiled the kind of smile that had always scared the crap out of Starlet. It reminded her of Meryl Streep in the movie *The Devil Wears Prada*.

"Well, of course you can do what you want," Kari said as she studied her manicured nails. "You don't have to listen to a manager with fifteen years' experience under her belt. Fifteen years of sweating it out with no-talents so that, when she finally found a person with a tiny bit of talent, she could mold and shape her into the kind of star who fills an auditorium." She waved her hand to encompass the coliseum before shrugging. "But...if you want a mediocre career that fizzles out after the first two albums, then you go right ahead and make your own decisions. I certainly won't stand in your way."

As always, Starlet conceded. "Okay, but I'll sing one of my other songs."

Kari shook her head. "'Good-bye Kiss' is your biggest hit—the one all these people have come to hear. If you leave it out, they'll charge the stage and trample you like a herd of angry elephants. So I suggest you pretend that the marine is one of the rodeo cowboys you seem to be so enthralled with and make the best of it." She turned without another word and walked down the stairs, leaving Starlet with no choice but to do as she said.

Downing the rest of the water, she walked back onstage.

"Well, hello again," she said when she reached the microphone. "I thought I'd slow things down a bit and sing a love song that you might recognize." The audience went wild. Once they'd quieted, she looked down at the front row. "But what's a love song if you don't have some-one to sing it to? What say we get one of the country's finest up here?"

Starlet's gaze ran over the marines. They were all dressed in camouflage pants and caps, green T-shirts, and lace-up desert boots. Most were standing and waving their hands to get her attention.

Except for one.

One arrogant marine who didn't seem to be that taken with Star Bentley. In fact, with the bill of his cap pulled low over his face and his booted feet stretched out and crossed at the ankles, he looked like Moses Tate napping on a park bench. Even ninety-year-old Moses had stayed awake during the concert she had done for the small town of Bramble, Texas.

Perturbed by the marine's audacity, Starlet had no problem pointing him out. "Now, when I said I was going to slow things down a bit, I didn't mean that you could go to sleep on me." She waved her hand. "Let's get Rip van Winkle up here and see if I can't wake him up."

The man didn't acknowledge her words, but the other marines did. With a loud whoop, they picked him up and lifted him over their heads, passing him along until he ended up onstage. He didn't fight them, but he didn't seem too happy about it either. Once the stagehands had him seated in a chair, he crossed his arms and stared down at his boots.

Starlet unhooked the microphone from the stand. "What do you say, soldier boy? You think you can stay awake long enough to listen to little ol' me?"

The audience laughed, but the marine remained mute. Starlet might've continued her teasing if a wave of dizziness hadn't hit her. Not a little wave, but the kind that made your head feel like it had been flipped in a blender and set on puree. The roar of the crowd sounded muffled and distorted, and the stage seemed to rock like the deck of a ship. Not wanting to fall on her butt in front of thousands of people, she improvised and sat down on the marine's lap.

Having dated her share of rodeo cowboys, Starlet wasn't a stranger to athletic bodies. But no cowboy she'd ever dated had a body like this one. Instead of long, lean muscles, this body had bunched, thick ones. Thighs like hard granite. A stomach like rippled steel. And arms with tight, knotted biceps as big as grapefruit.

Starlet loved grapefruits. In fact, they were the only things on Kari's starvation diet that she did love. Starlet had a half of one every morning—the juicy meat sectioned off and a sweet little cherry in the center.

"If you're going to sing, sing." The marine's hissed words cut into her grapefruit daydream.

She might've been ticked at his attitude if she hadn't

been distracted by his voice. It was familiar. Too familiar. She dipped her head to peek under the cap, but before she could get a good look, another wave of dizziness hit her. She blinked it away, along with the ridiculous notion that she knew this marine. The only marine she knew didn't have biceps the size of grapefruits and thighs like sculptured granite. He was a skinny nerd who worked some desk job at the Russian embassy. And even if he were in the States, he would never be caught dead at one of her concerts.

Which was just fine and dandy with Starlet.

What wasn't fine and dandy was this marine's arrogance and nonchalance. Starlet didn't care if he liked her, but he wasn't going to ignore her. Remaining on his lap just to spite him, she lifted the microphone to her mouth and started to sing.

It wasn't easy.

"Good-bye Kiss" was the first song Starlet had ever written for the first and only love she'd ever had. It seemed wrong to sing it to someone else. So she did what Kari suggested: She imagined the love of her life and let the words of the song flow from the heart. When she finished, tears rolled down her cheeks, and you could've heard a pin drop in the coliseum. The marine wasn't so moved. With a grumbled curse, he picked her up and set her on her feet before walking offstage.

Completely humiliated by his brush-off, she quickly lifted the microphone and ended the show.

"Thank y'all for coming. God Bless!"

As always, the closing riled the crowd and had them charging the stage, yelling for autographs and tossing up pink roses. Normally, she caught one and waved a good-bye. But tonight it took all her concentration to walk. The dizziness was back and worse than ever. She stumbled over a cord and would've fallen if the security guy hadn't appeared and taken her arm.

"This way, Miss Bentley."

Struggling to put one foot in front of the other, she followed him. He released her to jump down from the stage and then reached up to lift her off. It was then that she noticed where he had taken her. They weren't in the long corridor that led to her dressing room. They were at the back of the stage, behind the curtains and lights and amid all the technical cords and wires.

Now, why would he bring her back here?

"Wait—" It was the only thing she got out before a rag was stuffed in her mouth and her hands were jerked behind her back and tied. Still, it wasn't until he hefted her over his shoulder and headed for a side door that she figured out what was happening.

Star Bentley, the sweetheart of country music, was being kidnapped.

And Starlet Brubaker had no choice but to go along for the ride.

Chapter Two

BECKETT CATES HAD A HEADACHE. It wasn't unusual. Most days, he woke with a deep, throbbing pain pulsing in his temples and pressing against the backs of his eyes. The shrink at Camp Lejeune was convinced that it would go away in time. Of course, his shrink had also been convinced that driving to Charlotte and attending a Star Bentley concert would be good for Beckett. And look where that had landed him: onstage with a spoiled, snooty woman who had gotten much too big for her britches.

Not to say that Starlet Brubaker was bigger than the last time Beckett had seen her. In fact, she was a lot skinnier. Almost too skinny. If he hadn't seen her picture on the cover of numerous magazines, he might not have recognized her at all. The insecure, brown-eyed girl from Miss Hattie's Henhouse was long gone, replaced by a green-eyed blonde who was cockier than a special ops officer.

The only things that hadn't changed on Starlet were her breasts. They were still eyepoppers, which was hard not to notice when they had been snuggled against his chest like two warm kittens.

And speaking of eye-popping breasts.

A woman stepped out of one of the rooms along the backstage corridor. She wore painted-on jeans and a tight tank top that left little to the imagination. "You lost, good-lookin'?"

"No, ma'am." Beckett would've continued his search for an exit if she hadn't stepped in front of him and curled a hand around his bicep, bringing with her the scent of cigarette smoke and booze. While her body wasn't half-bad, her face told the story of a woman who had lived hard and wasn't done yet.

"You sure?" she said. "'Cause I wouldn't mind helping you find your way." She studied him with more than a little hunger in her big, brown eyes. Big, brown eyes that were a carbon copy of Starlet's before she ruined them with green contacts.

Beckett removed her hand from his arm. "Sorry, but I'm a pretty lost cause." He went to step around her when a hulk of a security guy came meandering down the corridor, an annoying female's voice blaring from the radio clipped to his black polo shirt.

"I want her found, Jed! And I want her found now! See if you can locate that rodeo cowboy. She's probably chasing after his chaps."

Jed took his time lifting the radio off his shirt and pushing the button on the side. "Will do. But you don't need to worry. If anyone can find her, I can." He looked at the woman standing next to Beckett. "I don't suppose that you've seen Star, Aunt Jaydeen?"

Before Aunt Jaydeen could answer, a midget of a man

in a Stetson and western suit stepped out of the room. "What's all the ruckus? Are we havin' a family meetin' and I wasn't invited? Now, that don't seem right, seein' as how I'm the head of the family."

"More like the ass of the family," Aunt Jaydeen grumbled. "It seems that Starlet has gone missing." She glanced over at Beckett. "Sorry, sweetie, but I'll have to catch you later. I need to go find my daugh— sister." She hurried down the corridor, her heels clicking against the concrete floor.

For being security, Jed didn't seem to be in quite as much of a hurry. He pulled a can of chewing tobacco out of his back pocket and took a dip before slowly moseying off in the direction he'd come from.

The midget cowboy watched him go and shook his head. "That boy has always been one apple short of a bushel." He glanced at Beckett and smiled broadly before holding out a hand. "Bernard Brubaker, at your service— but most folks call me Bernie. You Jaydeen's newest conquest?"

"Not hardly." Beckett shook his hand. "Beckett Cates." He stared down the corridor as his headache grew worse. He had no business getting involved. He had enough going on in his life. Especially when the squawking woman on the radio was probably right: Starlet was no doubt just meeting up with some cowboy.

Unfortunately, Beckett couldn't let it go until he knew for sure.

He turned to Bernie. "You wouldn't happen to know where the closest exit to the stage is, would you?"

"As a matter of fact, I do." Bernie quickly pulled a Sharpie pen from his pocket and signed the cap he held with Star Bentley's name. "Never hurts for a man to know how to get out of any given situation quickly." He tossed the pen and hat back into the room before leading the way down the corridor.

As they neared the stage, Beckett could see that pandemonium had broken out. Stagehands, security, and band members were racing around to the orders of a petite woman in a pink power suit with the same annoying voice as the one that had come from Jed's radio. Upon seeing the woman, Bernie pulled Beckett around to the back of the stage.

"It's best to keep your distance from the she-devil." He stepped over a tangle of black cable. "Kari is no doubt the reason my niece has run for the hills. The woman is a ballbuster if ever there was one. Very similar to my late wife." He took off his hat and covered his heart. "God rest her soul." His bald head gleamed in the stadium lighting. "Maybelline was the love of my life, but I spent most of our marriage in a bottle just trying to escape her bad temper. Since she died, I haven't touched a drop of liquor—leastways, not the hard stuff—which should tell you something. Here we are." He pushed open the side door.

The door led to a dark alley with three battered trash bins.

"You think Star's—?" Bernie started, but Beckett held his finger to his lips and shook his head.

Something had caught his attention by one of the Dumpsters. A flash of movement that had his senses alert and muscles tightening. He waved Bernie back and then slipped out the door and up against the wall of the coliseum. He was probably just being foolish. He had seen more than a few marines who had come off active duty being a little overly cautious. But something wasn't right. There was a shift in the air. An indistinguishable scent carried on the Carolina breeze that spoke of danger. The one time Beckett had ignored his basic instincts, bad things had happened. He wasn't willing to chance it again.

A few feet from the first trash bin, he paused and listened. There was a small whimper, then a distinctive click that had him hitting the ground just as a bullet whizzed over his head. The next gunshot had him rolling to his feet and ducking around the front of the Dumpster.

Beckett figured he had about ten seconds to make his move before the guy realized that he didn't have a gun and came out shooting. Looking around, he noticed the back end of a car parked on the other side of the bins. In one fluid motion, he leaned down and picked up a rock, chucking it as hard as he could at one of the car windows. Glass shattered, followed by rapid-fire gunshots. With the gunman's attention diverted, Beckett scaled over the top of the Dumpster and dove at the shadowy figure on the other side. They hit the ground hard, but Beckett didn't wait for his breath to rush back in before he made a grab for the gun.

The guy was no lightweight and refused to relinquish his hold, bringing his hand up and hitting Beckett in the chin with the butt of the revolver. Slightly stunned, Beckett allowed the man to get the upper hand and roll on top. His victory lasted for only a second before Beckett elbowed him hard in the throat. The jab caused the man to grunt and release the gun, and it skidded beneath the trash bin as Beckett rolled back on top. Unfortunately, he had no more than pinned the guy to the ground when someone clocked him over the head with a bottle. For a few seconds, he watched as amber glass rained down. Then there was nothing but darkness.

When Beckett came to, he was sprawled on his back in the alleyway with a headache the size of Texas. It took a moment and more than a few blinks to get his vision to clear. Amid a star-filled sky, three faces stared down at him.

"You'd think that a marine would be tougher than a bottle of Bud," Jed said.

"Beer has brought down more than a few good men," Bernie replied.

"And he is a good man." Jaydeen's eyes ran over him. "A real good man."

While Beckett tried to piece together what had happened, a cool hand stroked over his cheek and pressed him against an ample bosom. An ample bosom he identified as soon as the woman it belonged to spoke.

"I feel just terrible," Starlet said. "But it was dark, and I couldn't see a thing. First one guy was on top and then the other."

"It sounds like my last date," Jaydeen said.

"It's not funny, Mama!"

Beckett's head was pulled closer to Starlet's soft breasts. So close that he felt like he was suffocating. Which didn't explain why he wasn't protesting. Maybe because he could think of a lot worse ways to die than cocooned in a set of sweet breasts that smelled like lilacs and...bananas?

"Just think, I could've killed my hero," Starlet said in an overly dramatic voice. Of course, she had always been overly dramatic. Which was one of the reasons Beckett disliked her so much. He had trouble believing the sweet act she had cultivated. Especially when it had earned her a place in his family and enough money to pursue her career.

"Who said he was yours?" Jaydeen piped up. "I saw him first."

"Now, ladies—" Bernie started, but was cut off by the back door banging open. The noise caused Beckett's head to throb even more, and the high-pitched, screeching voice that followed the bang didn't help.

"What in the hell is going on out here?"

Beckett's head was released and plopped down to Starlet's lap. He looked up to see the petite woman in the power suit standing over them.

"Do you mean to tell me," she continued in the annoying voice, "that I've been racing around half worried sick while you've been cuddling with a marine in the alleyway?"

"I wouldn't call it cuddling, She-devi— Miz Jennings," Bernie said. "This here marine saved our little Star Baby's life."

That seemed to shut Starlet's manager up—at least for a few seconds. Once she digested the information, she turned back to Starlet. "Someone threatened your life?"

"I would've saved her, Kari," Jed said, "if this asshole hadn't jumped in. I was coming around the corner of the building when I heard the shots."

"But you didn't save my life. This wonderful man did." Starlet absently played with the lock of hair that had fallen over Beckett's forehead. Why that would send a shaft of desire spearing through him, he couldn't say. Or maybe he just didn't want to.

Jed snorted. "Your life wasn't in any danger."

"I don't know what you'd call it. The criminal trussed

your cousin up like a pig before slaughter," Bernie said, "and pert near killed this young marine with this here gun." He held up the revolver, completely unconcerned about ruining any possible fingerprints.

"Oh. My. God." Kari stared at the gun for just a second before pulling a cell phone from the pocket of her suit jacket and quickly punching in a number. Beckett expected her to start rattling off information to the police, but instead she spoke in an excited voice about something else entirely. "Deb, please tell me that the reporters are still lurking backstage." The answer made her shift excitedly from one high heel to the other like she had to take a leak. "Good." She started to pace. "Tell them that I have a scoop—" She stopped, her heels crunching the gravel. "No, wait! Don't tell them that. Just keep them and the photographers right where they are. I'll be in in a minute to explain everything." Without waiting for a reply, she hung up the phone and placed it back in her pocket before turning around.

"Are you two all right?" She hurried over, her voice no longer screeching but sugary and even more annoying than before.

"I'm fine," Starlet said, "but I'm worried about him. Shouldn't we call an ambulance?"

"I don't need an ambulance." Beckett sat up. His head hurt like a sonofabitch, but it wasn't anything he couldn't deal with. He got to his feet and touched a hand to the back of his head. There was a lump, but no blood. He shot an exasperated look at Starlet before directing his attention to the manager. "We need to call the police."

"Of course we do," Kari said. "And I will—just as soon as we get inside."

Having about as much as he could take, Beckett stared down at the petite woman and said one word. "Now."

Her shoulders stiffened for a split second before she nodded. "Fine." She glanced over at Jaydeen. "Could you please call the police while I get Star inside?" Starlet started to get to her feet, but she stopped her. "No. I don't want you walking. Not until we assess your injuries."

"She's right." Jed hurried over. "'I'll carry you."

"No!" Kari stepped in front of him. "I need you to take control of the situation inside. Let everyone know that Star is safe and sound. Then tell the stage and technical crew to get busy taking down the stage. And don't screw up. After what just happened, you're walking on thin ice."

Jed grumbled but did what she asked. Once the door closed behind him, Kari turned to Beckett. "I'm sure a big, strong marine like yourself wouldn't mind carrying Star inside?" She patted him on the chest. "I'm just going to run in and make sure the reporters don't go on a feeding frenzy."

Yeah, right. There was little doubt that she would be stirring up the feeding frenzy. Beckett waited for her to get inside before he turned to Starlet. He planned on telling her that he had no intentions of carrying her anywhere. Unfortunately, she was already climbing to her feet, and her legs were wobbling so badly that she had to grab on to the trash bin for support.

With an oath, Beckett walked over and scooped her up in his arms. Rather than protest, she looped her arms around his neck and snuggled close like the manipulative woman she was.

"So I'm assuming that the guy got away," Beckett said as he started for the door.

"Yes, sir." Bernie hustled over to open it. "By the time Jed and I got here, he was driving off in his beat-up Oldsmobile. Although I did get a license plate." He tapped his head. "Like a steel trap."

Beckett might've asked for the plate if he hadn't stepped through the door to the staccato clicks of a half-dozen cameras and a chorus of questions:

"What happened, Miss Bentley?"

"Was it an attempted kidnapping?"

"Was it a stalker?"

"Or just an overzealous lover?"

With her head tucked under his chin, Beckett could feel Starlet take an uneven breath and release it before lifting her head and smiling brightly for the cameras.

"I'm glad y'all are so concerned," she said. "But as you can see, I'm just fine and dandy. Thanks to the heroics of this marine."

That prompted a flood of questions and pictures, but it was Kari Jennings who raised her voice loud enough to be heard over the din.

"Why don't you give your hero a thank-you kiss, Star?"

The photographers catcalled their agreement. Before Beckett could dissuade her from the notion, Starlet's arms tightened around his neck, and he was pulled toward a pair of lips with a tiny mole at the corner, which he remembered all too well. The soft, full lips had barely brushed his when her eyes flashed open, and he found himself staring into a startled pair of green contacts.

The one word that slipped out of her mouth was the one word that Beckett had hoped he would never hear again.

"Becky?"

Chapter Three

"SO YOU DIDN'T RECOGNIZE THE MAN?" Brant Cates sat on the edge of the bed, his rugged good looks completely out of place in the pink, frilly bedroom of the tour bus.

Sleep-deprived and hungry, Starlet wished she could forgo the interrogation. But Brant wasn't the type of man who put off until tomorrow what could be done today. As soon as his brother, Beckett, tattled to him about the attempted kidnapping, Brant had contacted the doctors at the hospital and had Starlet kept overnight for observation, talked to the police and pushed for extra investigators on the case, and kept the buses from heading to the next stop on the tour. Being one of the wealthiest men in Texas—and the country—he had that kind of power.

But Starlet didn't see him as a wealthy, powerful man. To her, he was just Uncle Brant, the first man who had ever believed in her. Which was why it was so difficult to lie to him.

"No." She fidgeted with the stuffed Minnie Mouse sent by one of her fans. "I didn't recognize him."

"She's lying."

The words had her glaring at the man who lounged against the doorjamb as if he owned the bus instead of her. Beckett wore a similar outfit to the one he'd worn at the concert—minus the camouflage cap. His hair was military short on the sides, but longer on top. Long enough for one stray lock to curve over his forehead. Her gaze drifted down to his muscular chest. His body looked even more impressive in the predusk light that spilled in through the large windows. Of course, his new haircut and muscles didn't change the fact that, while she adored the other men in the Cates family, she could barely tolerate Beckett.

"Don't you have some terrorists to take care of, Becky?" she said. "Or do those jobs go to the real marines?"

His eyes darkened. It was the same look he'd given her years ago when she'd first used the nickname. And she couldn't help but send him a smug smile when Brant took her side.

"Tread carefully, Beckett. Starlet has been through enough, and I won't have you browbeating her. If she says she didn't know the man, she didn't know him."

"I'm not browbeating, big brother. I'm merely stating a fact." Beckett crossed his arms over his chest, which caused his biceps to strain against the short shirtsleeves like plump Georgia peaches. "Even though I'm not a 'real' marine, I've interrogated more than my share of prisoners and know the signs when someone's lying. Hell, she won't even look you in the eye."

"Watch your mouth," Brant warned before returning his attention to Starlet, who did have trouble looking him in the eye. "You're sure?"

Starlet crumbled like a crushed MoonPie. "Well,

maybe I'm not positive. I mean, I was drugged. And it was dark. And he was wearing a hat."

"Not the entire time," Beckett said. "The hat fell off during our fight, so you should've gotten a good look at him before he ran off. As for being drugged, that's debatable, seeing as how the bottle of water was never found, and there was only a slight trace of narcotics discovered in your bloodstream—something that doesn't surprise me, given your occupation." He paused before adding, "Or your family."

"I don't take drugs!" she snapped. Then, realizing that Brant was watching her, she cooled her temper. "And what about you, Becky? You were there too. So what did the guy look like?"

Beckett's eyes narrowed in thought for only a few seconds before he spoke with complete accuracy. "Around six two and two hundred pounds. Dark hair and eyes. Thick beard and broken nose."

Starlet's hand tightened on Minnie Mouse's bow, and it came right off in her hand. As if he heard the soft snap of thread, Beckett cocked an eyebrow at Minnie before continuing in his snooty voice. "But that's not what my brother asked you. He asked if you knew the man."

Obviously, Beckett's body had changed, but his personality was still as annoying as ever.

"And I said no!" Without thought, she threw bowless Minnie straight at Beckett's head. He ducked, and the stuffed animal sailed out the door and bounced off Jed's flat nose. For once, her cousin was a welcome sight.

"Everything okay in here?" he asked as he warily eyeballed Beckett. It was strange, but for always being the bully, Jed was the one who looked intimidated now.

"Of course everything's okay." Kari slipped past Jed,

trying her best to avoid contact in the narrow hallway of the bus. She wasn't as careful with Beckett. In fact, she wiggled her pixie body right up next to his as she scooted through the doorway. "The Cates are Star's family." She sent Beckett a smile that Starlet had never seen before—friendly with a hint of invitation. "And we are always happy to see family."

Beckett stared down at her with the same look he seemed to give everyone. A bored, arrogant, smarty-pants look that really grated on Starlet's last nerve. It didn't seem to bother Kari as much. She pressed against him for what seemed like an eternity before she turned to Brant.

"But as much as we love seeing family, Star needs to get busy writing songs for her new album, and we need to get on the road to our next concert."

Brant got to his feet and tucked the comforter around Starlet. "She doesn't need to worry about writing songs as much as getting some rest." He turned his steely gaze on Kari, who, to Starlet's delight, actually fidgeted. "And there's not going to be a next concert. After what happened, you need to cancel the rest of her tour—at least until we find out who was behind the kidnapping."

The Devil Wears Prada returned.

"I'm sorry, but we can't do that," she said. "The stadium in Atlanta is sold out, and we need to leave tonight if we want to get there in time. But I share in your concern and have hired extra security. And I promise that Jed won't let her out of his sight—nor will I."

Great. No MoonPies or rodeo cowboys for Starlet this week.

"Not good enough," Beckett butted in. "The man had a gun so he meant business. Next time, he might decide to forgo the kidnapping and just take a potshot."

A chill ran down Starlet's spine. As much as she hated to agree with Beckett on anything, he did have a point. One Kari wasn't about to concede.

"Now, why would a fan want to take a potshot at her?" Kari's gaze settled on Beckett's chest. "Besides, he no longer has a gun."

The disbelief on Beckett's face was almost comical. "Are you on drugs too? Because if a man has one gun, he usually has two. Or at least, knows how to get another one."

"Beckett is right," Brant said. "We can't chance it. Starlet is through with public appearances until we find this guy."

There was a moment when Starlet thought Kari might explode. Her pixie face turned red, and her big blue eyes almost popped out of their sockets. But Kari hadn't gotten where she was by losing her cool. Especially when she knew that she held the trump card. Or not a trump card as much as a pathetically weak country singer who was easily manipulated.

"Don't you think we should let *Star*"—Kari emphasized the name—"make her own decisions? After all, it's her career that's on the line." She paused. "Not to mention the careers of all the people who have worked so hard to make her concert tour a success."

Every eye in the room turned to her, and Starlet suddenly had an overwhelming craving for the MoonPie she'd hidden in the nightstand. But a MoonPie wouldn't change the fact that she was Star Bentley—not a real person, but a cooperation that was responsible for more than just Starlet Brubaker. As much as she wanted to cancel the concert, she knew she couldn't.

Even if her life was in danger.

"The show must go on," she said brightly before turning

to Brant and trying to ease his fears. "I know you're worried, Uncle Brant. But Kari's right. There's no need to be concerned when I'll be surrounded by security. Besides, this is the last concert before we head back to Nashville. Once there, I promise to keep my public appearances to a minimum until we catch the person responsible."

Brant studied her for a moment before nodding. "All right. But no taking water from anyone but family. And I plan to follow you to Atlanta and personally escort you onstage and off."

She smiled. "I'd love that."

Kari clapped her hands. "Now that we have that settled, we need to get on the road and let Star get to writing—" She sent Brant a smile. "I mean get some rest." She moved toward the door, but hesitated when she reached Beckett. "Since your brother is coming to the concert, I can only hope that you will too. I'm sure Star's fans would love to meet her hero."

"I'm afraid not. I have to get back to the base." Without a backward glance or a good-bye, Beckett disappeared down the hallway.

"If you'll excuse me, I need to have a word with my brother." Brant headed after him.

Once they were gone, Kari's face fell. "That's too bad that the marine isn't going to be there. The publicity shots we got of you two have caused quite the stir." She looked back at Starlet. "Are you sure there's not more to your relationship than you're letting on?"

Out the window, she could see Beckett striding across the parking lot. He no longer looked like the skinny nerd she'd first met at Miss Hattie's Henhouse. He looked like a muscled warrior headed off to battle. Again she wondered what he had been doing at her concert. Especially when he liked her about as much as she liked him.

"No," she said. "He's not my type at all."

Kari only shrugged before she left the room, sliding the pocket door closed behind her. A few moments later, the engine of the bus rumbled to life. But instead of writing new songs for her album or sleeping, Starlet picked up her cell phone and scrolled through her contact numbers until she found the one she wanted. The lazy drawl that answered would've made most women weak in the knees—which was exactly why Starlet had hired him.

"What were you doing at the concert telling Jed that I had invited you backstage and that I owed you money?" she said. "You're supposed to be in Bramble."

The drawl changed from sexy to annoyed. "I was in that Podunk town. And I did exactly what you wanted. And all I got for my efforts was a broken nose and dislocated shoulder."

"He beat you up?"

"Not him—her. You didn't tell me she was an ultimate fighter. That's why I showed up backstage at the concert. I think I deserve double the money for my hospital bills."

Starlet's shoulders slumped. Five men and five failed attempts.

"Fine," she said. "I'll send it to the address I sent the other check." She hung up without waiting for a reply.

Now even more depressed, she opened the drawer of the nightstand and pulled out an old, beat-up Bible. According to her mama, it and a pair of holey underwear were the only things her daddy had left behind when he'd run off. While Jaydeen cussed Ray Sparks out for not leaving money, Starlet thought the Bible a perfect parting gift. For years, it had fueled a fantasy of her father being a righteous Sir Lancelot who had been tricked into marriage with an evil queen. Not that her daddy had married her mama, but that was the best thing about a fantasy: It didn't have to be true. And it was a much better story than the one Jed told her about her father taking one look at his ugly newborn daughter and running for the hills.

Although deep down there was a part of her that believed Jed's story. She had been an ugly baby. Ugly enough that her daddy and mama had both wanted to abandon her. In fact, Starlet hadn't started feeling pretty until she had grown up and left home for Miss Hattie's Henhouse, the infamous house of ill repute where Starlet's great-great-aunt had once worked. The three old women— or "hens," as they preferred to be called—who lived there had taken Starlet under their wings and given her love and confidence. But they weren't the ones who made her feel beautiful. Only one man was responsible for that.

Fanning through the pages of the Bible, Starlet searched until she found the newspaper clipping. She carefully pulled it out, her gaze longingly devouring the picture of the heroic rodeo cowboy with the smile that melted her heart.

And made her extremely hungry.

She quickly found the other treasure she'd hidden in the Bible. The MoonPie was squashed flat, but still unbelievably delicious. She took her time eating it, savoring the banana icing and sticky marshmallow filling while she stared at the blue-eyed cowboy and strengthened her resolve.

Her plan would work. All she needed to do was find the right cowboy. She paused mid finger lick. And maybe that was her problem. Maybe instead of hiring the right cowboy, she needed to hire the right man. The kind of man who was better at getting women to say *yes*.

Her cell phone rang, jarring her from her thoughts and causing her to guiltily shove the MoonPie wrapper under her pillow before she picked up. She was about to say hello when her best friend, Brianne Hicks, started yelling. And since Brianne was the sister to the Cates brothers, she knew how to yell.

"Where have you been? And why haven't you returned my calls? Didn't you know that I'd be worried sick?"

"I'm sorry, but I couldn't." Starlet fanned through the Bible for another MoonPie but came up empty. "From the concert, I went to the hospital. And I've been surrounded by people ever since. Including your two brothers."

"I know. I talked with Brant a few minutes ago, but I'm a little confused about Beckett. I thought he was supposed to be in Russia. What was he doing there?"

"I don't have a clue. I was hoping you'd know the answer. And why didn't you tell me he'd gotten so..." Starlet pictured Beckett's body and tried to come up with the appropriate adjective, but Brianne beat her to it.

"Buff?" She laughed. "Maybe because I didn't think you cared. Although it looked like you more than cared in the picture I saw on the Internet."

"That was all a publicity stunt planned by Kari."

"I figured as much." A toilet flushed.

"Are you going to the bathroom while you're talking to me?" Starlet asked.

"If I want to have a conversation that's longer than two seconds, I have no choice," she said. "In the last month, my bladder has become the size of a dust mite—something all my sisters-in-law warned me about, but I never fully understood until now." She paused. "You're coming back for the birth, right? I mean, I can't be stuck in a birthing room alone with Dusty. The man has turned into a nervous Nellie, and I don't think he'll be much help."

There was nothing Starlet wanted more, but things had changed since the last time she'd spoken to Brianne. "The hens and your mama will be there."

"And you think that will be better? My mama will have the doctors jumping through hoops to take care of her baby girl. And you know the hens. I love the old gals, but they aren't exactly soothing. Look, if you can't make it, I'll understand. I just thought it would be nice to have my best friend there—especially when I'm a little scared about becoming a mama."

"I had planned to be there, Bri," she said, "but after what happened, I don't think it's a good idea. I couldn't stand the thought of putting the people I love in danger."

"Danger?" Brianne said. "What do you mean, Starlet? Do you think the kidnapper is still after you?"

Starlet took a deep breath, wondering how much she should reveal. Of course, Brianne knew how to keep a secret. She had proven that the first time Starlet had met her. And since this had to do with that exact secret, it seemed only right that she should know.

Clutching the phone to her ear, Starlet glanced around. Twilight crept in the tinted windows of the bus, casting the room in an eerie bluish haze. As she finally voiced the truth, she couldn't help the shiver of fear that had goose bumps rising on her arms.

"It was dark, so I can't be sure. But I think it was him, Bri. I think it was Alejandro."

Chapter Four

"Afghanistan?"

Brant's shocked reply prompted Beckett to be a smartass. "An Islamic sovereign state located west of China—"

"I know where it is, Beckett." Brant gave him a stern look. "What I want to know is what you were doing there."

It was a good question. Especially when Beckett had told his family that he was stationed at an embassy in Russia. It hadn't started out as a lie. With his computer skills, he had been offered a safe desk job at an embassy. But he had joined the marines because he was tired of being safe. Tired of being the sensitive geek of the family who couldn't beat his way out of a paper bag. Tired of being the one brother who fell far short of the Cates family name.

Unfortunately, no matter how much weight he could bench-press or how many times he'd beaten other recruits at obstacle courses, when it finally mattered, he still had fallen short. Except this time, it hadn't just been his ego on the line.

The pounding in Beckett's temples intensified, and he

downed the rest of the rum and Coke he'd ordered. But alcohol never eased the pain. In fact, it only loosened the tight restraint he held on the memories, causing them to flood back with gut-wrenching accuracy. Shoving away the steak dinner the waitress had just brought, he leaned back in the cushioned chair.

"Look, I'm sorry," he said. "I just didn't want the family to worry. Mom and Dad have done enough worrying with Beau's cancer and you losing..." He let the sentence trail off. Even though Brant had finally healed after the death of his wife and son, Beckett refused to bring up painful memories. He had plenty for both of them.

Brant stared at him, the expression on his face hard and unyielding. As a kid—hell, even as a teenager—the look had scared the crap out of Beckett. But after he'd lived through hell, there was little that scared him now. Although he did prepare to jump out of punching range.

"I'm getting damned sick of my brothers using that as an excuse for their lies," Brant said between gritted teeth. "Beau used those exact words when he decided to forgo more cancer tests."

"And look how well that turned out."

"I'm not amused, Beck."

No, his big brother was rarely amused, and Beckett figured you had to be stoic if you were the oldest Cates brother. Brant took his job of big brother seriously. But beneath the stern look, Beckett knew there was concern and love. This was confirmed when Brant released his breath and his anger quickly. "Maybe you're right. Maybe it's best that Mom and Dad didn't know where you were. And now that you're back safe and sound, it doesn't make much difference." He picked up his knife and fork and sliced off a piece of rare steak. "So where are they sending you now?"

Beckett looked around for the waitress. He had a feeling he was going to need another drink. Unfortunately, she was nowhere to be found. Two little boys at the table across from them caught his attention. Their parents seemed to be in an intense conversation while the boys were taking the opportunity to raise hell. Using their spoons and the edges of their plates, they were launching steamed broccoli at each other and trying to catch it in their mouths. Beckett grinned before he turned back to Brant.

"Actually, I'm going back to Afghanistan."

The fork with the sliver of steak halted inches from Brant's mouth. "Like hell."

"Pretty much," Beckett said. "The heat is about as close as you can get."

The fork clinked down to the plate as Brant stared at him. "So they're sending you back for another tour?"

"Yes," Beckett said, even though he wasn't sure. And wouldn't be sure until the investigation was completed. Of course, he should've known that his brother wouldn't take the news lying down.

"Well, I'm not having that." He pulled his phone from his suit pocket. "General Franks is a close friend, and I'm sure when—"

"No."

Beckett didn't know if it was the word or his tone that caused the surprised look on his brother's face. Probably both. Few people gave a firm "no" to Branston Cates. Beckett had done so only twice in his life—once when joining the marines and tonight.

"Put the phone away, Brant," he said. "I don't need you fighting my battles for me. Especially when I want to go back."

"You what? But why, Beckett? You've already done your duty. You served close to a year in a combat zone. That's more than enough."

It was more than enough for most marines. But most marines didn't have demons pounding away in their heads and voices keeping them up at night.

"I'm going back," he stated.

Brant stared at him for a long moment before he pocketed the phone. As a shrewd businessman, he knew when to let things go. "I hope to God you know what you're doing."

"Probably not, but it's my decision." He glanced back at the opposite table and noticed that one of the boys had finally hit his target. There was only one problem: The broccoli had lodged in his brother's throat, and it didn't look like he was breathing—something no one seemed to notice, including his celebratory brother.

Tossing his napkin down, Beckett got up and, in two strides, had the kid out of his chair and flipped over his arm. It took only one well-placed whack on the back to send the broccoli floret flying out of his mouth and onto his mother's plate.

"Way awesome!" his brother yelled as his parents stared at Beckett in shock. Beckett ignored them as he set the kid back down in his chair and knelt in front of him, checking his breathing and color.

"You okay?" he asked.

The kid nodded as his parents finally figured things out. The mother jumped up and pulled her son into her arms while the father pumped Beckett's hand and continued to thank him until Beckett was forced to pull away. He blushed as the entire restaurant broke out in applause, then made his way back to his table.

Brant smiled and shook his head. "I'm surprised you didn't become a doctor instead of a marine. You have always been good in a crisis situation. Remember the time you tried to stitch up Beau after he sliced open his finger with the pocketknife?" He chuckled. "You probably would've succeeded if Mama hadn't come in and jerked the needle and thread out of your hand."

The rest of the dinner was much less tense. Once they'd reminisced about their childhood, Brant filled Beckett in on the family. By the time the waitress came back to the table with the dessert menus, he had moved on to his concern over Starlet's kidnapping.

"I wish you'd come with me to Atlanta." He handed the menu back to the waitress and declined with a shake of his head. "The bodyguard she hired doesn't exactly instill confidence."

"I agree." Suddenly hungry, Beckett studied the menu a second more before handing it to the waitress and ordering bananas Foster.

Brant's eyebrows shot up. "Since when do you like bananas? I thought you hated them as a kid."

Beckett shrugged. "I thought I'd give them another try. So where did Starlet find that doofus of a bodyguard, anyway?"

"She didn't find him as much as he found her. He's her uncle Bernard's son." He tossed his napkin to the table. "The entire situation annoys the hell out of me. Her family didn't care that she moved to a house of ill repute, but they came out of the woodwork when she became famous and started making money."

"We both know that Miss Hattie's is no longer a house of ill repute. And hasn't been for years," Beckett said. "Although there have been a few times when I've had my doubts."

"Starlet's relatives didn't know that. And what kind of a family lets a young woman accept an invitation from a former madam of an infamous whorehouse?"

"They are a motley crew, aren't they?" Beckett laughed. "I caught her uncle shooting craps with the band members behind the bus. That wouldn't have been so bad if he hadn't been cheating with a rigged pair of dice he changed out whenever it was his turn."

Brant shook his head. "The man is disreputable, and I would've sent him packing long ago if not for Starlet. Regardless of her family's flaws, she seems to love them. Of course, Starlet loves everyone."

It was hard to contain his snort of derision. As far as Beckett was concerned, Starlet was no better than her uncle. She had scammed Beckett's entire family into believing that she was a sweet little angel who had arrived at Miss Hattie's Henhouse with the innocent desire to follow in her great-aunt's footsteps and become a Broadway star. But Beckett knew better. There was nothing innocent about Starlet. Something she had proved to him the night of her going-away party.

"I'm sure Starlet will be just fine," he said. "Especially since this is her last concert for the year."

"To be honest, I'm not worried about the concert as much as I'm worried about her going back to Nashville," Brant said. "She lives out on some massive ranch with her family."

"She has a security system, right?"

"Yes, but if the guy got past the security at the concert

without any problems, what makes you think he doesn't know how to get past a simple house alarm?"

Brant did have a point, but before they could discuss it further, dessert arrived. The banana Fosters made Beckett realize that he had gotten over his dislike of bananas. He polished the sweet confection off, then squabbled with Brant over who would pay the bill. The manager of the restaurant settled the argument by picking up the tab for Beckett's heroic actions.

The word "heroic" made Beckett's head throb even more. Or maybe it was the next topic of conversation that his brother brought up on their way to the parking lot.

"So you're doing okay financially?" Brant followed him to his car.

"As good as a lieutenant in the marines can be doing." He stopped in front of the brand-new Mustang and pulled the keys from his pocket.

Brant studied the car. "So this is what you pulled the money out of your trust fund for? When you told me that you wanted to withdraw some of your money, I had hoped that you planned to invest it."

Beckett hadn't withdrawn the money for the car—he'd borrowed the car from a buddy at Camp Lejeune—nor had he invested it. But he figured that he'd shared enough with his brother for one night.

"Yeah, well, I've never been as good at investing as you have." He pushed the unlock button on the key ring and went to open the door when Brant stopped him.

"So you're sure it's what you want, Beck?"

Beckett turned to his brother. "I'm sure. But I promise that after this, I'll let you pick me out a comfy desk job."

Brant only nodded before he leaned in and gave

Beckett a quick hug and thump on the back. "Stay safe, little brother."

"I will."

As it turned out, it was a promise Beckett could keep.

"What do you mean I'm being discharged?" Beckett got up from the chair positioned in front of the colonel's desk. A colonel who looked as somber and unmovable as Brant.

"I mean you're being discharged." Colonel Roland pointed a finger at the chair. "Now, sit down, Lieutenant."

For most of his life, Beckett had respected authority—his parents, his older brothers, teachers, commanding officers—but since returning to the States, he had discovered a belligerent side of himself. He remained standing.

"This has to do with my brother, doesn't it? He spoke with General Franks."

Colonel Roland chose to ignore his defiance. "I know nothing about a conversation with the general. This decision was made days ago. Once the investigation was complete, Major Martin and I thought it was for the best."

Beckett looked over at the major, who also happened to be the annoying psychiatrist who had been picking Beckett's brain since he got back from Afghanistan.

"So you think I'm nuts, sir?" he asked.

Major Martin fidgeted in his chair and refused to look at Beckett. "I didn't say that. I just think you need some time to heal after what happened. Especially with post-traumatic stress disorder."

"I don't have PTSD. What I have is a need to go back and serve my country." Beckett leaned closer, causing the doctor's eyes to widen. "I want to go back . . . sir."

"That will be quite enough, Lieutenant." Colonel

Roland looked at Major Martin. "You can go. I'll finish up with Cates."

The doctor got up and edged toward the door, keeping a safe distance from Beckett, who had a strong urge to grab the weasel by the throat for keeping him from what he wanted most. When the door closed behind him, the colonel nodded at the chair.

"I won't repeat myself."

Beckett sat down. "Does my discharge have anything to do with the investigation?"

The colonel leaned back and steepled his fingers against his chin. "No. There were no charges brought up against you. While you made an error in judgment, your presence wouldn't have changed the outcome." His eyes held more than concern; they held an understanding of what Beckett was going through. "There's no making it right, son."

It took a moment for Beckett to answer. "And you think that I don't know that?"

The colonel sat up and cupped his hands on the desk. "I think you've served your country well, Lieutenant Cates. And now it's time to move on with your life."

Beckett stared back at him, his gaze unwavering. "What life?"

Chapter Five

IF CINDY LYNN WOMACK hadn't already been sitting on a toilet in the bathroom of Josephine's Diner, she might've peed her pants with excitement. Gossip was the only thrilling thing in her life, and she prided herself on being the first to relay all the big news in Bramble, Texas. And what she had just overheard was definitely big news.

"Twins?" Faith Calhoun repeated.

"Shh," her twin sister, Hope, warned. There was a click of cowboy boots on tile, and Cindy Lynn quickly pulled up her feet. Hope must've just given the bottom of the stalls a quick glance because, within seconds, she was back to talking with her sister.

"You know what will happen when the townsfolk find out."

They'll have the biggest parade this side of the Pecos.

Cindy scowled. As excited as she was about being one of the first to get the news, she couldn't help but feel annoyed and jealous. Hope Lomax had been her biggest rival since high school. While Cindy had been popular, her popularity was nothing compared to Hope's. No matter how hard

Cindy tried to please the townsfolk—almost throwing out a hip to do the highest cheer kicks at the football games or, as president of the Ladies' Club, organizing every parade, shower, and wedding in town—she always came up short. And when Hope's twin sister, Faith, had arrived in Bramble, things got even worse. Now, instead of being runner-up to Miss Hog Caller of Haskins County, Cindy was second runner-up, which everyone knew was just another title for "the biggest loser."

Now here Hope was having twins while Cindy had popped out only one kid at a time. It was almost enough to make her want to lie down on the floor and throw a tantrum. But "what goes around, comes around," her mama used to say. And as Cindy continued to listen, things started coming around.

"Oh my gosh!" Faith released a small squeal of delight. "That is such wonderful..." Her voice dropped off as if she'd just figured something out. And she probably had. Hope and Faith had this weird thing going on where they could read each other's minds with one look.

Something that gave Cindy the willies.

"You aren't excited," Faith stated.

"I'm worried." Hope walked over to the sinks. "You know what happened the last time and how devastating it was. And you know that—" A blast of water cut off her next words, causing Cindy to almost fall off the toilet as she leaned forward to try to hear. Although she forgot all about finding out what was so devastating to Hope when the water cut off and Cindy heard her next words.

"...which is exactly why I'm thinking about dropping out of the mayoral race."

While Cindy Lynn held back her gasp, Faith showed

her own shock. "Not run for mayor? But you have to, Hope. The townsfolk are counting on you to take over when Uncle Harley retires."

Hope heaved a big sigh. "I know, but sometimes you have to put your family first. We both know how hard it is to take care of one newborn, let alone two. Not to mention how dangerous the pregnancy will be. It just makes sense that I'm there for—" The automatic paper towel dispenser cut her off before Faith picked up the conversation.

"But I'll help, Hope. And so will with Mama, Tessa, and Shirlene."

"With Mia off to college, Shirlene has her hands full with Jesse and her other two kids. Tessa lives in Lubbock. Mama works at the Feed and Seed. And you teach at the high school. How is that going to work?"

"I could take a year off," Faith said.

"No!" Hope snapped, and then her voice softened. "Look, I appreciate it, Faith. But your students love you too much for you to give up your job."

"Fine." Faith moved to the door. "But don't make any rash decisions. Think about it while we're camping in Red River. Maybe Uncle Harley would stay on until after the babies get here."

"I wouldn't do that to him," Hope said. "Not when he's so excited about retirement. Which means that I need to tell the town soon, so other candidates can step forward."

"Other candidates?" Faith said as the door squeaked open. "There's no one in Bramble who is interested in that job but you, sis."

Once the door closed behind them, Cindy set her feet down on the floor and smiled. There was one other person interested in the job. With a small squeal of excitement, she punched the air. This was her chance. Her chance to finally whup Hope Lomax at something. Or maybe not whup her—since Hope wasn't running—but holding a job Hope coveted was almost as good.

Cindy gave Hope and Faith plenty of time to rejoin their husbands and kids at their table before she slipped out the bathroom door and headed for the cashier counter. Rachel Dean, the diner's only waitress, met her there.

"Ed still fishin'?" she asked as she took the money from Cindy. "I swear that man has been gone more this summer than he's been home. Although with your kids spending time with your mama in Odessa, it must be nice to have a little freedom."

Cindy's excitement dimmed for just a second as she replied. "Real nice." Then she pushed the depression away and hurried out the door.

Her house was two blocks from the diner. At a flat-out run, it took her no more than two minutes to get home. First she would call Darla. Then she'd call the other officers of the Ladies' Club. If she was going to become the next mayor of Bramble, she would need their support. Just the thought had her giggling with glee. She was so caught up in her excitement that she didn't notice Gus the mailman standing on her porch until he spoke.

"Training for the Boston Marathon, Cindy?"

She came to a stop right next to the tractor mailbox her husband, Ed, had given her on her last birthday. At the time, she'd been ticked. No diamonds. No expensive perfume. Just a dumb mailbox that he had made from scrap lumber. But in the last month, she'd realized how thoughtful a gift it had been. Of course, now it was too late.

She stared at the large envelope in Gus's hand and

wiped the sweat from her brow. "Actually, I just need to take care of some important bid-ness for the Ladies' Club. What brings you here so close to quittin' time, Gus?"

"The mail. You got another registered letter. This is the third in less than a month." He held the envelope up as if to see through the thick manila paper.

Cindy quickly climbed the steps and snatched it out of his hands. She signed the form on his clipboard before making her excuses. "Well, I need to get to that bid-ness."

Not waiting for a reply, she hurried inside and closed the door behind her. Once she heard Gus's receding footsteps, she stared at the envelope and the name typed on the front. Cynthia Lynette Womack. Her gaze moved to the return address of the attorney's office in Houston, Texas. She had hoped that if she ignored the envelopes, Ed would give up. Like he had when he'd wanted to put the moose head over the fireplace. But it didn't look like he was going to give up this time.

She glanced at his empty recliner in the living room and felt the heavy wave of depression that she'd been fighting for the last couple months.

Divorce. How can Ed want to divorce me? Everyone in town knew that she had been the better catch. Even Ed. And why would you want to throw back a good catch? It made absolutely no sense whatsoever. Which is why she refused to sign the papers and return them. Ed would come to his senses eventually. All she had to do was wait him out. Just like she had waited out her chance to best Hope.

Carrying the envelope into the kitchen, she put it on the shelf with the other envelopes—right in between her *Betty Crocker Cookbook* and the Bramble phone directory. Then she picked up the phone and dialed Darla.

Darla answered on the first ring. "So did you hear?" she said in a hushed I've-got-some-great-gossip voice.

Some of Cindy's excitement fizzled out. Man, news traveled fast in a small town. "I know already. I heard it straight from the horse's mouth."

"Star Bentley's in town!" Darla said, sounding like an excited sixteen-year-old girl.

"Star Bentley? What are you talkin' about? I'm talkin' about Hope Lomax being pregnant with twins and droppin' out of the race for mayor."

A gasp came through the receiver. "No-o-o."

"Yes. I heard it with my own two ears. And just who do you think is going to take her place?"

"Rossie Owens?"

Cindy scowled. "No. Not Rossie Owens. The owner of the only bar in town wouldn't make a good mayor. Me. I'm going to run."

There was a long stretch of silence, followed by a very unexcited "Oh." Darla cleared her throat. "Are you sure you're up to it? I mean, it does take a lot of work."

"Of course I'm up to it. I've been the president of the Ladies' Club goin' on ten years. I don't know how much more 'up to it' you can get. Now, we need to make some plans." She opened a drawer to pull out a pen, but before she could grab one from the mishmash, a photograph caught her attention. A photograph of her, Ed, and the kids on their last vacation to Dollywood. She slammed the drawer closed and started making a list. "First we need to make some campaign signs and flyers. And I want you to help me design a float for the Fourth of July parade."

"But the parade is after the election."

"I know. But as the next mayor of Bramble, I'll be on

the first float in the parade. And I want it to be good." She rolled her eyes. Obviously, Darla didn't understand politics. "Now, what's this about Star Bentley?"

Darla seemed almost relieved to change the subject. "I guess some nut kidnapped Star Bentley by gunpoint. And you'll never guess who saved her—Beckett Cates. And remember how skinny he was a few years back? Well, he ain't skinny anymore." There was a click of knitting needles before she continued. "In the picture I saw, the man has a body that would melt butter. And speakin' of melting butter, I better get off and make Tad dinner. Is Ed back from fishin'?"

"Umm, no."

The knitting needles clicked. "I swear you're a better wife than I would be. If Tad went huntin' and fishin' as much as Ed, I'd divorce the man."

Cindy glanced at the shelf. "Well, hopefully, it won't come to that. Listen, I'll talk with you later."

She hung up and was about to place the phone back in its cradle when headlights flashed over the window. She hurried over and looked out, hoping to see Ed's red Ford pickup. But the headlights belonged to Owen Grieves. Owen and his wife, Kasey, had just moved in to the house next door. They were a young couple that hadn't been married for more than a few months. Cindy watched as the door to the house opened and Kasey came running out to greet Owen before he was even out of his car. They kissed passionately as Owen lifted his wife up in his arms and carried her back inside.

When was the last time Cindy had greeted Ed like that? The last time they'd kissed passionately? The last time he'd been happy to see her and she'd been happy to see him? It was sad that the only memories that popped up were from high school—before dreams of a perfect marriage had died beneath the reality of kids, housework, and mounting bills. Before she had started to resent him for ruining her life.

She looked around the kitchen. But what was so wrong with her life? She had a nice home, good friends, two beautiful children, and a kindhearted husband who made her a cute little tractor mailbox for her birthday. Or at least, she used to have a kindhearted husband. Now all she had was an empty recliner and the memory of the man who used to sit in it.

A tap on the kitchen screen door startled her out of her thoughts. She glanced over to see a stranger peeking in through the mesh. Not that she could see his face in the shadow of his cowboy hat, but no one in town wore a hat that spanking new.

"I'm sorry to bother you, ma'am," he said in a polite voice with a slight accent. New York, probably. Those New Yorkers had the weirdest accents. "But my truck broke down just a few miles back, and I was wondering if there was a gas station around here."

Cindy moved over to the door. "There's one on Main Street a couple blocks down. Did you need a ride?"

He shook his head. "No, thanks. I don't mind the walk—" The pop of a firecracker had him ducking behind a pyracantha bush. Yep, definitely a New Yorker.

"Sorry about that," she said as he peeked out. "That's just the neighborhood kids gettin' ready for the Fourth." She watched as the children raced down the street. And again, she wished that she hadn't let her mama talk her into taking the kids for the summer. If they were there, maybe the nights wouldn't be so lonely.

"You okay, ma'am?" the stranger asked.

She pinned on a smile. A smile she would need to practice if she was going to be the next mayor of Bramble. "Fine and dandy," she said. "And you don't need to call me ma'am. Cindy will do."

"Thank you, Cindy." He was halfway down the path before she called after him.

"And what's your name?"

He turned and stared down at the toes of his boots. "Cowboy. Just Cowboy."

Chapter Six

THE SPRAWLING MANSION SAT on a hundred acres of land that Starlet had never really looked at. She'd driven past it on her way to the house, but after weeks of traveling or hours spent in the recording studio, she was usually too exhausted to care that Kari had talked her into buying a piece of property that could easily be the setting for one of those horror movies where all the camping teenagers get hacked to death.

She cared now.

The view outside her balcony doors was nothing but thick woodlands that an ax murderer could easily hide in, topped with a spooky full moon that would send any vampire or werewolf into a killing spree.

Of course, she didn't have to worry about an ax murderer or a bloodthirsty Dracula. She had to worry about an angry Mexican drug lord who wanted his money back. Drug money that had accidentally been brought to the henhouse, from where Starlet had not so accidentally sent some of it to her mama for drug rehabilitation. Now that she was rich, she would gladly reimburse Alejandro. She stared out at the dark woods and shivered. She just didn't want to hand over the money personally.

A thump almost startled Starlet out of her slippers. She whirled around and found her cat, Hero, standing at the foot of the bed. The feline stretched lazily, his claws sinking into the plush carpet and his plump body arching up like an inflating hot air balloon. The cat had been a going-away gift from Brant's brother Beau, and Starlet loved it to death. It was too bad that the cat didn't feel the same way. When his eyes zeroed in on Starlet, he released a low, throaty growl and hunched down as if ready to pounce.

While she'd been on tour, it seemed that Hero had gotten slightly more aggressive—no doubt due to Starlet's housekeeper feeding him the appropriate daily serving of cat food. Dieting would make anyone cranky. Starlet had been in a bad mood ever since Charlotte. Not that she had growled at anyone. But she had wanted to. She had wanted to growl at Kari for the irritating green contacts she forced her to wear. Wanted to growl at her mama for getting smashed in Atlanta and making a scene in a local bar. And she'd wanted to growl at Jed just because he annoyed her.

But instead, she'd kept her anger hidden deep inside and had her drummer buy her a box of MoonPies when the bus stopped for gas in Chattanooga. She had gotten to enjoy exactly one before Kari discovered her stash. Which resulted in another hour-long lecture and a two-hour workout with the ThighMaster once they arrived home. Even now, her thighs ached and her stomach growled. But thanks to Kari hiring her Chef Healthnut, there wasn't a MoonPie or snack in the entire house.

But there were cans of cat food.

"Don't get your tail in a knot," she said as she inched around the cat. "I might not be able to eat, but you can."

Halfway down the stairs, Starlet realized that she should've turned on the hall light. The lower part of the house was dark and even creepier than the outside. Normally, there were numerous family members scattered around— Jed playing Xbox in the entertainment room, Uncle Bernie snoozing in his recliner in the study, and her mama wandering around the house looking for one of the spare bottles she'd stashed. But after the concert tour, her family had been sick of one another's company and had headed off in different directions. Although they would no doubt all end up at the same country bar by the end of the night.

At the bottom of the stairs, Starlet flipped on the light and turned toward the kitchen. But she stopped in her tracks when she noticed the front door. It was open. Not all the way open, but open enough for the wind to whistle through. Her breath halted as she tried to talk herself out of the fear that tiptoed down her spine.

It was no big deal. One of her family members had probably forgotten to close the door on their way out. Except her family never used the front door. They all went through the garage where they parked the cars and trucks she'd bought them. Of course, that didn't mean that one of the employees hadn't left it ajar. The housekeeper, the chef, the gardener, or the guy who took care of the horses Starlet was scared to death of could've easily forgotten to close it when they left their meetings with Kari earlier that day. Of course, if they had left it ajar, wouldn't the alarm have gone off when it was activated?

Starlet's gaze shot over to the alarm system. Activate the alarm! She knew there had been something she'd forgotten to do before she went to bed. Unfortunately, before she could correct her mistake, a muscled arm curved around her waist, completely lifting her off the floor. She started to scream, but a hand covered her mouth.

"Are you really that stupid?" a deep voice said next to her ear.

The familiar voice caused her muscles to relax as anger replaced fear. Pulling back her elbow, she jabbed Beckett as hard as she could in the stomach. Unfortunately, with his abs of steel, it hurt her more than it hurt him.

He hefted her higher, his biceps flexing. "Not only do you need some classes in self-defense, but you need to gain some weight. You're nothing but skin and bones." In a brief, fevered stroke, his thumb brushed the bottom swell of her breast. "Although there are a few soft spots."

"Mmm," she muttered against his hand.

"What's that?" He leaned closer, his stubbled jaw brushing her neck and sending goose bumps down her arms—and into her panties. "Are you a little upset at being held in this position?" He pulled her closer, making her well aware of just how hard a body he had. "Well, you'd be a helluva lot more upset if I happened to be Alejandro. Because from what I've learned about the man, he wouldn't just cop a feel."

At Alejandro's name, Starlet went perfectly still.

Beckett loosened his hold. "I see that finally got your attention—yowww!" He released her, and Starlet turned to find him shaking the leg Hero was attached to. He stumbled back before sitting down hard on the stairs. And still Hero hung on, his claws deeply embedded in Beckett's calf and a low growl emanating from his chest.

The humor of the situation struck Starlet, and she burst

out laughing. "What's the matter, Becky? Is the big, bad marine going to let a little puddy cat get the best of him?"

Beckett stopped trying to detach the cat and squinted up at her. "I don't like the name Becky."

Starlet shrugged her shoulders. "And I don't like being accosted in my own home by a man who thinks he's smarter than everyone else." She gave him a once-over, realizing for the first time that he wore civilian clothes. And not just civilian clothes, but western civilian clothes: a snap-down plaid western shirt, faded Wranglers, and boots that looked like they had been worn in as nicely as his jeans.

She lifted her eyebrows. "Don't tell me you've gone AWOL and expect me to hide you."

Pain skipped across his features before it disappeared beneath the usual arrogant scowl. "Get this thing off me." He glared at Hero.

Realizing that the fun was over, Starlet walked into the kitchen and grabbed a can of cat food out of the pantry. As soon as she pressed the button on the can opener, Hero came racing in and rubbed up against her legs. Beckett appeared only a second later with a cowboy hat in his hand and a slight limp in his walk.

"You're feeding him too much," he said in that know-it-all voice of his. "The cat has to be ten pounds overweight. No wonder he's so angry."

Rather than give Hero half the can like she'd planned, she dumped the entire can into his bowl before smiling sweetly at Beckett. "My house, my rules."

Beckett set his hat on the marble countertop. "One of those rules should be to turn on your alarm. Especially when you're being stalked by the Mexican cartel."

After tossing the can in the trash, she walked back

to the pantry, hoping that somehow Chef Healthnut had overlooked a banned snack. A MoonPie was preferable, but under the circumstances, any processed treat would do: Twinkie, Swiss roll, Ding Dong. Unfortunately, the only sweet she found was a bag of dried cranberries. Since beggars couldn't be choosers, she grabbed the bag and took a big handful before turning back to Beckett.

"So I guess Bri ratted me out."

His gaze seemed to be trained on the bottom half of her Disney nightshirt. She glanced down to see what he was looking at, but the nightshirt just looked like a nightshirt to her. And when she looked back, his blue-eyed gaze had moved over to Hero.

"I wouldn't call it ratting you out," he stated. "I'd call it doing the sensible, intelligent thing. Being nine months' pregnant, she couldn't exactly come check on you herself." He moved around the counter. In western clothes, he looked a little less intimidating than he had in fatigues. Less intimidating and much more...hot? She blinked at the word that had popped into her head as he continued. "And I wasn't about to give in to Brianne's pleas unless I had a good reason."

"So does Brant know?"

He shook his head as he squatted down to scratch Hero. "Bri made me promise to keep it a secret—although I think we should call the police."

Starlet choked on the cranberry she'd just tossed in her mouth. Before she could catch her breath, Beckett was holding out a glass of water. It took a few sips before she could talk. "We can't call the police. If we call the police, we'll have to give them a motive for why Alejandro is after me. And if they find out that Minnie kept the drug money a secret for months, she could go to jail. And I could go to jail for stealing it from Minnie's safe and sending it to my mother for her fake rehabilitation. Not to mention, Brianne going to jail for covering up my mistake."

Beckett studied her for a moment before releasing his breath. "Damn. Why do women ever think they can handle things on their own?"

Starlet puffed up. "We can handle things just fine on our own."

His exasperated look said it all. "Like protecting yourself, for example." He pointed a finger toward the front door. "I walked right in. Hell, the door wasn't even locked. How is that handling things?" While she tried to come up with a good answer for that, he started opening cupboard doors. "You wouldn't happen to have any aspirin, would you?"

"Did Hero hurt you that badly?"

"Hero?" He cocked an eyebrow at the cat before shaking his head. "No, not for my leg. I've got a headache."

"No doubt from that scowl you always wear." She opened the cupboard closest to her. "But I'm sure we've got a bottle somewhere."

"You don't know?"

"I don't really spend a lot of time here." She moved to the next cupboard. "I'm either on the road or in Nashville recording. Here!" She held up a bottle, but after shaking it, frowned. "Sorry. It's empty."

"If you don't have aspirin, how about something to drink?"

"Unless you're talking about green tea, you're out of luck. With my mom being an alcoholic, we don't keep liquor in the house. Although, if she were here, I'm sure she could direct you to a hidden bottle."

He glanced around. "Where is your posse, anyway?"

"Out."

He rolled his eyes. "Which makes a whole lot of sense, given your recent kidnapping. What you need is a professional security team—one that will install a proper security system with high fences, an electric gate, and surveillance cameras that are monitored twenty-four seven." He glanced at the picture of her uncle, mother, and Jed that someone had attached to the refrigerator with a magnet. "Not a group of losers who only want to mooch off you."

It wasn't like Starlet hadn't thought the same thing more than once since her family had moved in with her. But it was one thing for her to think it and another for an arrogant know-it-all to say it.

"They're not losers!" she snapped. "You're the loser. And speaking of mooching, I wouldn't be surprised if they kicked your butt out of the marines and you're here to volunteer your services as my security team."

"Mooch off you?" His eyes widened for a fraction of a second before he picked up his hat. "Look, I was just doing a favor for my sister. But screw it! If you're stupid enough to end up dead and buried in the woods, that's no skin off my nose." He tugged on his hat and headed for the door.

Starlet followed on his heels. "Talk about stupid. Alejandro doesn't want to kill me. He just wants his money. Which is exactly why he kidnapped me. If he'd wanted me dead, he would've put arsenic in my water instead of the tranquilizer."

Beckett pulled open the front door. "Then I guess you have nothing to worry about, do you?" Before she could say another word, he was gone.

For more than a few minutes, Starlet stood in the open doorway, the wind blowing back her blond extensions and fluttering the soft material of her nightshirt. It took head-lights sweeping over the porch for her to step back and close the door. She locked it with a snap, then set the alarm.

"What a complete jerk," she muttered. "A jerk that doesn't even know what he's talking about. Why would Alejandro want to kill me? I wasn't the one who took his money—at least not to begin with." She looked at Hero, who was sitting in the doorway of the kitchen licking his paws. "Right?"

The cat stopped licking and fixated on her, growling in a low, menacing way. For once, she didn't feel scared. Regardless of the scratches he gave her, it was nice having a guard cat in the house.

"Come on, my hero. Let's go to bed."

Of course, the cat didn't listen to her, and she was forced to entice him with a piece of turkey she pulled from the fridge. Not that she was scared of going up the stairs by herself. She just didn't want to leave Hero alone in the dark. Or at least, that's what she tried to tell herself. When she reached the shadowy upstairs hallway, she had to concede the fact that she might be a little scared. Of course, she blamed it all on Beckett. If he hadn't shown up and started spouting off about being killed and buried in the woods, she would be in bed right now, watching *Duck Dynasty*.

Holding out the piece of turkey so Hero would follow, she scurried across the hallway and into her brightly lit room. Once there, she heaved a sigh of relief. It got stuck in her throat when she noticed the open balcony door. If Beckett came in the front door, then who came in...?

Her gaze drifted over to the wall above her bed, and the scream Starlet released was filled with nothing but fear.

Chapter Seven

MOOCHING OFF HER?

Beckett thumped the steering wheel with his fist. He was so preoccupied with his anger that he barely noticed the chunk of plastic that fell from the steering wheel to his lap. As if he needed to mooch off Starlet Brubaker. He had plenty of money in the bank. Okay, maybe not plenty—especially after his last withdrawal. But he had enough to last him until he found a job. And where did the woman get off calling him stupid? Hell, she hadn't even gone to college, while he was only five credits and one dissertation away from getting his doctorate.

He pressed harder on the accelerator and shifted to a higher gear—or tried to. The piece-of-crap Nissan he'd bought from a corporal for two hundred bucks didn't seem to have a third gear. Before he could finagle it, the engine stalled and the car rolled to a stop just inside the arched wooden entry to the ranch. An entry with no security gate. No camera. And no guard.

And Starlet thought he was stupid?

He fumed for a few minutes more before he restarted the

truck. He had just popped the stick into first when a flash of lights had him looking toward the line of trees. Were those headlights? If so, what was a car doing off the main road?

An uneasy feeling prickled the back of his neck.

Shoving the gearshift into reverse, he turned around. Since the side passenger window had been knocked out, he heard the loud scream before he even reached the circular drive. He whipped the car up next to the porch steps, grabbed his revolver from the glove box, and jumped out. This time, the front door was locked tight. He tried kicking it in, but the solid mahogany wood held. With no other choice, he followed the high-pitched screaming to the open balcony on the other side of the house.

The vine-covered lattice served as a perfect ladder, and within seconds, Becket was jumping over the balcony railing and entering the bedroom. A bright pink bedroom with more satin and lace than a Victoria's Secret store. He glanced around for an assailant, but all he saw was Starlet hopping around the room with a cat attached to her leg.

At the ridiculous sight, he thought about turning right back around and leaving the exact way he came in. But then Starlet noticed him. In one leap, she hurled herself at his chest, cat and all.

She buried her face in his neck, her warm lips brushing his skin as she mumbled incoherently. "Thank God you didn't leave. I thought I was alone—and he would come back." She took a quivery breath. "And when I looked up and saw the blood, I couldn't stop screaming. And then Hero attacked me and wouldn't let go, and I don't know what I would've done if you hadn't come back."

Beckett tried to put a little space between his chest and the soft press of her breasts, but she wasn't having it. With a strength that surprised him, she pulled him back and snuggled closer. Since he'd been without female companionship for more than a year, it wasn't surprising that he rose to the occasion. Fortunately, she was too upset to notice.

"Calm down." Beckett didn't know if he spoke to Starlet or himself. Unfortunately, the only one to listen was the cat. He released Starlet's leg, then walked as daintily as a fat cat could over to the bed and jumped up. Beckett tried not to think about the bed or the long, bare legs pressed against his. He cleared his throat. "What blood are you talking about? Did your cat draw blood?"

She shook her head. "No. I'm not bleeding. It's the wall."

He glanced around until his gaze landed on the dripping, bloodred letters written above the plush pink velvet headboard.

You Owe Me.

Desire ebbed, and anger took its place. But this time, it was aimed at the sick bastard who had written the words. It grew more intense when Starlet lifted her head, and he read the fear in her eyes. Big, brown eyes that were much prettier without the contacts.

"You were right," she said in a small voice. "I didn't have enough security. Like you, he got in without me even knowing. In fact, he was right here when we were in the kitchen." A tremble racked her body as she looked at the door. "Which meant he was probably in the hallway when I walked down the stairs."

Beckett's headache returned. What had he been thinking? He should've checked out the house. He had no business leaving without making sure it was secure. In fact, he had no business leaving at all. Had he learned nothing from Afghanistan? A good soldier never let emotion get in the way of common sense. It didn't matter that Starlet had hurt his ego. What mattered was the promise he'd given his sister—a promise to keep Starlet safe.

If he wanted to keep that promise, he needed to pull his head out of his ass.

He took her by the arms and set her away from him. "Listen, Starlet, I need to check the rest of the house to be sure. And we need to call the police."

"No!" She shook her head. "We can't call the police."

"You don't have to tell them about the money, but they have to know that it's Alejandro they're looking for."

She pointed at the words on the wall. "And you don't think they're going to question why he wrote that?"

It was a good point. As much as he wanted Alejandro caught, Beckett wasn't willing to have his sister and Minnie thrown in jail in the process—not that both of them hadn't been there before.

"Fine," he said, "but you need to take this seriously. You need to hire a seasoned security team."

"First thing tomorrow." She held up three fingers. "Scout's honor." She finally noticed the gun resting against her arm. "Holy crap! Were you going to shoot him?" Her gaze lifted, her eyes soft and dreamy. "For me?"

With an exasperated groan, Beckett released her and moved toward the door. "Do you honestly think that everything revolves around you?"

"Now, that's laughable." She followed behind him. He thought about telling her to stay put while he checked out the house, but he figured that she wouldn't want to be left alone. And he didn't really want to leave her alone either—even if she was a bit of a chatterbox. "Nothing has ever revolved around me. Not as a child, and certainly not as an adult. The only time I felt remotely spoiled was at the henhouse."

"I find that hard to believe. After all, you're the sweetheart of country music." He pushed open the door to the first room that he came to and flipped on the light. Making sure Starlet stayed against the hallway wall, he moved in and checked under the bed and in the closet. When he came back out, she resumed the conversation.

"The sweetheart who does what everyone else wants her to. Wear this, wear that. Do this, do that. Say this, say that. Sometimes I feel like a puppet on a string."

"And your manager is the puppeteer?" He opened the next door.

"My manager. My family. Your brother."

He glanced back at her. "So tell them no and start making your own decisions."

A frown marred her forehead. "I would, but there's only one problem...I can't seem to say no."

Now, why that would turn him on, Beckett wasn't sure. One second, he was soft as a marshmallow, and the next, he was hard as granite. The erection stayed with him through the entire search. Probably because Starlet in her wispy, short nightshirt was never more than an arm's length away. That, and as he moved from room to room, he couldn't help thinking about all the naughty things she wouldn't say no to. By the time he had secured all the doors and windows and they arrived back in her bedroom, he was having trouble walking.

"Are you sure Hero didn't hurt your leg?" she asked. "You seem to be limping a lot more."

"I guess I hurt it climbing over the balcony," he lied. He stood at the foot of the bed and looked at the dripping paint on the wall. "You should probably sleep somewhere else until I can get this painted."

"You?" When he glanced over, she was stroking the cat's ears and smiling. "I didn't take you for a painter. Of course, I didn't take you for a big, bad marine who wields a gun either. What happened to the computer nerd?"

"Maybe he got tired of being the weakling Cates brother."

Instead of laughing, she nodded. "Yeah, I know what you mean. It's hard to be the odd man out."

"Or the odd woman." Beckett jerked the sheet off the bed, and moving up to the headboard, he tied one end to the ridiculous frilly canopy before holding out the other end to Starlet.

"Are you saying I'm odd?" She climbed up on the mattress and took the end of the sheet, draping it over the painted words on the wall and tying it to the other side of the canopy.

"You don't think that wearing skintight prom dresses and living at an infamous whorehouse with three old women was odd?" He waved his hand to encompass the room. "Not to mention your childish taste in decor."

She turned to him, her long legs braced and her hands on her hips. "Childish? Pink is not childish. Besides, I didn't pick this color. Kari did."

"I was referring to the color as much as the ruffles and menagerie of stuffed animals." He picked up a teddy bear in a pink tutu from the pile that surrounded her feet. "How do men find you in all this fake fur?"

Once the words were out, he wanted them back. He had no business bringing up her bed partners. Especially when his libido was urging him to be her next. His hard-on hadn't let up one iota, and he found it extremely annoying. She was not his type. She had never been his type. He liked petite, small-breasted college graduates—not tall, big-boobed country-western singers.

Which didn't explain what happened next.

"Men find me just fine!" She made a grab for the stuffed bear, but he pulled it away. The release of tension from the last few minutes made them both a little foolish, and a game of keep-away ensued, with Starlet lunging for the bear and Beckett keeping it just out of her reach.

"Too slow," he teased as he hid the stuffed animal behind his back. But his smile faded when she moved closer and made a grab for it over his shoulder, bringing her sweet breasts inches from his face. He might've been able to resist the temptation if he hadn't seen the jiggle of unfettered flesh beneath the thin cotton. A jiggle that beckoned like a cool, fresh-water pond on a hot summer day. Did they smell like bananas tonight? Or just heaven? The distance between him and the objects of his desire disappeared as he pressed his face between her breasts.

Starlet froze. Beckett should've stepped away. Except he couldn't. Not when being surrounded by her breasts was the closest thing to happiness he'd felt in a long time. He inhaled. She didn't smell like bananas. Instead, the soft scent of lilacs filled his lungs as her heart thumped soothingly against his ears. The V-neck of her nightshirt hung low enough that all he needed to do was turn his head ever so slightly to find sweet, heated skin and supple, abundant breast. He pressed his lips against the spot before tasting it with his tongue. She inhaled sharply, and her heart rate picked up, the cadence matching his own.

Needing much more, he used his teeth to tug down her neckline and reveal the entire plump gift from God. And it was a gift. A gift Beckett couldn't resist. Using just his mouth, he reconnoitered every inch of the sweet breast until he arrived, at last, to the cherry on top. A pink cherry the color of an east Texas sunrise. He kissed it once. Twice. Three times. Before he drew it into his mouth and suckled gently.

Starlet's hands lifted, and her fingers caressed his hair, sending contented shivers through his body as he moaned deep in his throat. He thought about dropping the bear and sliding his hands up those firm legs to test out the sweet cheeks beneath her nightshirt. But there was something so hot about using only his mouth to touch her that he kept his hands behind his back as Starlet manipulated his head to her other breast.

It was as pretty as the first, the tip already tight and begging for attention. He had just pulled it into his mouth when a blaring alarm went off. The loud noise had them jumping apart. For a split second, the sight of Starlet's sweet, jiggling breasts topped with wet, rosy nipples had Beckett seriously considering ignoring the alarm and going back to what he'd been doing. But common sense prevailed, and he reached for the gun he'd placed on the nightstand. His hand halted when he noticed the scattered stack of photographs next to the lamp. Photographs of men wearing nothing but a cowboy hat and a smile.

Suddenly, he didn't know who he was madder at— Starlet for enticing him or himself for allowing it. Obviously, one cowboy was as good as the other.

"Stay here," he growled as he headed for the door.

Of course, she didn't listen and caught up with him. As soon as they stepped out of the room, he could hear voices shouting above the alarm. Annoyingly familiar voices that caused his shoulders to relax as he slipped the gun into the waistband of his jeans.

"Just give me the right code, Bernie!" Starlet's mother bellowed.

"That was the right code!" Uncle Bernard yelled back. "And if you'd get out of the way—"

"I got it!" Starlet's mother said right before the alarm cut off.

Uncle Bernie laughed. "Even drunk, you're meaner than a junkyard dog, Jaydeen."

"Drunk?" Starlet hurried down the stairs. "After what happened in Atlanta, you promised me that you weren't going to drink tonight."

"Why, there's-s my girl." Jaydeen started forward, but tripped and sprawled out at Starlet's feet.

"Dang it, Mama." Starlet leaned down to help her up. "You have to stop doing this to yourself."

Beckett started to lend a hand when Jed came barreling in the front door all out of breath with his polo shirt ripped on the side. When he saw everyone standing there, he stopped in his tracks and got an exasperated look on his face.

"Where have you been?" Bernie asked. "I thought you were gonna meet me and Jaydeen at Charlie's Bar."

Jed's gaze landed on Beckett for a hard second before it came to rest on Starlet with a very un-cousin-like look. Beckett took off his shirt and slipped it around Starlet's shoulders before stepping in front of her.

"So where were you?" he asked.

Jed blinked. "That ain't any of your business. And what are you doing here? I thought we got rid of you in Charlotte."

"Not hardly. And we're not talking about me. We're talking about you completely ignoring your job—"

"It's okay," Starlet cut in. "That was my fault, not Jed's. I said he could go."

Beckett turned, and it was impossible not to take some of his anger out on her. Especially when the fool woman hadn't even taken the hint and put on his shirt. She stood there with it hooked on her shoulders like a cape, completely unaware that her hard nipples pressed enticingly against the soft fabric of her nightshirt.

Reaching out, he tugged the shirt closed and snapped the top snap. "Which only confirms that you're as ignorant as he is."

Starlet's eyes darkened, and her jaw set. "I guess you're back to being the arrogant, know-it-all Cates brother." She tugged open the snap and tossed the shirt in his face. "Thanks for the help, Becky, but I think my ignorant family and I can handle things from here."

It was only a nickname. And not even a very inventive one. But there was something about the way Starlet said it that could really piss Beckett off. So much so that he forgot all about Alejandro and his promise to Brianne and turned to the door. Unfortunately, his sister must've had some kind of sixth sense. He had no more than shoved Jed out of his way when his cell phone rang out with Brianne's ringtone. He thought about not answering it, but then changed his mind. Before he could even say hello, his sister's voice came through the receiver. At least, it sounded vaguely like Brianne.

A demon-possessed Brianne.

"Get your butt home, Beckett Cates, so you can tell Dusty and these stupid doctors that if I'm going to pop a baby out the size of a watermelon, I'm going to need more pain meds!"

Chapter Eight

"I DON'T WANT AN ICE CHIP. I want painkillers!" Bri shoved away the cup of ice her husband had just offered her before grabbing him by the front of his sheriff's uniform. "And stop panting like a fool. I am breathing!"

Starlet watched the jagged peaks of Bri's contraction rise on the monitoring machine and tried not to pass out. She had never been good with pain—her own or other people's. But her dizziness was quickly replaced with annoyance when Beckett spoke.

"After seeing this spectacle, if I were you, Dusty, I'd invest in some contraception."

Bri turned a mean glare on her brother, who was sprawled out on the sleeper chair with his cowboy hat tipped over his eyes. "If you love me, Beckett, you'll get me some painkillers!"

That's all it took for Starlet to head for the door. "I'll do it. I'll get you something for the pain." Except before she could grab the door handle, the contraction eased and her kindhearted friend returned.

"No, Starlet. I'm okay." Bri sent her a weak smile as

she stroked her huge stomach. "That one was just a doozy, is all."

Dusty stopped panting and fell back in his chair. "I'm starting to think that Starlet has the right idea, Brianne. Maybe we should get you something for the pain."

"No! I said I was going to have this baby naturally, and I am. You just can't listen to what I say during a contraction." She reached for his hand. "Promise?"

"Fine." Dusty leaned in and kissed her forehead. "But watching you suffer is one of the hardest things I've ever had to do."

Bri sent him an impish grin. "Harder than jumping out of an airplane?"

"Much harder." He glanced at the monitor and got up from his chair. "I'm going to check with the nurse. The last time she was in here, she said she was calling the doctor, and I'd like to know where the heck he is."

"That was only a few minutes ago, Dusty." Her gaze swept over to Starlet. "But you're right. You should check. And while you're at it, you can call Emmie and tell her that her baby brother is almost here and then stop by the waiting room and let everyone know that I'm doing just fine."

"I wouldn't say that being Jekyll and Hyde is fine, Bri," Beckett said. "I'm more than a little scared to be in the same room with you."

Dusty chuckled as he headed for the door. "I'll be back in just a minute." He glanced at Starlet. "Make sure she breathes."

Starlet really wasn't good at making sure anyone did anything, but she nodded and kept her eye on the monitor. At least, she did until the door swung closed behind Dusty, and Bri immediately started her interrogation.

"So what happened? I can tell by the look on your face that something's up. Is it Alejandro? Did he come back?"

Starlet and Beckett had agreed not to tell Bri about Alejandro painting her wall. A woman in labor had enough to worry about. Unfortunately, Starlet lied about as well as she took charge.

"Alejandro? *Psht.*" She flapped hand. "I'm sure he's long gone after your brother scared him off in Charlotte."

Bri's eyes widened with excitement. "So he did show back up. Where? Did he come to the concert in Atlanta? Follow your tour bus? Break into your house?" The line on the monitor started to climb, but Bri was so worked up about Alejandro that she didn't seem to notice the contraction. "I knew he wouldn't give up," she said as she pushed the button that raised the head of the bed. "The one and only time I met him, he didn't seem like the giving-up type. Now all we need to do is figure out how to take care of him."

Beckett rolled to his feet and sent Starlet an exasperated look. "No one is taking care of anyone. Especially not you."

"Then what are we going to do about him?" Bri asked. "We can't just let him stalk Starlet. Somehow, I don't think he's only after his money."

Starlet had to agree. The words painted on her wall were more than a request for money. They were a threat. A threat that even now caused goose bumps to rise on her arms.

"Maybe we should go to the Feds," Bri continued. "I'd rather go to jail than let anything happen to you, Starlet."

"No one is going to jail." Beckett picked up a blanket from the stack on the shelf and draped it around Starlet's shoulders. After the long night, he should've looked as tired and mussed as Starlet. Instead, he looked as hot as the pictures of the models the escort agency had sent her. With him standing so close, it was hard not to think about what had taken place in her bedroom. Of course, it was just a freak incident brought on by the events of the evening. Hot or not, Beckett wasn't her type. Which didn't explain why her breathing increased and her nipples hardened when his hand accidentally brushed her collarbone.

"What she needs is security around her house." Beckett moved over to the bed and checked his sister's pulse as if he knew what he was doing. "Something I plan to have Brant take up with her manager ASAP." He glanced at Starlet. "Bri's contraction is over, so you can stop panting. You sound like your fat cat right before he threw up all over Brant's new plane. Although the cat didn't get as sick as your mama."

His obvious dislike for her family and pet regulated her breathing. Unfortunately, her nipples stayed as hard as two creek pebbles.

"Hero can't help it if he gets motion sickness. Which is one of the reasons I can't take him on tour. As for Mama, that's exactly what you get for bullying all of us onto the plane."

"I only bullied you, and only to please my demanding sister who was in labor. I didn't realize you wouldn't come without your screwed-up posse."

"They are not—"

"Both of you be quiet," Bri cut in. "The demanding sister in labor wants to talk about something besides cat puke. Let's get back to the subject of Alejandro. I agree that we need to up Starlet's security. In fact, I think she needs a full-time bodyguard."

"If you are thinking what I think you're thinking, you can get it out of your head right now." Beckett moved away from the monitor, and Starlet saw that another contraction had started. But obviously, adrenaline worked better than painkillers, because Bri didn't display any signs of pain besides the slight tightening of her mouth.

"But you told me that you had decided not to sign up for another tour of duty and were considering other options," she said. "Why couldn't you do your considering while you guard Starlet?"

"Not a chance. I'm not a babysitter. Especially for a 'Star Baby.'"

The way he said her uncle's nickname made Starlet want to reach out and slug him. Her annoyance must've shown, because a flash of delight registered in the deep blue of his irises. But before she could come back with a snide remark, the door opened and Olive Washburn slipped in. Or not slipped as much as charged. Olive was a big woman who never did anything subtly or quietly. Something Starlet admired. She had arrived at the hen-house after Starlet and still lived there with the original hens.

"It's shore nice to see my two favorite chicks back together," she said with a broad smile. She winked at Bri. "So how you doin', little missy? That bouncin' baby boy ready to come out yet?"

"Hopefully—" Bri started, but was cut off when Uncle Bernie strutted in.

While her mother and Jed had complained the entire trip to Bramble, her uncle had acted like it was an exciting adventure. He grew even more excited when they walked into the hospital and his eyes landed on Olive. His obvious infatuation didn't surprise Starlet. Aunt Maybelline had been a big woman who liked tattoos and ignoring the law. But while her aunt had been cruel and mean-spirited, beneath Olive's hard exterior was a heart of gold.

Not that she had shown that side to Starlet's uncle.

"There you are, my little tulip bulb," Uncle Bernie said.

"I ain't a tulip bulb," Olive snapped, "and I shore ain't little."

"You're right." Uncle Bernie took off his hat and covered his heart. "You're a big chunk of heaven that I long to immerse myself in."

Starlet might've giggled if Olive's eyes hadn't turned so mean.

"You ain't e-mersin' yourself in anything, Mister. I've had enough losers in my lifetime to know one when I see one. And if you weren't Starlet's uncle, I would've already laid you low." She shook a fist under his nose.

"As delicate as a blossom." Uncle Bernie leaned down and kissed a knuckle, which had Olive huffing and jerking her hand away—but not before she turned a deep shade of pink.

"Enough, Uncle Bernie," Starlet said. "You're embarrassing Olive. Besides, you shouldn't be in here."

Uncle Bernie tipped his hat at Bri. "My apologies to the mother-to-be. May your child be born with a head of hair and brains beneath—because Lord only knows that Jed was born as bald and empty as a cracked egg." He winked at Olive. "I'll see you later, my little tiger lily." Placing his hat on his head, he strutted out the door, sidestepping the cute doctor with the stethoscope around his neck.

"Well, Mrs. Hicks, it looks like you're—" The doctor glanced up from the chart he'd been reading, and his eyes widened. "Star Bentley? *The* Star Bentley?"

Because Beckett was standing there watching, Starlet laid Star Bentley on thick, offering the doctor a dazzling smile and an exaggerated country twang. "Why, that would be me. And you are?"

The doctor held out a hand. "Dr. James Hollister. It is such an honor to meet you, Miss Bentley. I'm a huge fan."

"Well, isn't that sweet." She took his hand and gave it a gentle squeeze. "And please call me Star."

Dr. Hollister looked about ready to pass out from happiness. "Do you think I could get an autograph, Star?" He held out the chart and pen. Starlet had no more than scrawled her name on the bottom when another contraction hit Bri, and she bellowed.

"And after everyone has gotten everyone's autograph, maybe somebody can get this baby out of me!"

With a look of apology, the doctor pulled back the chart and turned to Bri. "Actually, Mrs. Hicks, that's exactly why I'm here. It's time to meet your son."

"Which means that it's time for me to go." Beckett started for the door, but Bri reached out and grabbed his arm.

"Oh, no, you don't." She spoke through clenched teeth. "Not until we get Starlet's situation settled. You promised, Beckett."

"I promised to keep her safe last night." He held a hand out to Starlet. "And as you can see, she's safe and sound. Now, if you'll excuse me, Ms. Hyde"—he unclenched her fingers from his arm—"I'll go get your husband and wait for the arrival of my nephew in the waiting room with the rest of the family."

While Bri loudly verbalized her displeasure, he walked to the door and pulled it open. Seeing her chance for escape, Starlet offered Bri a weak smile and "Luv you" before she scurried out ahead of him.

"You really are a chicken, aren't you?" Beckett said as soon as they stepped into the hallway.

"You should talk. You couldn't wait to get out of there."

"Only because I didn't want to make any promises I have no intentions of keeping." He waved a hand at Dusty, who had just stepped out of the waiting room. "It's time, big daddy." Dusty halted in his tracks for only a split second before he sprinted down the hall and into the room with his hollering wife.

Starlet stared at the closed door. "She's going to be okay, right?"

"Of course, she's going to be okay. Don't you remember how loudly Brant's wife, Elizabeth, yelled when she delivered Bobby?"

Starlet smiled. "She did yell pretty loudly. Especially for a soft-spoken librarian." She glanced at him. "I'm surprised you remember that I was at the hospital for Bobby's birth. You never once acknowledged me."

He smoothed back the lock of hair on his forehead before pulling on his hat. "When you have my entire family twisted around your little finger, why would you care if I acknowledge you?"

"You're right. I don't."

From beneath the brim of his hat, his blue eyes were uncomfortably direct. "And I think you're lying. I think you want everyone twisted around your little finger, Miss Bentley, and you're willing to do whatever it takes to achieve that—playing the sweet, innocent victim for my

family or the sweet, little ol' country girl for your fans.
And people like the good doctor fall for your act hook,
line, and sinker." He pointed a finger at his chest. "Well,
I'm not falling for it, Star Baby. You can manipulate the
hell out of other people, but you're not going to manipulate me. I've got better things to do with my time."

He turned on a boot heel and headed down the hospital
corridor while Starlet struggled to find words to deny his
accusation. But she couldn't find a one. Probably because
Beckett was right. She was a fraud. A skinny, blond,
green-eyed fraud who had manipulated her fans into loving someone who didn't exist. Unfortunately, there was no
way out of the charade now. Starlet Brubaker had disappeared. And if Star Bentley did, too, there would be nothing left.

Nothing at all.

Chapter Nine

AFTER TWENTY-FOUR YEARS, THE office chair still squeaked. The framed map of Texas still hung at a lopsided angle, no matter how many times you straightened it. And the air conditioner still wheezed like an old woman on an incline. But the view from the window was the prettiest sight Mayor Harley Sutter had ever seen.

When seated behind the hundred-year-old desk in his town hall office, Harley could see almost all of Main Street. In the distance, the sign in front of Bootlegger's Bar advertised half-off beer at happy hour. Across the street, the First Baptist Church advertised Vacation Bible School. Next door to the church, the American and Texas flags flapped over the pitched roof of the library. And to the right of the library, Mickey Owens maneuvered his John Deere lawn mower around the flower beds of the gazebo in Confederate Park, lifting his hand in greeting to Josephine, who was just slipping in the back door of Josephine's Diner.

This early in the morning, the pink caboose of a diner was a good hour away from opening its doors, but

Josephine always let Harley in early so they could chat while she cranked up the burners on the stove and started the homemade biscuits. When Rachel Dean arrived, Harley would move to his regular stool at the counter and enjoy his usual breakfast of two over easy eggs, three sausage links, and a short stack of pancakes. But today he might bypass breakfast at the diner and drive the extra ten miles to the truck stop. Harley was tired of hearing the townsfolk throw out suggestions of what he could do once he retired. As if he hadn't already investigated all his options and found nothing appealing.

Fishing was a lonely business for a person who enjoyed socializing as much as he did. Model trains were just as boring. And with twelve years in the military, he'd gotten his fair share of traveling. Which was exactly why he wasn't looking forward to Election Day. But he had little choice in the matter. At sixty-six, he was well past his prime. Or at least well past the ability to learn newfangled technology.

He glanced over at the laptop that sat on his desk. A laptop Hope Lomax had bought him for his birthday the year before. The sleek, silver computer looked completely out of place on the old, scarred desk. As out of place as Harley felt in the world of technology. After hours of trying to figure out how to navigate on the dang computer, he'd given up and left all the e-mailing and social networking to Hope. Which was just another reason that she would make a darned fine mayor.

The click of boots against tile floor had Harley pulling his feet off the desk and sitting up with a squeak of rusty springs. Kenny Gene appeared in the doorway, his mirrored sunglasses identical to the ones worn by Sheriff

Dusty Hicks. Unfortunately, his law-enforcement skills didn't even come close.

"Hey there, Harley," Kenny said as he strode into the room, the multitude of gadgets he had attached to his belt jangling. "I was wonderin' if you had a key to the gun cabinet in the sheriff's office. Cora Lee said she couldn't find it, and since Dusty is off in Lubbock baby birthin', I figure there better be one armed officer of the law to keep Bramble safe."

Anyone who knew Kenny Gene knew that Bramble would be much safer if he wasn't armed. And spending most of his life as a politician, Harley had learned the skill of beating around the bush.

"The key? Hmm? Well, it must be around here somewhere." He pulled open a desk drawer and pretended to look inside as Kenny continued.

"Dusty was shore riled up. For a man who don't like me usin' the si-reen, he used it quick enough when he got the news that Brianne was in labor." Kenny picked up the motor home magazine Rossie Owens had dropped by. "So are you gonna buy one of them big Winnie-Bagos when you retire, Harley, and travel around the country like Tyler's daddy and mama? If I was you, I'd get me one with a toy hauler. That way you could buy a motorbike to go with it." He pointed a finger. "Hey, maybe Colt would give you a good deal on one of his custom choppers."

Harley shook his head and opened the next drawer. "I've never been one to go for motorbikes."

"Four-wheelers?"

"Nope."

"What about that bicycle you used to ride around when you was gettin' in shape for becomin' our next governor?"

"It's long gone. When I realized that I could never

leave Bramble, I sold it to Jesse Cates for twenty dollars." He opened another drawer, wondering if he should just give Kenny the key to get rid of him. He wasn't in the mood to listen to his nonstop chatter today.

"Well, I guess you'll have plenty of time to figure out what you want to do." Kenny played with the handcuffs on his belt. "Seein' as how you won't have to come into work ever again, you could spend all day thinkin' about it in that big, old house your granddaddy left you." He closed the handcuff around his wrist with a click. "And I guess you heard about the bang-up retirement party the Ladies' Club is plannin' on throwin' you. Josephine is gonna make you a big ol' armadillo cake with candles for every year you was mayor, and Wilbur's band is plannin' on playin' 'For He's a Jolly Good—'"

Harley slammed the drawer closed with a bang. "I don't want a retirement party," he snapped. Since he had never raised his voice for more than quieting down a town meeting, Kenny froze with the handcuff still cuffed to his wrist. He stared at Harley with those mirrored lenses. In them, Harley saw exactly what he was—a man who had reached the end of his career and wasn't willing to accept it. It wasn't Kenny's fault that he was scared.

Once the thought popped into his head, Harley realized it was the truth. He *was* scared of giving up a position he'd held for more than twenty years. Scared of having nothing to do but sit in his old house watching *The Price Is Right* and doing crossword puzzles. And scared of becoming useless to the people of a town he loved.

It was a funny thing. But now that he had finally acknowledged his fears, they didn't seem quite as insurmountable. And hadn't a great Texan once said, "There is nothing to fear but fear itself"? Or if it wasn't a Texan who had said it, it should've been. Texans weren't ones to cower in the corner, waiting for the bomb to drop. Being a Texan by birth, it was time for Harley to quit feeling sorry for himself and accept the fact that Hope Lomax was the best choice for Bramble. She was strong, dedicated, and smart enough to figure out technology.

"I'm sorry, Kenny Gene," he said. "I guess I'm just not myself until I've had my first cup of Josephine's coffee. I appreciate Cindy Lynn and the Ladies' Club puttin' together a retirement party for me."

"It won't be Cindy Lynn puttin' it together," Kenny said. "Now that she's throwin' her hat into the ring for mayor, she don't have time for party plannin'."

Harley almost fell out of his chair. "Cindy is runnin' for mayor? Since when?"

"Twyla heard it from Darla, and Darla heard it straight from the horse's mouth. I went over just this mornin' and found Cindy in the garage makin' signs to put up around town. She sure got upset when I asked her why Ed wasn't makin' them for her, seein' as he's so handy with a hammer. In fact, she hurried me off so quickly I didn't even get a chance to talk with him about his fishin' trip."

"Well, I shore hate to see that girl waste her time," Harley said. "Everyone knows that Hope is going to be the next mayor of Bramble."

"Not now that she's havin' twins." Kenny tugged on the handcuffs.

"Twins! What do you mean twins?"

"You didn't hear that Hope is pregnant with twins? That's why she can't be mayor." Kenny shook his head. "You need to get out more, Harley."

Obviously, Kenny was right. Harley had been so busy feeling sorry for himself that he hadn't paid attention to the most important part of his job—listening to town gossip.

"Here they are." Kenny reached in the drawer Harley had just opened and held up the ring of spare keys triumphantly. "Although it's gonna take me a month of Sundays to figure out which one goes to the gun cabinet."

Figuring that Kenny was right, Harley decided to let him take the keys. Dusty would be back before Kenny found the right one. And his next words proved it.

"And I shore hope an extra pair of handcuff keys are in here." Kenny tugged on the handcuffs still attached to his belt and wrist.

"I'd look for those first," Harley said as he got to his feet. "But for now, I need to get back to work."

Forgetting about the handcuffs, Kenny flashed a grin. "I'm gonna stop by the beauty salon and tell Twyla that I get to carry a loaded gun."

"Give Twyla my love."

"Will do," Kenny said before he disappeared out the door.

Once he was gone, Harley sat down in his chair, more than a little overwhelmed by all the information Kenny had given him. Hope wasn't running for mayor. And Cindy Lynn was.

Harley shook his head. He liked Cindy Lynn, but he couldn't let her become the next mayor of Bramble. A mayor had to be calm and levelheaded. Not flighty and the worst gossip in town. And if Hope wasn't running, the best person for the job was...

He looked at the laptop and smiled. If Rachel Dean

could learn how to use Josephine's newfangled cash register, Harley could learn how to use a computer. All he had to do was buck up and take technology by the horns.

Two hours later, Harley felt like he'd been gored to death. He had gotten the darned laptop turned on but didn't have a clue how to use the touch pad at the bottom and get the little arrow to land on what he wanted. Frustrated, he flopped back in his chair and stared out the window. A stranger walked by. A stranger wearing western duds that looked like they were straight off the rack. Since no stranger had ever arrived in Bramble without being greeted by the mayor, Harley got up and headed for the door.

The man was halfway down the street by the time Harley came hustling out and called to him. "Hey there! You new in town?"

The man stopped suddenly and slowly turned. When he saw Harley, he cleared his throat like he was about to make a speech. As it turned out, that's exactly what he did.

"Dammit straight, I am," he said in a twangy accent that Harley had never heard before in his life. "I'm a rodeo cowboy straight from Big D itself." He whipped off his brand-spanking new hat and slapped it against his leg, revealing a handsome face and a big toothy smile. "I thought I'd stop by this little town and check out your bulls. I love a good bull ride."

Harley squinted at the young man. "Well, we don't have a lot of bulls, but Lowell's got a couple wild horses he'd probably let you ride if you asked."

The man seemed to be stunned by the offer. He stopped flapping his mouth and stared at Harley as if he couldn't quite believe his ears. His response just reaffirmed Harley's belief that a big city didn't hold a candle to a small town.

"Come on, son." Harley hooked an arm around the man's shoulders. "I'll drive you over to Lowell's myself."

"Uhh..." the man started, but Harley cut him off.

"No need to say thanks. Here in Bramble, we believe in welcomin' folks with open arms."

As he walked the cowboy to his truck, Harley couldn't help feeling a little bit proud. He might not be able to work a computer, but he could still help out a stranger. And that's exactly what a good mayor should do.

Chapter Ten

THE FARM WAS SMALL but well cared for. The house and barn looked freshly painted, the weeds had been cut back, and the garden thrived. A man was working amid the leafy plants and vines, his shoulders hunched as he hoed his way down the even rows. When Beckett pulled into the dirt drive, he stopped working and rested his weight on the handle of the hoe, his eyes shielded by a battered straw cowboy hat.

This was the fifth stop Beckett had made since returning to the States. The first three had taken place on weekend furloughs while he had still been at Camp Lejeune. The fourth, right after he'd been discharged, on his way to check on Starlet. After this, he had only one more.

He thought they would get easier, but as he reached for the door handle, his hand shook and his throat seized up. And once he stepped down from the monster truck his brother Billy had loaned him, he had trouble keeping his knees from buckling. He pulled off his cowboy hat, and the man in the garden straightened, his hold on the hoe more like a tight grip.

Beckett swallowed the bile that rose to his throat. "Mr.

Monroe?" The man continued to stare at him. "I'm Beckett Cates. I was stationed in Afghanistan with your son."

Still, the man said nothing.

"Sir, I wanted to stop by to offer my condolences. As far as I'm concerned, Sergeant Monroe was the best sergeant in the marines. He loved his job, and he loved his country."

The hoe dropped to the ground, scaring the cat that had been snoozing beneath an overgrown tomato plant. In a rustle of leaves, the cat streaked toward the house, disappearing beneath the front porch steps. Mr. Monroe watched it before turning to Beckett.

"You knew my Thomas?"

Beckett nodded.

Mr. Monroe picked up the hoe and stepped closer, moving much too slowly for a man no older than Beckett's own father. "So you were there with him?" When Beckett nodded, he squinted out at an open field for a moment before voicing his next question. "Did he suffer?"

The image that Beckett had been struggling to erase filled his vision, and for a moment, he thought he might be sick. Instead, he took a deep breath and forced the words from his closing throat. "No, sir. He didn't have time to be scared or suffer." He paused. "The IED exploded without warning."

Mr. Monroe leaned heavily on the hoe as if legs couldn't hold him up anymore. Beckett knew how he felt. "Good," he whispered. "I couldn't stand the thought of my boy suffering."

Before Beckett could find his next words, a screen door slammed, drawing their attention to the house. A slender woman stood on the porch, one hand on her hip and the other holding a dish towel.

"Who is that, Joshua? Why don't you two get out of the heat and come in for iced tea."

The man became instantly alert and pinned on the kind of practiced smile Beckett had been giving to his family. "I already offered, Cathy," he yelled back, "but it seems the young man's just stopped for directions." When he looked back at Beckett, the smile was still intact, but the eyes beneath the brim of the hat were pain-filled. "It was honorable of you to stop by, son, but it's a little too soon for my wife."

Feeling anything but honorable, Beckett nodded and pulled the folded check from his back pocket. He held out his hand and pressed it into Mr. Monroe's palm. The man's eyes registered confusion for a brief second before he glanced back at the house and discretely slipped the check into the pocket of his overalls. He waited until Beckett got back in the truck before he moved closer to the open window and asked, "What is it?"

It took a moment for Beckett to find the right words. "A plea for forgiveness."

After leaving the Monroes', Beckett didn't know where to go. Since Brianne and her son, Bryson, had been discharged from the hospital, he had planned on following his parents back to Dogwood. But his daddy would want answers, and the last thing Beckett wanted to talk about was his time in the marines. Which eliminated his brothers' homes as well. Brianne was the only one who knew when to leave well enough alone. But Beckett wasn't about to butt his nose into a new family. What he really needed was a drink. And since he knew of only one bar in the vicinity, he headed for it.

On a Monday night, Bootlegger's was almost empty. Within seconds of Beckett sitting down, the bartender came over and took his order.

"Patrón," Beckett said. "And bring the bottle."

While he waited for his drink, he looked around. There seemed to be some kind of entertainment going on at the very end of the bar. Deputy Kenny Gene and three other men huddled around something that held their attention.

"Why, that is just like magic," one of the men said. "I could've swore that peanut was under that middle walnut shell."

"Not magic," a voice Beckett recognized instantly answered. "The hands are just quicker than the eye... unless you have a quick eye."

"Being a law-enforcement officer," Kenny Gene said, "my eye is lightnin' fast. Let me have a try."

Uncle Bernie chuckled. "Since I've never been one to argue with the law, Deputy, step right up. Just set your five dollars down there on the bar."

The men shifted places so Kenny could get closer. In doing so, they revealed Starlet's grinning uncle perched on a bar stool like an elf in Santa's workshop. Once the money was down, Uncle Bernie held up the peanut and showed it to everyone before placing it under one of the three walnut shells on the bar.

"Watch closely, gentlemen." He slid the shells around and then leaned back. "Make your choice, Deputy Kenny." Kenny Gene took his good sweet time before lifting the first one. Of course, the peanut wasn't there. "Sorry, my man." Uncle Bernie picked up the money and shoved it into the breast pocket of his western jacket. "Better luck next time."

"You sure it's luck?" Beckett asked as the bartender set down the bottle of tequila and a shot glass.

Uncle Bernie looked over, and his smile got twice as big. "Pardon me, gentlemen, but a friend has just arrived who looks like he needs someone to share with." The men seemed thoroughly disappointed until he added, "Feel free to keep my nuts and continue to play." He jumped down from his stool. Once he reached Beckett, he took a seat next to him and waved at the bartender. "Another shot glass."

Beckett poured himself a shot and downed it in one swallow.

"Ahh," Bernie said as he accepted the glass from the bartender, "you're not lookin' to savor. Just lookin' for a little relief from life's tragedies." He poured himself a shot and took a sip, wrinkling his nose. "So tell me, my friend, what tragedy has left you with a hollow space that you think alcohol can fill—an unobtainable goal? A broken heart? Or death and taxes?"

It was surprising how accurate Starlet's uncle's words were. Beckett did have a space that needed filling. And tequila might not fill it, but it could numb it enough to lessen the pain. He downed another shot before he answered. "All but taxes. What brings you here? I thought Starlet and her entourage were staying at Miss Hattie's before heading back to Nashville."

"We are, but I'm a firm believer in the old adage that 'absence makes the heart grow fonder.' "

Beckett chuckled. "I guess Olive gave you the shaft."

Bernie grinned. "More like kicked me out and locked the door. That one is quite a sassy pants."

"I'm surprised Starlet didn't let you back in."

"She would've if I'd caused a ruckus. Star Baby does take good care of me. Although I can't figure out why she bothers." He stared down into his shot glass of tequila. "I didn't make her life an easy one. Not that I abused her like my ornery wife, but I didn't stand up for her either."

The word "abused" didn't sit well with Beckett. Since his brothers doted on Starlet, he had always thought of her as a manipulative, spoiled brat. But now he realized that Starlet had had a life before the henhouse. And it didn't sound like it had been an easy one.

"What kind of abuse?" he asked.

Bernie pushed his shot glass away. "You mind if I order something else? Strong spirits no longer agree with me." He waved a hand at the bartender. "A glass of your best bubbly, my man." When the bartender acknowledged the order with a nod, Bernie returned to the question. "Not physical—although Maybelline could give you some pretty good swats if she took a notion. But with Starlet, it was more snide remarks about her looks and her ability. I think Maybelline was jealous that Starlet was prettier and more accomplished." He shook his head. "Not to mention sweeter. Star Baby took all the verbal abuse in stride. I can't remember her ever saying one mean word to her aunt. She took it, and then one day, she was gone." He smiled. "Just like Cinderella, she finally got her castle."

The bottle of champagne arrived, and Beckett watched as the bartender popped the cork and poured a glass. Since Bernie was quite the con man, it would be easy to discount his Cinderella story. But for some reason, Beckett believed it. Not that it changed the fact that Starlet had manipulated her way into his family, but he now understood why she had.

Bernie lifted his glass. "To the hens and your brother for giving Starlet her dream. And to my new love, Olive Washburn. With any luck, in the next few days, she'll succumb to my charm."

Beckett started to lift his shot glass when Bernie's

words registered. "The next few days? I thought you were headed back to Nashville tomorrow."

"Nope. Starlet has decided to stay longer."

"Damn it!" He pulled out his wallet and threw some money on the bar. "Starlet is supposed to go back to Nashville, where Kari has hired more bodyguards and upped the security around her mansion, not stay in a house that Alejandro knows like the back of his hand."

"Alejandro?" Bernie looked over at him. "So you don't think that the kidnapper was some overenthusiastic fan, I take it?" When Beckett didn't answer, his smile finally dropped. "I was afraid of that. 'Course, I don't know what we'll do about it. For some reason, this time, Star Baby seems set on doing what she wants. She's even taken to ignoring the she-devil's calls."

Beckett didn't know the reason either, but he was going to find out.

"I'm headed out to the henhouse," he said as he pulled on his cowboy hat. "You coming?"

"Nope." Bernie tapped the rim of his champagne glass. "Women like Olive are similar to a fine champagne. A man should never jump in and start guzzling. Instead, you should let them sit for a bit and enjoy the fizzle."

Miss Hattie's Henhouse was located a good fifty miles from Bramble. Having once been the most notorious whorehouse in Texas, it made sense that it was located close enough to civilization to be profitable but far enough away to be ignored by the law and prudish citizens. Upon first seeing Miss Hattie's, Beckett had understood Brant's and Beau's infatuation with the house. Sitting amid miles upon miles of mesquite, the large farmhouse stood out like an oasis in a dry, barren desert. The cottonwoods were huge and shady, the porch wide and welcoming. Which explained why his brothers and the old "hens" who lived there had been able to turn it into a popular bed-and-breakfast.

Although it didn't look that popular tonight. When Beckett pulled up in the circular drive, the house was dark and quiet—he glanced at his watch—which made sense, considering that it was close to midnight. If he hadn't worked himself into a fine lather, he might've waited until morning to yell at Starlet. But he was pissed, and the fact that the front door wasn't even locked made him that much angrier.

When Starlet had lived there, she'd slept in a room on the main level with the rest of the hens. But somehow Beckett didn't think that was where she'd be sleeping tonight. There was only one room that the hens would think fit for the sweetheart of country music.

Miss Hattie's.

Taking the massive staircase two steps at a time, he climbed to the second level. On the off chance that he was mistaken, he tapped lightly on the double doors. When a few moments passed and no one answered, he tried the door handle. It too was unlocked, and he didn't hesitate to ease the door open. The room was dark except for the shaft of light that came from the closet and fell over the huge canopied bed where Hero was sleeping next to an open suitcase.

The cat hissed a warning, but Beckett ignored him as he checked the bathroom and then the closet. When they both turned up empty, he pulled out his cell phone with every intention of calling Dusty. The faint music stopped him. Music that seemed to be coming from the closet. He shoved aside the row of dresses to reveal a small door that was cracked open.

Beckett knew about the secret door. In fact, he'd used it on the night of Starlet's going-away party. That night he had followed Starlet through the secret passage from his room to Miss Hattie's. Tonight he went in the opposite direction, following the music down a flight of stairs to an open door at the bottom.

As soon as he stepped inside the room, he knew where he was. The Jungle Room was located in the basement of the henhouse. It had been built as a sort of "break room" for the women who worked there. Now it was more of an entertainment room for the hens and his family. Although the decor looked more like a sixties movie set: shag carpet, furry furniture, plastic plants, lava lamps, and a dance floor complete with mirrored disco ball. Which, not surprisingly, was exactly where he found Starlet.

She stood in the very center of the floor, the tiny dots of light from the disco ball dancing all around her. At first he thought she was practicing some song for her next concert, but then a jazz singer's voice came through the overhead speakers. It sounded nothing like Starlet's sweet country twang.

As the song continued, Starlet started to move. For the first time, Beckett noticed what she had on: a feathery dress that flared out on either side and reached to her knees. With the dress, she wore spiked heels that made her legs look a mile long as she swayed to the beat of the music. Even when she had weighed more than a bushel of apples, she'd been a good dancer. The night of her going-away party, he had watched from the sidelines while one man after the other had swept her across the ballroom floor. Back then, he had been impressed. Now he was more than a little turned on. There was something about

the way she moved that was as seductive as the jazz singer's voice. Something about the way she held her eyes at
half-mast as her arms came out to her sides—

Beckett's eyes widened as the feathers of the dress
parted for a split second and then fluttered back into
place. Suddenly, he realized that it wasn't a dress she was
wearing but two large feather fans. Two large fans that
she proceeded to manipulate around her body in a swirl
of white as she twirled and spun around the dance floor.

Beau had told him about Miss Hattie's infamous fan
dance. The dance had been performed for the very first
time by Miss Hattie Ladue herself right here in this house.
Of course, according to his brother's story, Miss Hattie
had been stark raving naked—

The fans lifted again, and Beckett's heart did a half
gainer and ended up stuck in his throat. He'd definitely
seen skin. Creamy, white skin. He swallowed and, without thought, stepped closer. But Starlet didn't notice. Her
eyes were closed and her head thrown back as if the music
had consumed her.

Beckett wasn't far behind. With each sweep of the
fans, with each flutter of feathers, he became hypno-
tized. He forgot all about his purpose for being there,
but mostly, he forgot all about what had taken place in
Afghanistan. Since the horrific image had been with him
night and day, being without it was like stepping into a
spring of cool, clear water after a hot, dry trek across the
desert. And he was willing to do anything to keep that
image at bay.

Even something really stupid.

Chapter Eleven

THE STRESS OF THE concert tour and being stalked by Alejandro had finally caught up to Starlet. After spending the entire night at the hospital with Bri, she should be soundly sleeping in Miss Hattie's bed. Instead, she had climbed down the stairs to the Jungle Room, stripped naked, and proceeded to dance around like a loon. The really weird part about it was that it felt right. In fact, it felt more right than anything she'd done in a long time.

Maybe it wasn't the fan dance as much as just being back at the henhouse. Walking through the peaceful lilac garden. Eating dinner with the old hens, Minnie, Baby, and Sunshine—and the newer hen, Olive. Or sitting on the front porch watching a Texas sunset stripe the horizon with deep oranges and reds. She had lived with her uncle and aunt for most of her life. But this would always be her home. The first place she had ever felt loved and safe.

At this moment, she needed to feel loved and safe more than she'd ever needed anything. She was scared. Not just scared of Alejandro, but scared of having lost herself—and most important, her music.

In the last couple months, she had used the stress of the tour as an excuse for her writing block. But tonight, in the quiet of Miss Hattie's room, she'd acknowledged the fact that the tour had nothing to do with it. Stress had never affected her songwriting before. Regardless of what was going on around her, music had played in her head constantly. But now there was no melody inside her. No words. Not even a single note. Just deafening silence. And if Starlet Brubaker didn't have her music, she had nothing.

Trying to push down her fear, she slowly swirled around the dance floor to the song that played through the speakers. "Someone to Watch Over Me" was a favorite of the hens. As Starlet twirled on her heels and swept the fans in wide circles around her, she sang along with Ella Fitzgerald. Surprisingly, the words to the song echoed her feelings to a tee. She felt like a little lamb that had been lost in the woods. A lamb that would be "good" to someone who would watch over her.

"How good?"

The deeply spoken words had Starlet stopping so quickly that her body outdistanced her feet. She would've fallen flat on her face if she hadn't dropped one fan and grabbed on to the edge of the piano that sat just off the dance floor. With her entire backside exposed to the room, she hoped that the deep-voiced question had been just a weird fluke brought on by stress, lack of sleep, and too many helpings of Baby's banana cream pie. But she should've known that her luck wasn't that good.

There was the soft click of boot heels on wood flooring, followed by a shift in the air, before the question was repeated. This time right next to her ear.

"How good?"

Starlet might've turned around if Beckett hadn't

stopped so close. So close that she could feel the brush of denim against her bare bottom. She shivered and couldn't help but wonder what part of his blue-jeaned-covered lower body stuck out more than the rest.

"I was just…" she started, but her words trailed off when his warm fingers closed around her waist.

"Dancing?" The brim of his hat came into view and brushed her cheek as he placed his lips on the curve of her shoulder. He took a long sip before lifting his head, his warm breath falling on the wet spot his mouth had just made. "No. I wouldn't call it dancing. Tempting." He kissed the side of her neck. "Seducing." He kissed the edge of her ear. "Driving the most sane man completely crazy."

Crazy? She had driven Beckett crazy? The thought might've made her gloat if she hadn't felt so crazy herself. She had no business standing there letting him kiss her. He didn't even like her. And she certainly didn't like him. And yet she couldn't seem to move as his hand slipped from her waist and curled around her bare hip, bringing her back against his denim-covered hardness.

With the contact, his breath hissed between his teeth, fanning out over her shoulder and breast. Her nipple pebbled, and desire settled heavily inside her. He flexed his hips, and she released the moan that had been sitting at the edge of her throat. But still, she didn't move. She just stood there and let him do what he would. She should've known that what Beckett Cates did wouldn't be like any other man.

After only a second's hesitation, he released her hip and took the fan from her hand. He stepped back, taking the heat with him, before speaking in a soft, raw whisper.

"Bend over."

This was where any sensible girl would turn tail and

head for the hills. But Starlet had never been sensible. Nor able to ignore a plea. And that's what the words were. Not a command, but a plea.

Bending over, she pressed her breasts and stomach against the cool, hard wood of the piano while her fingers spread out on the polished lacquered finish. The anticipation of his first touch caused her nerves to twitch. She didn't know what she expected, but it wasn't the soft, titillating brush of feathers. Starting at one ankle, he slowly worked his way up her leg to the top of her thigh. Then, with only the slightest tickle in the place she wanted him to touch the most, he stroked his way back down before moving to her other leg. When he had her shaky-kneed and panting, he placed the fan between her shoulder blades and swept the feathers down her spine, tickling each buttock with a teasing swirl. Then he repeated the pattern. Leg. Leg. Back. Bottom.

"Spread 'em," he said in a voice that sounded as breathless as she felt.

Lust-loopy and wobbly-kneed, she had to hold on to the piano for support as she slowly slid her feet apart.

The fan tickled the insides of her thighs. "Wider."

She bit down on her lip and moved her feet a few more inches. Then she waited. And waited. And waited. The song had long since ended, and all she could hear was her own labored breathing. One would think that the reprieve would've cooled her down. But the opposite was true. The silence seemed to heighten her desire. Until she wondered if she was going to reach orgasm without being touched at all.

Then it came again. The gentle sweep of feathers. In one long stroke, he swept them down her spine and in between her legs. The sensation seemed almost too wicked—too invasive. She tried to bring her legs together, but he stepped closer and stopped her with the toes of his boots. He stroked her two more times with the fan before he dropped it to the floor.

Placing his hands on her hips, he brought her up against the front of his jeans. There was no mistaking his passion. The bulge beneath his zipper felt hard and mammoth. He slid it back and forth a few times before his fingers took up where the fan had left off, caressing her spine, circling each buttock, and tracing the crevice between the two. When she moaned in frustration, he dipped his fingers between her legs and tested the throbbing nub of her clitoris and the slick heat beneath.

It probably would've taken only a couple strokes to send her skyrocketing into an amazing orgasm, but being the obstinate man he was, Beckett only gave her one teasing stroke before he pulled away.

He bent over her, his hard-on pressing, his lips close to her ear. "Wait for me, Star Baby." She could finally hear his ragged breathing over her own. "Please wait for me."

She waited. Clinging to the piano like a shipwrecked victim to a raft, she listened to the quick pop of a snap, the whisper of his lowering zipper, the soft tear of plastic. Then he was back and something much harder than feathers replaced his fingers. The fit was snug, and he allowed her vaginal walls to adjust before he started to move—a slow withdrawal followed by a deep reseating that had her entire body quivering with need. With each thrust, she could feel the whisper of denim on the inside of her thighs, the flex of bare muscle against her bottom, the pulse of his desire deep inside of her.

While one hand held her in place, the other reached around to stroke her clitoris. He played her like a fine instrument. And with each strum, she became part of his music.

Sweet, beautiful music that filled her head and consumed her body, lifting her higher. And higher. When she thought she couldn't take one more note of ecstasy, her orgasm crashed over her like the crescendo of a hundred-piece orchestra.

In that moment, that one beautiful moment, everything was right in her world.

Which turned out to be a sex-induced hallucination. Because once Beckett groaned out his orgasm and the last little tingles of desire melted away, Starlet was left with nothing but the cold, stark reality of being naked as a jaybird and bent over a piano. Which was wrong. So wrong. Especially with a man who hadn't even stopped to remove his clothes before he'd taken advantage of her.

Okay, so maybe he hadn't taken advantage of her. In fact, she had only herself to blame. Sunshine had warned her about the seductive effects of the fan dance. Obviously, she'd been right. Which meant that Starlet should be the one to apologize. Except it was hard to apologize when you were pinned against a piano like a fly-swatted insect to a window. Beckett was barely standing. His boots still held her feet apart, but his body had slumped over her, his shirt snaps digging in to her spine and his face snuggled between her shoulder and neck.

Starlet cleared her throat, but he didn't move a muscle.

"E-excuse me," she said breathlessly. Not because she was turned on, but because his weight had squeezed all the air out of her lungs and she was having a hard time getting it back. Had the man fallen asleep on her? His breathing did seem nice and even. And was he drooling?

"Excuse me," she tried again, this time a little louder.

There was a tightening of muscles before he lifted his head.

"What?" he said rather grumpily.

What? What did he mean "what"? She might've brought this on herself, but it wasn't like he hadn't enjoyed it. In fact, even now, she felt him harden inside of her. And if he thought they were going for round two, he had another think coming.

"Get off me!"

His breath released in something that sounded a little like a chuckle before he braced his hands on either side of her shoulders and lifted his upper body. Unfortunately, his lower half still pinned her to the piano.

"Are we feeling a little testy?" he asked, his breath falling against the side of her face. For the first time, she noticed that he smelled like her mama did…pretty much all the time.

"You're drunk." She did a weak push-up and found herself cocooned in sculptured muscle and man. And yep, he got even harder. Which caused a heated tingle to course through her body. She might've reconsidered round two if he hadn't spoken.

"Would there be any other explanation for what just happened?"

The tingle quickly fizzled, and she lifted her foot and sank a high heel into the toe of one boot.

"Sonofabitch!" He stepped away from her.

Once free, Starlet straightened on wobbly legs and reached for the fan. With a flick, she opened it and held it in front of her as she edged over to the bar to get her night-shirt. Beckett continued to hop around on the dance floor. With the mirrored reflections of the disco ball glittering around him, he looked like he was doing a bad rendition of the "Cotton-Eye Joe" line dance.

"For someone who is drunk," she said as she slipped on her nightshirt, "you have great balance." She sent him one last disgusted look before she headed for the door that led to the secret stairs.

There was no lock on the door in the closet, so she walked into the bathroom and locked it. Once the door was secured, she took off her nightshirt and turned on the faucet to the claw-foot bathtub. She had just sunk down in the soothing water when the doorknob rattled.

"Open the door," his annoying voice said through the crack.

She ignored it and picked up the bar of soap.

"I mean it, Starlet. Open this door, or I'm going to kick it down."

"Go ahead. But do you really want the hens and guests knowing what a Neanderthal you are? Not to mention a real jerk." She lathered her arm and started to hum. It was the melody that had been playing in her head right before her orgasm. Not the jazz song "Someone to Watch Over Me." Her sudsy hand paused on her shoulder. In fact, it wasn't a song that had ever been published.

It was a new song.

Her new song.

While she sat there stunned, Beckett finally decided to apologize.

"Okay," he yelled through the crack. "I admit it. It was a stupid thing to say. I'm not drunk—at least, not that drunk."

Barely paying attention to his words, Starlet quickly rinsed off and jumped out of the tub.

"But you can't really blame me for what happened," Beckett continued as she pulled the robe off the hook on the back of the door and put it on. "I mean, I show up here to get after you for staying at the henhouse without security, and I find you dancing around in nothing but a feather dress—"

She opened the door and shoved past him. "Fans," she said absently as she raced over to her suitcase and rifled through it. "Feather fans."

"Feather fans—a feather dress? What difference does it make? Do you know what could've happened if Alejandro had found you instead of me?" He moved closer to the bed, his voice taking on a hard edge. But it barely registered. Starlet was too busy dumping out the contents of her suitcase, causing Hero to growl and jump off the bed. When she didn't find a pen and paper, she moved over to the nightstand. But thc only things in those drawers were a bunch of antique sex toys.

"Pen and paper." She pointed a wicked-looking dildo at him. "I need a pen and paper."

Beckett blinked and shook his head as if he couldn't quite believe her. "You need a keeper. Not to mention a security team."

Starlet groaned in frustration before she remembered the notebook she kept in her purse. Her purse. Where was her purse? She found it under the pile of clothes she'd tossed on the bed. Once she found the notebook and a pen, she quickly sat on the bed, sketched out five staff lines, and wrote down the musical notes that were dancing in her head. Although now they weren't dancing as much as sluggishly tiptoeing. And it didn't help that Beckett kept talking.

"If you're not going to listen to me and get better security, I'm going to call Dusty and have him bring in the Feds. I mean it, Starlet. This is crazy."

She jumped up and grabbed his arm, pulling him toward the door. "Okay. I'll get better security first thing in the morning."

"Not better," he stubbornly said. "A good, experienced team with weapons."

"Fine." She pulled open the door. "I'll get an army of Van Dammes carrying Glocks, machetes, and machine guns."

He paused in the doorway. "A machete would be pretty useless—"

"Shut up!" she yelled louder than she had ever yelled in her life.

"Excuse me?" The expression on his face registered surprise mixed with anger before it softened to the know-it-all look. "So you *are* upset about the sex thing."

If she hadn't been in such a hurry to get rid of him, she might've been pissed off about the entire "sex thing." But her music always beat out her ego.

"No. I'm not upset about what happened. Although it was stupidity at its finest and will never happen again." While he looked slightly stunned, she shoved him out the door. "So thanks a bunch and have a safe trip back to Dogwood."

She slammed the door and locked it, then raced back to the notebook and pen. Within fifteen minutes, she had the melody. And within an hour, she had the lyrics to the song. Not just *a* song, but a great song. The type of song that would hit the charts like a tornado at full steam and race straight to the number one spot.

There was only one problem.

When Starlet picked up her guitar and started to sing, she found herself picturing one man. And it wasn't the handsome rodeo cowboy she usually pictured when she sang her love songs.

It was an annoying ex-marine who had a way with feathers.

Chapter Twelve

THE CACOPHONY OF DUDLEY Murdock's hound dogs barking alerted Rachel Dean. Throwing back the covers, she hurried as fast as her bunions would allow to the bathroom, where she quickly removed the sponge rollers from her hair, then did a lightning-fast mouth rinse with Scope. By the time a tap came on the window, she was tucked back in bed with her hands folded over her chest like Old Lady Tucker on the day of her funeral.

The tap came again, and Rachel tried to slow down the beating of her heart. But just the sound of the man softly calling her name was enough to make the fickle muscle thump like the base drum in the Bramble High band.

"Rachel."

She took a deep breath before she slowly climbed out of bed and made her way to the window, smoothing out the wrinkles of her nightgown and wondering too late if she wore her good panties or the ones with the stretched-out elastic. She tugged up the window, and the cool night air drifted in, along with the scent of Old Spice aftershave. A scent she'd become quite partial to. Of course, in her lifetime, she'd been partial to a variety of men's cologne. And look where that had landed her—living all alone in the tiny house she grew up in without a husband or a child.

Which might've explained her rather snide reception.

"Well, if it isn't Rossie Owens. Now, what brings you out on this pretty June night?"

"Would you step out of the way and let me in, woman? I'm gettin' eaten up by mosquitoes." He scratched at his arm to prove it. "And I don't know why I can't just enter through the front door like any normal person."

She glanced over at the alarm clock on her nightstand. "Normal people come callin' at twelve forty-two at night, do they?"

He huffed out a breath. "What has your tail feathers in a ruffle? You know I don't close down the bar until twelve thirty on weeknights. And I'd come calling at a decent hour on my night off if you'd let me. But you don't want people talkin', so I'm forced to slink over here like a fox in the henhouse whenever I want to see my woman."

The words "my woman" sent a flush of heat spiraling through her body. But at fifty-eight, she'd learned how to control untrustworthy emotions.

"Your woman?" She placed a hand on her hip. "Who said I was your woman?"

"Damn it, Rachel Dean." He took off his cowboy hat and swatted it against his leg. "I might've promised you that when we're in public, I'd treat you like my good friend. But after five years of this craziness"—he waved his hat around—"I figure I've earned the right to call you my woman. Now move out of the way and let me in."

There was something about a man taking the bull

by the horns that had always gotten to Rachel. Without another word, she stepped back and allowed him entry, chuckling under her breath when he had a hard time getting his leg over the windowsill.

"It isn't funny," he grumbled. "One of these nights, I'm going to pull a groin muscle, and you won't be laughing then."

She giggled again, but it was cut short when Rossie captured her in his arms and kissed the daylights out of her. When he pulled back, his dark eyes twinkled in the moonlight. "Darn ornery woman," he mumbled before he kissed her again.

Being the waitress at the only restaurant in Bramble, Texas, Rachel got to hear more than her fair share of gossip. Men liked to gossip about the weather, the price of grain, and their fishing and hunting expertise, while women liked to gossip about the townsfolk, their men, and sex. Because of the latter, Rachel knew that most women her age didn't enjoy sex. Some blamed menopause, while others blamed their oversexed husbands or their hectic lifestyles. At one point in her life, Rachel would've agreed wholeheartedly with them—her first two husbands had made sex more of a chore than fun.

But Rossie Owens had changed all that.

Even after five years of twice-a-week rendezvouses, Rachel couldn't seem to get enough of Rossie's love-making. The man had a slow hand and a heated touch that never failed to send her over the moon. Tonight was no different. Amid soft kisses and gentle caresses, he swept away her nightgown and panties—plus all her reservations—and lowered her down to the mattress.

Thirty minutes later, she was snuggled up next to his

naked body as sated and content as an alley cat after mid-night. The quiet time after was almost as good as the sex. Almost.

"Just when I think it couldn't get any better"—he kissed the top of her head—"it does. I think you're the best-kept secret in Bramble, Texas."

She blushed and swatted his chest. "Go on with you."

"I'm not jokin'. For years, I just thought you were a pretty waitress who was a good conversationalist. If I'd know about the hot woman beneath the apron, I would've tried to get under it much sooner."

The afterglow dimmed, and she lifted her head. "I thought we decided from the beginnin' that we weren't gonna lie to each other. I got plenty of that with my first two husbands. I ain't pretty, Rossie. I got my mama's small eyes and wide mouth and my daddy's big bones and hands." He started to say something, but she held up a big hand. "You don't have to feel sorry for me. I might not be pretty, but I'm a hard worker and an honest woman." She winked. "And a damn good lover."

He chuckled. "That you are." His expression turned serious. "But my mama always told me that beauty was in the eye of the beholder, and when I look at you, Rach, I see a beautiful woman with a heart of gold."

No, her heart wasn't made of gold. Gold was hard, cold, and heavy as a stone. And right now, Rachel's heart felt soft, warm, and light as air. But if she was anything, she was a realist. In the dark, they were just two lonely people looking for a little warmth and comfort. But in the light of day, they were a handsome business owner who had graduated from college and a homely waitress who had barely made it out of high school. Rossie might think he didn't care if the townsfolk knew he was courting her now, but once their secret was out and people started pointing out their differences, he would care. And Rachel wasn't about to go back to watching Jimmy Kimmel and soaking her bunions on Tuesday and Thursday nights.

"Enough of this nonsense," she said as she sat up. "You better get goin'. It's already almost two, and I need to be at Josephine's in just a few hours."

He leaned up and gave her a kiss that brought on a major hot flash. "What about if I stayed until you take your afternoon break? We've never made love in the light of day, and I can't think of anything I'd like more."

Just the thought of her body being displayed in the full light of day cooled Rachel down, and she pulled out of his arms and got to her feet. Grabbing her nightie, she slipped it on, covering breasts and a butt that had as little elasticity as her panties. Once she was covered, she turned back to him.

"You know that I don't take an afternoon break, Rossie."

He released a sigh as he rolled to his feet. "Fine, woman. Then what about Saturday night?" He pulled on his undershorts. "I hired someone to help out Manny on the weekends so I could get here a little earlier."

She shook her head. "Too many folks are up and around on a Saturday night. So who did you hire?"

"The new guy in town. Says his name is Cowboy."

"Real good-lookin' with a bright smile?"

"Can't say how good-lookin' he is. He keeps his hat pulled low and spends most of his time staring at his scuffed boots." He sent her a disgruntled look as he snapped his shirt. "And just what are you doing noticin' another man's looks?"

She flapped a hand at him. "Lord, he's too young for me. And a little too cocky. He told me he was a rodeo cowboy, but Wilma Tate heard that he got thrown off Lowell's wild mustang before he even got a foot in the stirrup."

"Hmm?" Rossie's brow crinkled. "That sure doesn't sound like the Cowboy I hired." He shrugged. "But speaking of Wilma, I heard some gossip tonight at Bootlegger's that you might be interested in. I guess she's decided to jump into the mayoral race."

"I figured it wouldn't be long before she hopped on the bandwagon with Cindy Lynn," she said. "Like Cindy, Wilma has always wanted to be in charge. And now that her husband, Elmer, has sobered up, she's must be lookin' for another cause." She shook her head. "I'm tickled pink that Hope is pregnant with twins, but it shore put a wrench in things."

Rossie pulled up the window. "I wonder how Jenna Jay is taking the news. It can't be easy for her after what happened. It was a crying shame when she lost that baby."

As always, just thinking about Jenna Jay's baby brought back painful memories of Rachel's own loss. Of course, not a day went by that she didn't think about her precious, little Johnny. When she didn't reply, Rossie turned around with sadness brimming in his eyes.

"I'm sorry, Rach. I shouldn't have brought that up"

She shook her head. "I figure God had His reasons. Maybe He knew that I would have enough on my hands just dealing with all the crazy folks in Bramble. Which brings us back to findin' a good person to take over the job of mayor. It certainly can't be Cindy Lynn or Wilma."

"Without Hope, who could we possibly get to run this town the way it should be run?"

Rachel grinned widely before she remembered the gap between her front teeth and pulled her lips together. "What about you?"

"Me?"

"Of course, you. You've lived in this town for most of your life. You own a successful business. You're smart as a whip. Not to mention, handsome as any politician in Texas."

An arrogant grin spread over his face. "You think I'm handsome, do you?" He leaned over and kissed her. A gentle, slow kiss that made her stomach feel like the Fourth of July. When he pulled back, he was smiling. "Okay."

Stunned by the kiss, she didn't have a clue what he was talking about. "Okay what?"

"Okay, I'll run for mayor. But on one condition— no make that two, being that the mayor of Bramble is a tough job."

She shook her head. "Fine. What are your conditions?"

Before he answered, he lifted a leg over the sill and climbed out. When he was standing outside the window, he leaned in and held up a finger. "One, you make love to me in the light of day so I can see that gorgeous body of yours." He grinned impishly and held up another finger. "And two, you marry me."

Chapter Thirteen

BECKETT STARED OUT THE window of his brother's sprawling mansion. Not at his niece and nephew who frolicked in the swimming pool. Nor at his sister-in-law Shirlene who lounged in a chair next to the pool. Nor at the miles of mesquite that surrounded the property. No, Beckett might be staring out the window, but he wasn't seeing. Instead, his mind was replaying over and over again the X-rated scene from the night before. A scene complete with a baby grand piano, a feather fan, and a sweet, little ass so tempting that he—

"Hey! Are you two knuckleheads listening to me?"

Beckett turned from the window and looked at his next-to-oldest brother. Billy looked like he had been rode hard and put away wet. There were dark circles beneath his eyes, and his thick hair stuck up in tufts. Of course, he looked no better than Beau, who sat in the chair across from Beckett doing his own staring out the window.

"Yes, I'm listening," Beckett said. "You were talking about Jesse failing geometry and having to take summer school."

"Not just failing geometry, but his entire attitude about school." Billy ran his hand through his mussed hair. "The kid doesn't understand the importance of education. He's convinced that he'll do just fine without it. And the sad truth is that he probably will." He shook his head. "Did you realize that he has more than twenty thousand dollars saved up in his bank account? All from the wheeling and dealing he's done with the townsfolk."

Damn. That was twice as much as Beckett had left in his.

Billy released a sigh and leaned back on the edge of his desk. "So you think I should tan the kid's hide?"

Beckett shrugged. "Would it help?"

"No. It would probably only make Jesse run off for good. Besides, I doubt I could bring myself to do it. He's suffered enough pain in his lifetime, what with all the foster homes he lived in." He looked at Beau. "What do you think, Beau?"

His brother turned from the window, a vacant look in his eyes. "I thought she was over losing the baby." Both Beckett and Billy exchanged looks. Obviously, Beau hadn't been listening to their conversation. And Beckett couldn't blame him when he had his own problems to deal with. Jenna Jay had been six months' pregnant when the doctors discovered that something was wrong. The baby had died in the womb, and close to two years later, it looked as if Jenna still hadn't come to terms with it.

Or Beau for that matter.

"I thought things were better," Beau said. "Not normal, but better. And then suddenly she starts pulling away from my touch, and she doesn't want sex anymore. The other night I walked in on her undressing, and by her reaction, you would've thought that I was some kind of stranger."

"It takes time," Beckett said.

"Bullshit!" Beau got to his feet. "Something isn't right. And I'm going to figure out what." He headed for the door. "I'll talk with you later."

When he was gone, Billy ran a hand through his hair. "Damn, I didn't even think about the baby when I was spouting off about Jesse. It was almost like I was thumbing my kids beneath Beau's nose. Maybe I should go after him."

"I'd wait. You don't want to get in the middle of his marital problems."

Billy released his breath. "You're right. For now, I need to concentrate on getting Jesse through summer school. I won't have my son becoming a high school dropout. Slate has offered to work with him this summer, in hopes that football might motivate him to go to class. But Shirlene is convinced that he needs a tutor."

"Good luck with that." Beckett picked up the *Field & Stream* magazine on the end table. "It would have to be one hell of a tutor to get Jesse to learn if he doesn't want to. I tutored in high school, and it was hard enough teaching the kids who wanted to learn." He leafed through the magazine but found nothing of interest. Unlike Billy, Beckett wasn't much of the outdoors type. He'd never been any good at killing things.

Until Afghanistan.

The thought had him closing the magazine. He would've dropped it back down on the table if another magazine hadn't caught his attention. It was one of those celebrity magazines—the kind that divulged the dirty secrets of the rich and famous. And damned if there wasn't a picture of Starlet on the cover. Not a full-page picture—one of the Kardashians had claimed the headline. No, this was just a small corner picture of Starlet cuddled up against some dopey-looking cowboy with a championship belt buckle the size of a standard-issue canteen.

Star Bentley Hired Me to Lure a Wife Away from her Husband.

The caption was ridiculous. And there was little doubt that the story would be too. Which didn't explain why he exchanged magazines and pulled the pair of reading glasses from his pocket. He got through only the first paragraph of the article before Billy stopped him.

"That's it!"

He glanced up to find his brother looking like he'd just reeled in a ten-pound trout. His eyes sparkled over a wide grin as he pointed a finger at Beckett.

"You can tutor Jesse."

"Oh, no." Beckett went back to the article. "I'm not tutoring a delinquent."

"Why the hell not?" Billy walked over and jerked the magazine away from him. "Since you quit the marines, you don't have anything better to do. And Jesse's not a delinquent. He's just a little ornery."

"Ornery?" Beckett took off his glasses and got to his feet. "Dusty told me that besides ditching class, he stole the statue of the school mascot and placed it on top of the gazebo in Confederate Park. He has more than a few speeding tickets. And he almost burned down the First Baptist when he snuck a cigarette while playing a shepherd in the Christmas live nativity scene. If that's not a delinquent, I don't know what is." He made a grab for the magazine, but Billy tucked it behind his back.

"I'll give you the school mascot thing," he said, "but he hasn't gotten a ticket in more than a year."

"Only because you took his driving privileges away."

Billy's face fell. "There is some truth to that, but we've all gotten our fair share of speeding tickets—well, maybe not you, Beck—but the rest of us have. And as for the smoking, that was just a middle school phase he was going through. He felt real bad about what happened and didn't argue for a second when I made him take money out of his account and replace the burned-down nativity stable. In fact, he shopped all over the Internet until he found a used one complete with a pulley to hoist Kenny Gene when he plays the Angel of the Lord."

"I'll still have to pass on the tutoring." Beckett held out his hand. "Now, if you'll give me back the magazine, I'm going to go join Shirlene and the kids by the pool."

Billy released his breath. "You're probably right. A tutor isn't going to change Jesse's mind. I'm beginning to think that nothing will." He went to hand over the magazine, but Beckett had no more than closed his hand around the glossy cover when his brother jerked it back. "An ex-marine doesn't want some girlie magazine to read. I just got a new *Popular Science*—"

"I want that one!" Beckett's words came out sounding just a little too desperate. He realized his mistake the second the competitive sparkle entered Billy's eyes. Being the youngest of four brothers, it was a sparkle Beckett had seen more times than he could count.

"This magazine?" Billy waved it in front of his nose.

Beckett made a grab for it, and the brotherly tussle

began. Usually, it ended with Beckett facedown on the ground, getting the Cates brothers' signature Russian Noggin Rub. But that was when Beckett was a good twenty pounds lighter, and when he hadn't spent months in self-defense training—honing his reflexes to stay alive. Billy had no more than curled an arm around his neck to pull him into a headlock before Beckett had his brother facedown on the desk with his hand pinned behind his back.

But instead of giving him a noggin rub, he released him and quickly stepped away. It took Billy a little longer to move. Slowly, he straightened and cracked his neck. When he turned, his eyes held surprise, pride, and humor.

"Why did you wimp out, Beck?" he said with a contagious grin. "You had me."

Beckett might've laughed with relief if he hadn't noticed the red welt on his brother's cheek where it had hit the desk.

"I'm sorry, Billy. Are you okay?"

Within seconds, Billy had his head tipped back with laughter. "For being such a badass marine, you are still a marshmallow inside." He thumped Beckett on the shoulder before he handed him the magazine and pushed him toward the door. "Of course, being that you're my little brother, I went easy on you. If it had been a real contest, there's no doubt who would've won."

Beckett sat at Billy and Shirlene's dining room table, picking at his enchiladas and offering up one-word replies to their questions about his time in the military. The magazine article had made him bad company—or maybe it was the pictures that had done it. He knew that most of the story was a pile of crap made up just to sell copies, but six different pictures of Starlet with rodeo cowboys meant there was some grain of truth in it. He didn't know what annoyed him more. Starlet's awestruck face as she looked at the bull riders. Or the bull riders' awestruck faces as they looked at Starlet.

It was like a mutual admiration club. And what really bothered him was that not once had she ever given him a look even close to the ones she gave the cowboys. Not even after he'd given her an amazing orgasm.

Not that he knew for certain that he had given her an amazing orgasm. He was just basing it off his orgasm... which had been pretty damned amazing. But if hers had been all that special, then why had she kicked him out of her room without a backward glance?

And why the hell had he let her?

"I think you got a little too much sun this afternoon, Beckett." Shirlene cut into his thoughts. "Your face is as red as Cristina's beet salad."

"I guess I forgot to wear sunscreen," he hedged as he picked up his glass of iced tea and took a few deep gulps to try to cool his anger.

"That's just like what happened to Daddy when he took Mommy on a trip to Hawaii," his five-year-old niece, Adeline, said around a mouthful of chicken enchilada. "'Cept he got a bad burn on his wee-wee."

Billy choked and then stared at his daughter in horror. "Where did you hear that, Addie?"

Adeline looked at Shirlene. "I heard Mommy telling Auntie Hope that you got a real bad blister. But, Daddy, how did you get burned through your swimmin' trunks?"

While Beckett hid his laughter behind his napkin, Billy turned to his wife. "You told Hope about that?"

She shrugged. "Now, honey, you have to admit it was kind of funny. And I didn't have a clue Addie was listening in." She looked at her daughter. "Eavesdropping is not becoming of a lady."

"Then how come you do it when Dad's secretary calls?" Brody, their eight-year-old son piped up. Brody had a face like an angel and a voice like a thirty-year-old chain smoker—deep and gravelly.

Billy's eyes widened as he stared at his wife. "You're worried about Delia? She's fifty with grandkids."

"And has a Facebook page filled with half-naked cowboys who suspiciously resemble you."

A teasing light entered his brother's eyes. "Are you jealous, Shirley Girl?"

Shirlene sent him an exasperated look before pointing her fork at him. "Hush up and eat your supper before it gets cold."

Billy looked like he was about to continue his teasing when the front door slammed, and a sweaty-looking Jesse appeared. It had been a while since Beckett had seen Jesse. The kid had added at least five inches in height, but he was still whipcord thin.

"I ain't doin' it!" He threw the football helmet he carried to the floor with a clatter. "I don't care what you say. I'm not going to run around on a field while eleven assholes try to squash me like a cockroach."

"Jesse!" Billy got to his feet. "You'll watch your mouth."

"Watch my mouth! Watch my manners! Watch my grades!" Jesse threw up his arms. "Well, I'm tired of watchin' everything I do." He whirled and headed out of the room with the thump of his running shoes.

When he was gone, there was complete silence at the table. Figuring it was past time for him to retire to the guesthouse, Beckett pushed back his chair. "I sure thank you for the wonderful dinner, Shirlene, but I think I'll call it a night."

"There's no need to run off, Beckett." Shirlene cast worried eyes at the doorway. "This isn't the first tantrum Jesse has thrown, and it won't be the last. Once he cools off, he usually comes back downstairs and apologizes. In fact, why don't I just go get dessert? Once Jesse smells apple cobbler, he won't be able to resist coming down."

"As much as I love apple cobbler, I'm going to have to pass." Beckett got to his feet. "I haven't gotten much sleep in the last few nights, and I'm done in." It was an understatement. Between Brianne having the baby and his inability to sleep after Starlet's brush-off, he *was* more than done in. He ruffled Brody's hair as he moved around the table. "I'll just get my bag out of the truck and go around to the guesthouse." Once he hugged Shirlene and Adeline, he thumped Billy on the back. His brother looked so depressed he couldn't help trying to comfort him. "Jesse is going to be okay, Billy. Like you said, he's just doing a little rebelling."

Unfortunately, when Beckett walked out the front door and found Jesse trying to hot-wire Billy's monster truck, he had to rethink his words. Especially when the kid succeeded in starting the vehicle.

"Hot damn," drifted out the open passenger window, and Beckett barely had time to pull open the door and hop in before the truck took off out of the driveway. Of course, Jesse slammed to a stop soon enough, almost giving Beckett whiplash in the process.

"Uncle Beckett." The words came out of the kid's mouth like a curse.

"In the flesh." Beckett clicked his seat belt closed. "So where are we going?"

Jesse thumped the steering wheel and slumped back in the seat. "Nowhere now."

"Where were you planning on going?"

"Anywhere but here," Jesse grumbled. "Can't anyone see that I don't belong here? I'm not a Cates. I don't have the looks, the manners, the muscle, or the talk. I'm just a trailer-trash orphan who sucks at school."

Beckett might not have a lot of experience dealing with the teenage psyche, but he did understand being the outcast. While his brothers had excelled at sports, he had excelled at academics. So much so that he'd been labeled a geek from day one of his freshman year. And the thing he remembered hating the most was when his father or mother minimized his complaints of not fitting in.

"Okay," he said. "I get it. You don't want to be here. But you can't just run off half-cocked."

"I'm not runnin' off half-cocked," Jesse groused.

"So you have a plan? Money?"

Jesse's bottom lip protruded. "I had money until Daddy put it into an account I can't get to without his signature." He glanced over, and his face lit up. "Unless you could spot me, Uncle Beckett. I'm good for it."

"I wish I could, but I'm running a little low on money as it is."

"What about your trust fund?"

Smart kid. "Yeah, well, I sorta spent it."

"Damn. Does Uncle Brant know?"

Beckett shook his head. "And when he finds out, the shit is going to hit the fan." Which was putting it mildly.

"You could always get a job and try to pay it back," Jesse suggested. Obviously, the kid didn't have a clue how much money had been in Beckett's trust fund. "I had a job at Jones's Garage until Daddy made me quit and pay more attention to school. 'Course, I make more money fixing up junk and selling it than I did working there."

"That's what I heard." Beckett reached over and slipped the key in the ignition, turning off the engine before taking it back out. "So if you're so good at wheeling and dealing, why don't you make a deal with your parents?"

Jesse perked up. "What kind of deal?"

Beckett knew he was getting involved in something he had no business getting involved in, and yet he couldn't seem to stop himself.

"Summer school only lasts a couple months, right?" When Jesse nodded, Beckett continued. "What about if you promise to attend every day and pass all your classes in exchange for some of the money in your bank account? Then, when you turn eighteen in September, you won't need your parents' permission to drop out of school and you'll have some money to get started with." Even in the dark, Beckett could see the spark of interest in the kid's eyes. Although it died quickly enough.

"There's no way I can pass geometry," he said. "I don't have enough brains."

Beckett unsnapped his seat belt. "It's not about brains as much as it's about learning how to work the system."

"Work the system? You mean cheat?"

"Not cheating. Just a few tricks." Beckett opened

the door. "But you're probably right. You aren't smart enough." Ignoring Jesse's stiff shoulders and sullen glare, he got out and grabbed his duffel from the bed of the truck before leaning back in the open window. "Well, good luck, Jesse. Of course, you know if you take the truck, I'm going to have to tell your daddy. Then he'll have to call Dusty, who will have to leave your new baby cousin to track you down." He paused. "But the choice is yours. I think I'm going to go back inside and help myself to some of that apple cobbler."

"Cristina made apple cobbler?"

"Apple cobbler and the best darned chicken enchiladas I've had since heading for boot camp." He turned and started for the house, listening intently for the sound of the truck starting. Instead he heard the truck door slam, and when he glanced back, he saw Jesse strutting toward him.

"I figure anyone can pass geometry with a D," he said. "But I'm not waiting for September. As soon as summer school's out, I'm gone."

Beckett grinned. Of course, he didn't know why he was so happy. Since it was his plan, it was now up to him to change Jesse's mind about dropping out of school and leaving.

Chapter Fourteen

"SO IT LOOKS LIKE you're loading up on traveling munchies?" The middle-aged woman behind the cash register rang up Starlet's groceries. "Nothing like a road trip to give you an excuse to eat sugar."

Starlet adjusted her sunglasses and glanced down at the pile of snackies. But before she could feel more than a slight twinge of guilt, the woman handed her the Snickers bar she'd just scanned.

"You might want to eat that now, honey. In this heat, it will be nothin' but a gooey mess by the time you get to the car." She wiped an arm across her forehead. "It's the hottest June I can remember. Which only makes you wonder if those scientific folks ain't right and them icebergs are meltin'." Her eyes squinted in thought. "Although I don't have a clue what meltin' icebergs have to do with the weather in west Texas."

Starlet peeled back the candy bar wrapper and took a big bite. The chocolate, caramel, and nuts did a cha-cha on her tongue and jazz hands down her throat, before ending with a happy dance in her tummy.

"Now these"—the cashier lifted the box of banana MoonPies—"these ain't gonna melt in a little heat. I swear that they would survive a nuclear blast." Her gaze drifted over to Starlet, and she tipped the box at her. "It's hard to tell with those big sunglasses, but have you been to Bramble before?"

Starlet froze with the candy bar halfway to her mouth, wondering if the wig she'd borrowed from Miss Minnie was still on straight. "Once or twice," she squeaked out.

The woman studied her for a moment longer before she nodded. "Well, welcome back."

Starlet's shoulders wilted. "Thank you, ma'am."

"We still don't have a hotel, but if you need a place to stay, you might want to talk to our old librarian, Ms. Murphy—who is now Mrs. Brant Cates. She hasn't been able to sell her house, and I bet if you were to ask, she'd rent it out to you for a few days."

Starlet couldn't stay a few days. She shouldn't even be there now. She'd left the henhouse early that morning with the intention of taking a little drive. Before she knew it, she was driving past the WELCOME TO BRAMBLE sign.

"I appreciate it," she said as she paid the woman. "But I need to be going."

"Well, you come back soon, honey." The woman handed her the bag of goodies. "I love a woman who knows how to eat." She gave Starlet the once-over. "Although where you store all that sugar on your skinny little body is beyond me."

Once outside, Starlet hooked the bag over her arm and headed down the street toward the spot where she'd parked the henhouse van. She hadn't spent a lot of time in Bramble. On the few occasions that she had left the henhouse, she had preferred going to the town of Culver, which had more shopping, movie theaters, and restaurants. But after living in a big city, she could now see the appeal of the small town. There was a cozy quaintness about the shops that lined the street and a welcoming warmth from the people who greeted her. Although she had trouble remembering all their names, she recognized quite a few of them from the Cateses' weddings.

On the way down the street, she took note of all the campaign posters taped and tacked to every available light post and storefront window. It seemed that the town had quite a selection of mayoral candidates to choose from. Starlet had counted ten different candidates before her cell phone rang. Juggling the bag, she pulled the phone from her purse and answered it, realizing too late her error in not checking caller ID first.

"Ahh, I see that your cell phone finally has good reception, sweetie." Kari's sugary voice came through the receiver. "Isn't it interesting how you can't seem to get reception at the henhouse, but Jed doesn't have any problems?"

"That is strange, isn't it?" Starlet said. "He must have a different phone carrier."

There was a long pause. "Well, it doesn't matter. By the end of the day, you'll be back in Nashville, and we'll have plenty of time to talk. I have a helicopter picking you up in two hours to take you to the airport in Houston."

Two hours? Starlet shoved the rest of the candy bar in her mouth and hurried down the street.

"Star?" Kari said. "You'll be ready, right? Because you have dinner with the reporter from *Country Music* magazine tonight and a photo shoot and meeting with the executives of your music label tomorrow."

"Of course." Starlet tried to speak around the mouthful of caramel and chocolate.

"What are you eating?"

"Eating?" She swallowed hard. "What else would I be eating for breakfast? Grapefruit and oatmeal."

There was another pause, as if Kari knew she was lying through her teeth. "Fine. I'll meet you at the airport and we can go straight to dinner from there. How is the songwriting coming?"

"Good." Or it had been going good. Starlet had had no problems writing the first song, but since then, not a note had entered her head. Which was strange. Usually, once her creative juices started flowing, they didn't stop until she had a full album. But she had spent the entire day yesterday trying to write another song with no luck whatsoever. All she kept thinking about were the darned feather fans and the piano.

"I'm glad to hear it," Kari said. "We want as many hits on this next album as you had on your last. Now I'll let you finish your . . . oatmeal, and I'll see you this afternoon."

The phone clicked, and Starlet placed it back in her purse and took out the van keys. Since the old white van was twice the length of a car, she'd been forced to park it in the alleyway next to Sutter's Pharmacy. She had just started toward it when male laughter had her freezing in her tracks.

Time seemed to stand still as she slowly turned and looked across the street. When she saw him, it was like the sun split in two—one remained hovering in the blue west Texas sky and the other stood in the parking lot of Josephine's Diner talking with Mayor Sutter.

Beau.

Just the sight of his silver hair and handsome face filled her with such love and longing that it took all her willpower to keep from running across the street and diving into his arms. Which was one of the reasons she'd avoided him and kept all their communication to brief phone conversations. When she was with Beau, she couldn't hide her true feelings. It had been more than a year since she'd seen him in person. More than a year of waiting and hoping for a miracle to happen.

Not that she hadn't tried to help that miracle along. Even now, there was a cowboy on his way to Bramble—if he wasn't already there.

Some subtle movement must've alerted Beau to her presence, and he glanced across the street. She couldn't see the color of his eyes, but she didn't need to. The pure sapphire blue was, and always would be, her favorite color.

He lifted a hand in casual greeting. "Good mornin'." Just hearing his voice caused her breath to release in a whoosh of air. She smiled and lifted her hand, but it froze when the door of the diner opened and Beckett stepped out.

It was strange, but Beckett looked bigger than Beau. When had he gotten bigger? And his hair was thicker. Or was that just the way the wind swept it across his forehead? Beau said something to him, and he smiled. And it must've been the angle of the sun, because it looked even brighter than Beau's. But that made no sense. How could his smile be brighter than Beau's?

She shook her head. It had to be her imagination. Beau was still the love of her life. Beckett was just a man she'd had sex—

Her eyes widened, and she dropped the bag, the goodies spilling around her feet. The noise pulled Beckett's gaze over to her. But all she could do was stand there as the realization of what she'd done slammed into her.

She'd had sex with Beau's brother.

Beau's brother!

Just that quickly, the fantasy of marrying her rodeo cowboy hero melted like the chocolate bars on the hot pavement. She might've melted down to the sidewalk, too, if Beckett hadn't spoken.

"Starlet?"

Her name pulled her out of her misery, and she took one last look at Beau's shocked face before she turned and sprinted down the alleyway. She needed to be alone. Alone to sob out her depression at realizing that her dream was over. All because of a piano and a man who knew how to wield a feather fan.

Jumping in the van, she started the engine just as Beckett came running down the alley.

"Have you lost your mind, woman?" he yelled.

Tears coursed down her cheeks. No, she hadn't lost her mind. She'd just lost her Beau. She popped the van into drive and took off, forcing Beckett to jump out of the way. She expected that to stop him. She should've known better. As she headed down the alleyway toward Main Street, she glanced in the rearview mirror and saw that he was still giving chase. And for a muscle-bound guy in cowboy boots, he could flat-out run. Which caused her to smash down on the accelerator. She was so intent on watching Beckett that she almost ran over Cousin Jed, who jumped out of nowhere.

"Don't panic!" he yelled. "I'll save you."

She swerved just in the nick of time, taking out a row of trash cans. Suddenly realizing that she was going too fast to take the corner on Main Street, she applied the brakes. Unfortunately, the pedal went straight down to the floor without any resistance whatsoever. And without slowing the van down one iota.

Now she wasn't worried about losing Beau as much as losing her life. She pumped on the brakes as the back tire jumped the curb, almost taking out the park bench Moses Tate slept on. And Minnie would never forgive her if she killed her boyfriend.

In her panic, Starlet overcorrected and veered to the other side of the street, taking out the petunias that lined the sidewalk in front of the library. But the flowers didn't bother her as much as Jenna Jay, who seemed completely unaware of the runaway van heading straight at her. Starlet might've wanted Jenna out of the picture, but she had never wanted her dead. She jerked on the wheel and headed straight toward the town hall. The van hopped the curb, sailed over the lawn, past the huge maple, and right into the bronze statue of William Cates. Her sunglasses went flying off before her head bopped the steering wheel. Then all she saw was darkness. Which didn't explain why she could still hear Beckett's annoying voice.

"Starlet!"

She turned toward the sound, but couldn't see a thing. "Oh my God. I've gone blind," she sobbed. There was an exasperated grunt before the wig was jerked off her head. She blinked until Beckett's face came into focus. She expected to see pissed-off blue eyes. Instead, they were filled with concern.

"You okay?" He cradled her chin and gently touched

the spot right above her nose. She barely noticed the slight discomfort. She was too focused on the banjo that started playing in her head. A plucky tune that grew louder when Beckett smoothed back her bangs. "Are you dizzy? Sick to your stomach?"

She hadn't been dizzy, but she felt kind of dizzy now. Dizzy with music.

"I need a pen and paper," she whispered.

"You need a doctor—or a psychiatrist." He reached in and unhooked her seat belt, then lifted her out of the van. A crowd had gathered around the crash site, the townsfolk speaking in excited whispers when they recognized her.

"Well, I'll be a monkey's uncle; that's Star Bentley," a man said.

A woman with high, teased hair pushed her way to the front of the group. "Hey there, Miss Bentley! Remember me? Cindy Lynn. Welcome to Bramble."

Mayor Sutter appeared, hiking his pants up over his big stomach. "Watch your manners, Cindy Lynn. Welcomin' people to Bramble is still my job and will be even after the elections." He tipped his hat. "Welcome to Bramble, Miss Bentley." His gaze moved over to the statue of William Cates and the bumper that curved around it. "Did we have a little accident?"

Before Starlet could say how sorry she was, Beckett jumped in. "I'm sure Miss Bentley will take care of all the damages. Now, where's the doctor's office?"

"This way, Beckett." Beau's voice had Starlet ducking her head against Beckett's shoulder. The banjo music returned. This time with a steel guitar. The music continued playing all the way to the doctor's office. Starlet desperately wanted a pen and paper—or better yet a guitar. Her fingers were just itching to strum the notes that bounced around in her head.

The doctor's office was located just off Main Street in a converted residential house. Beau held open the door, but before Beckett maneuvered through it, he stopped on the porch and turned to the townsfolk who had followed them down the street.

"I'm sure you folks know how fast news can travel. And if word gets out that Miss Bentley is visiting Bramble, she'll have to deal with a lot of reporters and fans—"

"Say no more," Mayor Sutter said. "The folks of Bramble know how to keep a secret." He looked around the crowd. "Don't we, folks?" There was a chorus of loudly voiced agreement.

"Don't you worry about a thing, Miss Bentley. Mum's the word."

"My lips are sealed tighter than foil on a tater."

"Zipped and locked."

"We won't let no foreign reporters bother one of our own."

Starlet didn't know why their words brought tears to her eyes. Maybe because it had been a long time since she felt like she belonged. She smiled weakly and waved to the townsfolk as Beckett carried her inside.

Being as arrogant as he was, he bypassed the shocked receptionist and carried her straight into a room and set her on the table. But his arrogance didn't bother her as much as what happened as soon as he took his hands off her.

The music stopped, and there was nothing. Not one note. Not one banjo strum. Nada.

"Look directly at the light." He pointed an instrument

at her with a pinpoint beam of light, but she was so concerned about what had just happened that she didn't listen.

"Doc's on his way." Beau came into the room. "He was out at Ethan's helping to deliver a breech calf." He walked over and took Starlet's hand. "Are you okay, Starlet?"

Starlet looked down at his hand, then up into his clear blue eyes. With his silver hair and perfect features, he was still the most beautiful man she'd ever seen. She had the strong desire to apologize for ruining their happily-ever-after, but before she could make a complete fool of herself, Beckett took her chin and turned her face to the light. Just like that the music came back, and with it, a startling realization that dried her tears and had her staring at the arrogant man in front of her in horror.

Beauregard Cates might be the love of her life, but it seemed that Beckett Cates was her muse.

Chapter Fifteen

"I can't believe you didn't tell me, Brianne. If anyone should realize how dangerous the man is, you should."

Beckett could tell by Dusty's hard look that he really wanted to yell at his wife. The two things that kept him from it were the newborn cradled in his arms and Moses Tate napping on the couch.

"I'm sorry, Dusty," Bri said. "But I didn't want to put you in a bad position. I know how you like to follow the law to the letter." She held up her hand and sent him a look that was anything but innocent. "So do you want to handcuff me now or later?"

Dusty blushed before he turned to Minnie. "While we're on the topic of illegal behavior. You had no business keeping that money from the Feds, Miz Minnie."

Sitting in her wheelchair behind the large desk that took up a third of the henhouse library, Minnie looked like a frail old woman. But anyone who knew the head hen realized that her physical appearance was deceptive. Beneath the wrinkled skin and fading eyes was a tough old bird who had seduced outlaws, manipulated senators, and held the entire Cates family in the palm of her gnarled hand.

She shrugged as she pulled a Dum Dum sucker from a desk drawer. "I just didn't want it collecting dust on an evidence shelf when it could've gone to helping folks out. And I'm not talkin' about Starlet's mama—that woman doesn't need money as much as a slap upside the head."

"But it wasn't your money to keep." Dusty's voice rose enough to cause Bryson to fuss.

Beckett glanced over at his sister and was surprised that she wasn't jumping up to take Bryson. In fact, now that he thought about it, she hadn't held Bryson once since arriving at the henhouse.

"Well, it makes no difference now," Minnie said. "The money is back with the Feds, and Alejandro thinks Starlet owes him." Her eyes narrowed. "Which doesn't explain why he cut the brake line on the van. If she's dead, she can't give him money."

"You're right," Beckett said. "It doesn't make any sense. If he had wanted her dead, why didn't he kill her in Charlotte or at her house in Nashville?" Olive's cat, Jiggers, brushed against his legs, and he reached down and absently stroked his matted fur. For being so big and mean-looking, Jiggers wasn't half as ornery as Starlet's cat. Although, Hero wasn't ornery enough to mess with Jiggers. Even now, the fat cat was hiding upstairs with Starlet while she recovered from her head injury. A head injury that still had Beckett more than a little concerned.

Dusty handed the baby off to Bri, who suddenly looked terrified. She held Bryson like a loaf of hot bread as her husband pulled out his cell phone. "Beckett, do you remember the name of the officer who was in charge of Scarlet's kidnapping case?"

"Doyle. Officer Doyle."

Dusty dialed a number and then walked out of the room, closing the door behind him. Once he was gone, Bri tried to hand the baby off to Beckett. Beckett would've taken him if Minnie hadn't spoken up.

"Let Brianne get used to her new son, Beckett. It looks to me as if Dusty has been doing all the bonding. And given that this isn't his first time, I can understand him being more comfortable. But you won't get over your fear, Brianne, if you don't face it."

Bri looked down at her fussing son. "But what if I hurt him?"

"You're not going to hurt him. Although you might want to stop holding him like he's a load of dirty laundry. From the sounds of that cry, I think he's getting hungry. Why don't you take him down to the Jungle Room and nurse him?"

"By myself?"

Minnie laughed. "I think you can figure it out without Dusty's supervision. In fact, a little alone time is exactly what you two need."

Bri looked like she wanted to argue, but when Bryson's cries got even louder, she awkwardly tucked him in her arm and headed for the door. When she was gone, Minnie smiled at Beckett.

"Don't worry. She'll figure it out soon enough. Just look at what a great mother she is to Dusty's daughter, Emmie." She tossed the sucker at the trash. It landed dead center. "So what happened?"

Beckett leaned back in his chair. "I've told you

everything I know. Starlet showed up in town wearing some crazy wig and glasses and ended up running into William Cates's statue. Although knocking over that thing would've been a blessing. It looks nothing like my great-grandfather and exactly like Billy on a bad fishing day."

For a woman who usually found life humorous, Minnie looked dead serious. "I wasn't talking about what happened today. I was talking about what happened in Afghanistan."

Without hesitation, Beckett got up from the chair, stepping over Jiggers, who had fallen asleep at his feet. He walked to the window and looked out, refusing to talk about a subject he wanted to forget. The hum of Minnie's battery-powered wheelchair alerted him, and he glanced back to see her sitting behind him.

"So I guess what they say is true. War is hell."

As far as Beckett was concerned, that was an understatement. Hell had to be better than what he'd seen. When he still didn't say anything, she continued.

"I can't begin to imagine what you've been through, Beckett. But you're one of the lucky ones. You came back to an entire family who loves you. And I figure when the time is right, you'll release that huge burden you're carrying and let love heal."

"I don't know if I can heal, Miss Minnie."

"You can, and you will." She smiled. "The Cates boys are made of pretty tough stuff."

There was a part of him that wanted to believe Minnie, but the other part feared that he would have to live with this hole in his heart for the rest of his life. Before Beckett could voice his fears, Dusty came back into the room.

"I've got some good news." He glanced around. "Where's Brianne?"

Minnie turned her chair to face him. "She's nursing the baby." She zipped back behind the desk. "It's nice that you've taken time off work to help, Dusty, but Brianne needs to learn how to be a mama, and she can't do that if you're doing all the mothering. Now, what's the good news?"

Dusty glanced back at the door for only a second before answering the question. "Detective Doyle located the guy who kidnapped Starlet, and he isn't Alejandro. He's some street thug."

"Could Alejandro have hired him?" Beckett asked as he moved away from the window.

"Doubtful. The guy said he was hired by some big dude in a bar the night before."

"Hired to do what?"

"According to the thug, he had strict orders not to hurt her. He was just supposed to take her to his car and wait for the guy to show up. When you came out of the stadium instead, he got scared and fired off a few warning shots."

"They seemed like more than just warning shots to me," Beckett said. "Do you think it was one of Alejandro's men who hired the thug?"

"I thought so at first. But according to one of my connections at the FBI, Alejandro has been cut off from the cartel and hung out to dry. The man has no money or connections in Mexico or here. Last they heard, he was in Panama, living off some prostitute." Dusty sat down on the arm of the couch next to Moses's stocking feet. "Which still leaves us with the question of who hired the thug and what he wants with Starlet."

"Sounds like he just wants to scare her," Minnie cut in. "Especially since he didn't want her hurt."

"I would agree, if not for the cut brake lines," Beckett said. "That was more than just scaring."

"Unless he was plannin' on stoppin' things before she got hurt."

Everyone in the room turned to Moses. After only a moment's pause, the crushed cowboy hat was lifted and a wizened old face peeked out.

"Well, don't keep us in suspense, Mo," Minnie said. "What in blue blazes are you talking about?"

With the creak of bones, he sat up on the couch and smoothed back the white hair sticking up on his head. "I'm talkin' about the feller that cut the brake lines."

Beckett stepped closer and stared down at the old man. "You saw him? Why didn't you say anything?"

"Whelp, because I never like to point a finger at a man until I have all the facts." He reached for the Solo cup sitting on the coffee table and spit a healthy dose of tobacco in it. "After what I saw today before I almost got run over, and after listening to y'all yammer, I figure I've got enough to start pointin'."

"And who is it, Moses?" Dusty asked. "Was it Alejandro?"

"Now, I haven't seen any pictures of this Alejandro feller, so I couldn't tell ya. But the feller I saw didn't look like no Alejandro to me. He looked like a big oaf who couldn't coordinate his feet, which was probably why he had trouble catchin' the van."

"Jed," Beckett said. With the name came a multitude of memories. Jed's nonchalance when Starlet was kidnapped. Jed showing up at her house after the break-in with his shirt torn. Jed suddenly appearing in town and chasing after the van.

For being the coolheaded Cates, Beckett was so pissed off he saw stars. With a muttered curse, he charged out the door. He found Jed in the kitchen scarfing down on Baby's cooking. When he looked up and saw Beckett, he dropped his fork and headed for the back door. He made it only to the edge of Miss Hattie's lilac garden before Beckett grabbed his shirt and jerked him around.

"You sonofabitch!" The punch Beckett threw had Jed reeling to the ground. Beckett would've jerked him up and hit him again if Dusty hadn't grabbed him.

"That's enough, Beck!"

Still steaming, Beckett jerked away and pointed a finger at Jed, who refused to get up off the ground. "He was the one who hired the guy to kidnap Starlet, the one who painted the sign on her bedroom wall, the one who cut the brake line and almost killed her!"

"I wasn't going to kill her," Jed whined as he held his nose, which was spouting blood. "I just wanted to rescue her."

"Rescue her?" Beckett stared at him in disbelief.

"Yeah, rescue her. I figured if I rescued her, Kari could never fire me because Starlet would feel like she owed me. And she does owe me. I would've had all my mama's attention if she hadn't come along."

A loud snort came from behind the huge cottonwood tree, followed by the creak of hammock ropes before Uncle Bernie appeared. His hat and jacket were missing, and the hair on the sides of his head was mussed.

"Now, boy, that's an out-and-out lie if ever I heard one. Starlet had nothin' to do with your mama's lack of attention." His expression turned sad. "What have you done, son?"

"Don't call me *son*!" Jed snapped. "We both know that I was never your son. My daddy was the best WWF wrestler that ever lived."

Uncle Bernie sighed. "And the meanest sonofabitch you'd ever want to meet. I was hopin' you didn't get his blood. But I guess the apple don't fall far from the tree."

Dusty pulled out his cell phone. "I'll call the sheriff of Culver County and have him head out."

"I'm not goin' to jail!" Jed scrambled up and started to run. Beckett and Dusty would've gone after him if Olive hadn't appeared from behind the cottonwood tree and tackled him to the ground.

Thirty minutes later, Beckett watched from the front porch as Jed was being driven away in the sheriff's car.

"It's a cryin' shame," Bernie said. "I married his mama when she was three months' pregnant and always thought of Jed as my own. I knew he was a few cards short of a deck, but I didn't think he'd hurt his own kin."

"Well, I don't feel the least bit sorry for the rascal," Olive said. "He should be horsewhipped for what he did to little Starlet. Speaking of which, I better go up to Miss Hattie's room and check on her."

"I'll go with you, buttercup."

"I ain't your buttercup," she snapped and swatted at the hand he tried to place around her thick waist. "And don't you forget it, you no-account flimflam man." They continued to spar as they walked in the door.

Dusty chuckled before looking at Beckett. "Well, I guess that takes care of any concerns about Alejandro." The whirl of helicopter blades had him looking up at the sky. "Is Brant coming in?"

"That's not Brant's chopper," Minnie said as she rolled

her chair closer to the edge of the porch. "That's the same one that came for Starlet this morning. I hope Starlet isn't thinking about traveling back to Nashville after her head injury."

"She's not going anywhere." Beckett moved next to Minnie and waited for the helicopter to land in the cleared field that the henhouse used as a parking lot. The blades had no more than stopped moving when Kari climbed out and came charging toward the porch.

"Where is she? Where is Star?" Her gaze pinned Beckett, and her eyes narrowed. "I should've known that you would be here. Ever since you showed up, Starlet has become an unruly brat. Now, where is she?"

Beckett crossed his arms over his chest. "She's resting right now."

"I don't care if she's sound asleep." Kari climbed the porch steps. "She's got an interview in Nashville tonight." She tried to step around Minnie's wheelchair, but the old woman zipped back and blocked her path, barely missing the toes of Kari's high heels.

"That isn't going to happen," Minnie said. "And if you aren't a registered guest, I think you need to leave."

Kari's face turned a bright red, and Beckett figured she was about to throw a tantrum. But before she could, lively banjo music came out the screen door. Since the only one who knew how to play the banjo was the same person who was supposed to be resting, Beckett forgot about Kari and headed inside.

He found Starlet in the ballroom. It was the same room she'd had her going-away party in, and Beckett couldn't help but remember how beautiful she'd looked that night in the gold gown that had slipped off her body so easily.

But she wasn't dressed in a gold gown tonight. She was dressed in a Minnie Mouse nightshirt as she plucked out a tune on the banjo.

She stopped suddenly and picked up a pencil, scribbling something down on the notebook propped on the piano. A piano very similar to the one that continued to haunt Beckett's dreams.

"A new song?" Kari came clicking into the room. "You're writing a new song when you should be on your way to Nashville?"

Starlet glanced up, her brown eyes unfocused behind the lenses of the black-framed glasses. It was the first time Beckett had seen her in glasses, and the sight made him feel more than a little turned on. "Oh. I didn't realize you were here."

"Of course, I'm here," Kari snapped. "What did you expect when you wouldn't come back—"

Starlet held up a finger. "Just one second."

Since Starlet had probably never interrupted Kari in her life, her manager was struck mute. In fact, everyone shut up and watched as Starlet scribbled down a few more notes before plucking them out on the banjo.

"No." She stopped playing and shook her head. "That's not right." Her brow knotted before her gaze drifted over to Beckett. She cocked her head. "Becky—I mean, Beckett—would you mind helping me over to the chair by the window?" She put the back of her hand to her head. "I'm suddenly feeling a little dizzy."

"You should be back in bed," he said.

"Of course I'll go back to bed. I just need to get the refrain right." She batted her eyelashes at him. "Please."

Rather than help her to her feet, he picked her up banjo

and all, hesitating so she could retrieve the pencil and notebook from the piano music rack. "Fine, but you better make it quick."

"For once Beckett is right." Kari came striding over as soon as Beckett settled Starlet in the chair. "You need to hurry so we can get back to Nashville. You have the interview—"

"No!" Starlet's voice echoed around the cavernous room and had Kari taking a step back and Beckett smiling. "I'm sorry, but I can't go back to Nashville right now. Not when... Texas seems to have my creative juices flowing. At the rate I'm going, I should have a complete album in another week." She went back to scribbling down notes.

Kari started to argue, but then stopped, obviously realizing what a new album meant for both their careers. With a grumbled oath, she turned on a heel and walked out. Chuckling, Miss Minnie followed behind her. Beckett would've joined them if Starlet hadn't grabbed on to his sleeve and hung on as if her life depended on it. When he glanced down, she smiled sweetly. Almost too sweetly.

"Not you. You need to stay right here."

Chapter Sixteen

TWYLA JENNINGS LEANED CLOSER to the mirror over her styling station and used the end of her teasing comb to point out the culprit. Yep, it was a gray hair. A coarse, steel-colored strand that stood out from her blond dye job like a zit on prom night. Catching it between the tips of her artificial nails, she viciously yanked it out. But she knew there would be more. As a beautician, she had watched it happen to each and every woman of Bramble after they turned forty.

And in less than two months, Twyla would turn forty—a secret she'd kept from the entire town. They all thought she would be thirty-five. Only her family, who lived in Austin, knew the truth. Forty years old. Twice as old as her baby sister, Tracy Ann, who had just gotten married last month to a cute repo man from Laredo. Now all five of her younger sisters were happily married to their first husbands, while Twyla remained single after three.

Her last husband, Dab, said it was because she hung on too tightly. Which made no sense at all to Twyla. If you didn't hang on, then you let go. And that's exactly the mistake her mama had made with her daddy. She had just up and let him leave without once making an effort to save their marriage.

Twyla had tried to save all three of her marriages. Unfortunately, no matter how much she overlooked the cheating, gambling, and drinking—no matter how hard she worked to smile and be the perfect wife—it hadn't been enough. And she was starting to wonder if there wasn't something wrong with her. Maybe she wasn't meant to be married. Maybe she was meant to be Bramble's next old maid.

She looked at her reflection in the mirror and searched for flaws. Her gaze swept over the sky-high, teased blond hair. The artfully applied black eyeliner and blue shadow. The just-about-perfect nose and lips and the nice set of breasts that stretched out her COWGIRLS DO IT BETTER T-shirt. She shook her head. Who was she kidding? She could no more be an old maid than Shirlene Cates. Some women were just too good-looking for their own good.

Of course, some men just needed to be reminded of that.

Swerving the chair away from the mirror, she lifted her cell phone and speed-dialed Kenny Gene. His cheerful voice had her heart thumping in overtime.

"Hey, Twyla. How you doin', darlin'? I wish I had time to talk, but I'm still lookin' for the right key to the gun cabinet. Besides, Dusty gave me strict orders not to chitchat on my personal cell phone unless it was an emergency."

She glanced down at the gray hair that curled around her finger before she shook it off. "Well, this is an emergency. I waited until your shoulder healed up after that villain Alejandro shot you. Then I waited for you to finish goin' to that deputy school. Then I waited while you learned 'the ropes' of bein' a new deputy. But I am tellin' you now, Kenny Gene, that I am through waitin'.'"

"Now, Twyla, honey, you don't mean that."

"I most certainly do. I'm the best thing that ever happened to you, and if you can't figure that out, then I'm through with you."

There was a long pause. "All right, then, Twyla. You can set a date for next summer."

"No. Not next summer. Or next spring. Or this fall. You'll slip a weddin' band on my finger by August fifteenth, or I'll get somebody else to do it."

There was a muffled sound like he'd dropped the phone before he finally spoke. "August fifteenth! But that's only two months away. There is no way I can get things taken care of by then."

"Things taken care of? What things taken care of?"

"Uhh..." he stuttered. "I gotta go." The phone clicked dead.

Twyla stared at it for only a second before she started bawling like a calf that had been separated from its mama. Some people might think that, after three weddings, she was more interested in the ceremony than the man. But the truth was that Twyla loved Kenny Gene. She loved how he separated big words by syllables and thought Scooby-Doo was the smartest, funniest dog ever. She loved his long stories and the way he line danced with one shoulder lowered and a thumb hooked in his belt loop. She loved him being a deputy and his bright smile. But most of all, she loved the way he looked at each day as if it were a big ol' present that he couldn't wait to unwrap. Which was exactly why she'd waited eight long years. When Kenny slipped a wedding band on her finger, it would be forever.

"Oh, for the love of Pete."

Sniffing, Twyla turned to the door. Jenna Jay Cates stood there with an exasperated look on her face. Jenna had always scared Twyla. Not only because she didn't beat around the bush verbally, but also because she had no problem making her point physically. Something that more than a few men in town had figured out the hard way.

"So let me guess. Kenny Gene still refuses to set a date," Jenna said as she crossed her arms over her chest. Usually she dressed in tight Wranglers and cute, tucked-in western shirts. But lately she had taken to wearing leggings and long, loose-fitting shirts. Some women just gave up on fashion when they got married.

Twyla grabbed a tissue from the box on her cutting station. "I guess you think I'm stupid for puttin' up with him for this long."

After only a second's hesitation, Jenna's shoulders slumped. "No. Love can turn even the strongest woman into a sniveling wimp."

"Amen," Twyla said before blowing her nose loudly. "If you're lookin' for Brianne, she's on maternity leave until next month."

"Which is exactly why I'm here." Jenna walked over and picked up a pair of shears. "With Brianne gone, there won't be anyone to stop me."

"Stop you from what?"

Jenna handed her the scissors. "From cutting off all my hair."

Twyla didn't know if she gasped because Jenna wanted to cut off her long, beautiful locks or because she was willing to let Twyla do it. Most of the younger women preferred Brianne to cut their hair. Although Twyla had yet to figure out why.

"Are you sure?" she asked.

"Positive. I want something short and easy to take care of." Jenna nudged her out of the chair and sat down. "And I want to donate it to Locks of Love, so make it short."

"You really are a good person, Jenna." Twyla ran her fingers through the thick, blond mane and shivered with delight. "And don't you worry. I'll do right by you." She stood back and put a finger to her mouth. "I'm thinking I'll give you somethin' my mama used to call the Dorothy Hamill after that cute little Olympic figure skater."

Jenna shrugged. "Whatever."

The haircut didn't turn out to be as much fun as Twyla thought it would be. Jenna watched her every move and told her exactly what to cut and how. Not wanting to end up in a headlock, Twyla followed her instructions to a tee. When she was finished, she had to admit that it looked darned good. The short haircut made Jenna's blue eyes look twice as big and framed her pretty features. Of course, just because Twyla liked her haircuts didn't mean her clients did. She held her breath as Jenna looked in the mirror, swiveling the chair first one way and then the other. Finally, she smiled.

"I like it."

Twyla's shoulders relaxed. "Me too." She studied her own reflection. "Maybe I should cut my hair. Maybe that would wring a proposal out of Kenny."

Jenna took off the cape and handed it to her. "Why don't you try giving Kenny a little competition? I'm not so sure that my ex-boyfriend Davy's proposal didn't prompt Beau's."

"You think?"

"It couldn't hurt."

Twyla smiled. "Why, Jenna Jay, I didn't realize how devious you could be."

"I guess I'm as devious as any other woman who wants to catch a man...or keep him from being hurt," Jenna said. Twyla was just about to ask her what she meant when the screen door squeaked open. They both turned to find a handsome cowboy with a bright smile.

Twyla had heard gossip about the new stranger in town, but the gossip she'd heard was about a shy, mannerly cowboy who didn't talk much. This cowboy didn't quite fit the description.

"Dammit straight, I do love devious women," he said with an exaggerated wink as he strutted into the salon.

Jenna got up from the chair and sighed. "Not again. I thought she would've given up by now."

"Who would give up?" Twyla asked.

But Jenna ignored the question and walked over to the man. "We can make this easy. Or we can make this hard."

"I've always liked it hard."

Jenna glanced over her shoulder. "Thanks, Twyla. How much do I owe you?"

"Not a penny. It was my pleasure." She stared at the cowboy, then back at Jenna. "Do you two know each other?"

"No," the cowboy said. "But I'm hoping to change that."

"I'm sure you are. But it's not going to happen." Jenna tried to walk past the cowboy, but he grabbed her arm and pulled her close.

"So, you were talking about hard."

In two seconds flat, he got it hard. Jenna Jay kneed him so hard in the crotch that he doubled over and knelt down on the floor. Then, as if she were on a Sunday stroll, she walked right out the door. Once she was gone, Twyla stared at the handsome man who was gasping for breath. After talking with Jenna, she figured that a little healthy jealousy was exactly what Kenny Gene needed to get him to the altar. And this cowboy had practically dropped in her lap.

"Come this way, sugar." She took his arm and helped him to his feet before leading him over to the styling chair. "Twyla will have you fixed up in no time. You ever heard of the Dorothy Hamill?"

Chapter Seventeen

THE KEY THAT MISS Minnie had given her didn't seem to work. Starlet had been standing on the porch in the late-afternoon sun for the last ten minutes, trying to open the door of the pretty, picket-fenced house with no success. It didn't help that Hero sat at her feet with smug disdain in his bright green eyes. Or that her drunken mama lounged in the swing, singing Starlet's latest hit at the top of her lungs. Or that her uncle Bernie had yet to stop talking about Olive.

"Olive might've looked like she was happy to see me go, but that woman don't fool me a bit. And that kiss I snuck from her plump, luscious lips proves that I'm growin' on her." He chuckled. "Sorta like Beckett is growin' on you."

Starlet dropped the key and turned to stare at him. "Beckett is not growing on me."

Uncle Bernie grinned from ear to ear. "I don't know what you'd call it, Star Baby. You wouldn't let the man out of your sight last night."

Since it was the truth, she ignored the comment and went back to trying to open the door. Although Beckett hadn't grown on her. In fact, he still annoyed the heck out of her. But he also happened to be her muse. Something she had finally accepted.

It had been a hard pill to swallow. Unfortunately, creative people couldn't pick and choose what inspired them. She had once read an article about a painter who was inspired by a guinea pig. If his pig wasn't sitting on his lap, he couldn't paint. It looked like Starlet had the same problem. Beckett had to be within touching distance before she could hear music.

Which explained what she was doing renting Elizabeth Murphy Cates's house. Since Kari would allow Starlet only so much time before she forced her back to Nashville, Starlet couldn't mess around. Two songs were not enough for an album. She needed at least five or six original songs. Which meant she had to be as close to Beckett as she could get.

"I'm just a simple country gal," her mama sang in an off-key voice. *"Love my chickens. Love my boots."* She changed the lyrics to Starlet's song. *"Love a cowboy with plenty of loot."*

Starlet cringed. Of course, putting up with Beckett couldn't be harder than putting up with her family. Not that she had to worry about Jed anymore. Just the thought of her cousin made her sad. She knew Jed had been resentful over her making it big. She just hadn't realize how resentful. And once she'd thought about it, she couldn't hold it against him. If having Maybelline as a mama hadn't been bad enough, he'd had Kari as a boss. Which was why Starlet had decided not to press charges. Besides a bump on her head and a badly painted bedroom wall, Jed really hadn't hurt her.

"You have business at Ms. Murphy's?"

Starlet stopped fiddling with the lock and turned to see a stout woman in a bad hat standing on the sidewalk next to a skinny man in overalls. Starlet couldn't remember the woman's name, but the man's name was Elmer. He had gotten drunk at every wedding Starlet had ever attended and ended up embarrassing himself. Although with her mama singing at the top of her lungs, Starlet didn't have room to talk.

"Well, hello, folks." Uncle Bernie trotted down the porch steps and reached over the picket fence to shake their hands. "I'm Bernard Brubaker, and this here is my niece, Star Bentley."

"Star Bentley?" The woman gasped, completely ignoring Uncle Bernie's hand. "Why, I heard you were in town, but I didn't believe it."

Her mama stopped singing and bellowed at the top of her lungs, "Well, believe it! The amazing Star Bentley is stayin' right here in your dumpy neighborhood."

"Oh my Lord." The woman placed a hand on her chest. "This is exactly what I need to win the election—Star Bentley as a neighbor and supporter. I gotta call Myra!" She hustled off.

When she was gone, Elmer shook his head. "Crazy as a loon." He hooked his hands in the front of his overalls and nodded at the door. "You havin' problems with Ms. Murphy's lock?" Before Starlet could reply, he pushed open the gate and started up the path. Without even taking the key, he twisted the knob and gave it a jiggle, then pushed open the door. "Just needs a little finaglin'."

After Elmer and Uncle Bernie helped her carry in the luggage, Elmer showed her how to turn on the swamp cooler, light the pilot on the old gas stove, and gave her directions to the First Baptist Church—just in case her mama might want to stop by his AA meeting. Since her mama was now passed out on the couch, it was a good suggestion.

Elizabeth's old house was even smaller than the hotel suites Starlet stayed in when traveling, but there was something about the comfortable furniture and cozy rooms that made Starlet feel content and happy. So content and happy that she felt like singing. Once she helped Bernie put her mama to bed, she went out on the porch with her guitar.

First she played the two new songs she'd written. They were good. Real good. She tried working on a third. Unfortunately, without her muse, the music refused to come. Giving up, she strummed the chords to "The Good-bye Kiss."

Since the accident, she hadn't had much time to think about Beau. Her mind had been too full of music. But she thought about him now. She thought about his silver hair and pretty blue eyes. About his dazzling smile and upbeat personality. About how sweet he'd been to her when she'd first arrived at the henhouse. She loved Beau. She would always love Beau. And she was sad about losing him forever. But she wasn't as sad as she thought she'd be. In fact, while strumming the song, she didn't cry one single tear. When she was finished, all she felt was hungry.

It was a nice walk into town. The sun had set and washed the sky in bright pinks and oranges. Since Starlet no longer wore a wig or glasses, she figured she'd have to deal with more than a few exuberant fans. But to her amazement, instead of asking her for an autograph or to pose for a picture, they just smiled and told her that they hoped she enjoyed her stay. Because of this, she took her time, stopping at the Dairy Treat for a hot dog and fries before buying some MoonPies at the Food Mart. While enjoying her banana treat, she strolled down the street, looking in the windows of the closed stores and stopping to covet a blue prom dress in the window of the clothing store Duds 'N Such.

She had just decided to head back home when she noticed the full parking lot of Bootlegger's Bar. She'd always had a special place in her heart for country honky-tonks. They were her first venues. The first crowds that had loved her music. Because of this, she was drawn across the street.

The bar was dark, loud, and looked to be filled with the entire town of Bramble. A live band performed on a small stage in front of a dance floor that was filled to over-flowing with two-stepping couples.

Starlet sat down on the only vacant bar stool and, within minutes, was ordering a beer from the bartender who seemed too busy to fuss over a famous country singer. Once she had her beer, she sipped it and watched as the bartender took orders, juggled bottles, and mixed drinks. The band had made it through three songs before he finally let a glass of draft beer slip through his fingers. It had barely hit the floor when another man appeared and mopped it up.

"Thanks, Cowboy," the bartender said as he continued to pour drinks. Cowboy's cowboy hat dipped in acknowl-edgment before he grabbed a crate of dirty glasses and carried them toward the back room. There was something about the way he walked that seemed vaguely familiar. But before Starlet could figure out who the man reminded her of, Mayor Sutter sat down next to her.

"That Cowboy has shore turned out to be a good addi-tion to our little town. I hate for bad things to happen to folks, but it was a blessin' when his truck broke down." His handlebar mustache twitched as he sent her a smile. "I hope you're enjoyin' your stay in Bramble, Miss Bentley. Once I found out that you'd be rentin' Ms. Murphy's, I gave the town strict orders to mind their manners and let you enjoy your vacation."

"I certainly appreciate it," Starlet said.

"Yep, I bet a big star like you gets pretty tired of people buggin' you for autographs...and favors." He stared off for a second before he continued. "'Course, bein' in a parade wouldn't be a favor as much as just fun. Everyone loves a parade."

Starlet knew a hint when she heard one, and since the townsfolk were going out of their way to give her a peaceful stay, she couldn't decline. Besides, she *had* always loved parades. "If I'm still in town, I would be happy to be in your parade."

His eyes widened. "No kiddin'? Because you bein' in our Fourth of July Extravaganza Parade would be like icin' on the cake of me winnin' the race for mayor."

Kenny Gene appeared out of nowhere and slapped the mayor on the back, sloshing the glass of beer he held in his hand. "And seein' as how Dusty is headed to his parents' house for the Fourth, I get to lead the parade in my patrol car. Ain't that right, Harley?"

"Now, I didn't say nothin' about you leadin' the parade, Kenny," the mayor said. "I think the new mayor of Bramble should start it off—hopefully with Miss Bentley here."

Kenny's eyes crinkled in confusion. "But how is Miss Bentley gonna fit in your little bitty clown car?" He looked at Starlet. "Wouldn't you much rather ride in a car with flashin' red lights, Miss Bentley?"

Before she could answer, another man at the bar joined in the conversation. "And just maybe you won't be startin' the parade, Harley. Maybe the folks of Bramble think that it's time to try someone new—like Rossie Owens." He nodded at the attractive older man working the cash register behind the bar.

"Like hell," another man jumped in. "I just heard that Tom Long has thrown his hat into the ring. And seein' as how Tom is a rancher and so good with cattle, I figure he should be able to corral the people of Bramble."

That set off a chorus of other names being tossed out. Not wanting to be in the middle of a town fight, Starlet slipped off the stool with every intention of heading for the door.

Unfortunately, before she could reach it, a cowboy grabbed her arm and pulled her over to the dark corner next to the cigarette machine. Or not a cowboy as much as a poseur. His jeans weren't worn in. His shirt looked like it had come straight off the rack with no starch whatsoever. And his cowboy hat wasn't shaped to his head.

"Excuse me," she said as she tried to pull away, "but if you want an autograph—"

He cut her off. "I don't want an autograph. I want my hair back!" He whipped off his hat to reveal the worse haircut Starlet had ever seen. The bowl cut made him look like the lead in a stage production of *Peter Pan*. But it wasn't the hair that had Starlet's mouth dropping open in shock as much as his picture-perfect features.

"Vance?"

"Nice to meet you, Miss Bentley," he said. Although he didn't sound like it was nice at all.

"What are you doing here?" she asked.

"I saw you walk in and followed you so we could

have a little chat." He glared at her. "You told me that all I had to do was seduce some woman away from her husband."

Starlet glanced around. "Would you be quiet?"

He followed her gaze over to the crowd of arguing townsfolk. "I don't know what you're worried about. The tabloids already published the story from the last model you hired."

It was true. Except Rowdy hadn't been the last model she'd hired. He'd been the first rodeo cowboy she'd hired. But he hadn't wanted money as much as sex with a country singer. When Starlet wouldn't give it to him, he spilled the beans. Fortunately, no one believed his story. Probably because it was hard to believe that the sweetheart of country music would be so low as to hire someone to seduce a woman away from her husband.

And it was low. Starlet didn't make any bones about it. It was possibly as low as a woman could get. But when your heart belonged to a man, you would do just about anything to have him. And Starlet's heart belonged to Beauregard Cates. Or at least it had.

"I'm sorry," she said. "But there's been a change of plans. I won't be needing your services anymore. Of course, I'll still pay you, along with extra for your..." Her gaze drifted up to his bangs, which looked like they had been curled under with a curling iron. "What happened?"

He tried to smooth out the curl. "Some scissor-happy broad attacked my hair. Before that I got kneed in the nuts by the woman you sent me to seduce, and before that the friendly mayor got me thrown off a horse." Starlet cringed. "And dammit straight, you'll pay me extra."

She squinted at him. "I believe it's 'damn straight.'"

"Whatever. Just give me my money so I can get the hell out of this crazy town."

She rifled through her jeans pockets, but all she came up with was seven dollars and change. "I'm afraid I don't have a lot of cash on me." She held up the grocery bag that was still on her arm. "MoonPie?" When he looked confused, she shook her head. "Never mind. I'll send you a check—"

"Hide me." Vance ducked behind her and grabbed on to her waist, maneuvering her so she faced the doorway of the pool room. "The fat blonde in the tight jeans," he hissed next to her ear. "That's the one who ruined my hair and tried to get me to take her out on a date so she could make her boyfriend jealous. What is up with manipulative women these days?"

Starlet looked in the pool room and saw Twyla standing at a table chatting it up with a cowboy who was getting ready to take his shot. While Vance looked like Peter Pan in cowboy duds, the youngest Cates brother looked like the real McCoy. Beckett's straw hat curved just enough over his forehead to shadow his eyes. His shirt had just enough starch to emphasize his broad shoulders. And his jeans had just enough wear to make a woman want to run her hands over every square inch—especially the worn pockets on his fine butt.

Which was exactly what Twyla looked like she wanted to do. That didn't seem right. Not right at all. If Beckett Cates was going to give his music to anyone, it was going to be Starlet.

Chapter Eighteen

"So ARE YOU SURE you don't dance, honey?" Twyla said for the umpteenth time since joining Beckett at the pool table. "Because if you was to dance with me, that might just be enough to get things rollin'."

He didn't know what the woman was talking about, and he didn't care. As he leaned over the table to take a shot, his attention wasn't on Twyla's ramblings or the six ball he'd planned on hitting into the corner pocket. No, his attention was solely on the cowboy's hands wrapped around Starlet's waist. The same cowboy he'd seen in the picture on Starlet's nightstand.

Beckett's hands tightened on the pool stick before he pulled back and rammed it at the cue ball with so much force that it bypassed the green six ball and jumped over the bumper of the table. It hit the cement floor with a resounding crack and then rolled straight toward Starlet and her cowboy lover. Ignoring it, Beckett used the eight ball as a cue and set up for another shot.

"My, but you suck at pool," Twyla said. "Kenny Gene is really good at pool." She glanced back over her shoulder, and her expression turned sad. "Are you sure you don't want to dance?"

"Beckett doesn't dance." Starlet appeared on the other side of the table. Without the cowboy. In fact, the man was sprinting out the front door. Something that drew Twyla's attention and got her moving.

"Excuse me, y'all, but I just saw someone I know." She hurried out.

When she was gone, Starlet dropped the cue ball on the table. "I'm not sure, but I think you're supposed to hit them in the pockets."

Beckett took the ball and lined it up with the six. "So what happened to your boyfriend?"

"He's not my boyfriend. He's just an acquaintance." Her gaze traveled to his ass, which had Beckett completely missing his shot. As soon as the ball ricocheted off the corner, she walked around the table, her finger trailing along the wood. While she usually wore loose-fitting, almost girlish dresses, tonight she wore tight jeans with little rhinestones and studs running along the front pockets and a silky tank top with a scooped neckline that showed just enough cleavage to have him grabbing his beer and taking a deep swallow. "How's Billy and Shirlene?" she asked. "You're staying at their guesthouse, aren't you?"

"Yes." He watched her finger move closer. "But not for long. I plan on leaving tomorrow."

Her finger stopped. "Tomorrow? But you can't leave tomorrow."

He lifted his gaze from her finger to her face. Her hair had been pulled back in a ponytail, and she wore little or no makeup. But she didn't need any. Her cheeks were full and flushed. Her lashes dark and long.

"And why can't I leave tomorrow?" he asked.

She blinked those long lashes a couple times. "Because... because your brothers have missed you while you were in the marines."

"I've visited with them enough. Besides, I need to see my parents."

"Well, why don't you invite them here? Then your entire family would be together for the Fourth of July—and speaking of the Fourth, if you leave now, you'll miss the big parade!"

He tipped his head and studied her. "What's going on, Starlet? Why do you want me to stay? And don't tell me that you're worried about Jed coming back. Because if you were so worried about him, why didn't you press charges?" He leaned the cue stick against the table and crossed his arms over his chest. "Well?"

She swallowed. "Well, maybe I want you to stay because I—"

Mayor Sutter peeked his head into the room. "Miss Bentley, the band was wonderin' if you'd maybe join them for a few songs. 'Course, if you're too busy..."

"No!" Starlet said. "I'd love to join them for a couple sets." She handed a grocery bag to Beckett. "Don't go anywhere. I'll be right back."

The smart thing for Beckett to do would be to head back to Shirlene and Billy's. Instead, he followed after Starlet. Partly because he wanted to hear the rest of what she had been about to say, and partly because he just couldn't stop himself.

Once Starlet got onstage, she seemed to become a different person. A confident country girl who teased the band and pretty much charmed the entire town. Then she started to sing, and instead of charming the crowd, she seduced them. And not just the crowd but Beckett. There was something about her voice that reeled him in and refused to let go. It was like she understood every emotion he'd ever felt and had put it into words. Once she finished one song, she quickly moved to another. After it, she asked for the use of a guitar and strapped it on before stepping back to the microphone.

"With your permission, I'd like to sing you a song I just wrote. Feel free to tell me what you think—unless you don't like it; then you can keep that to yourself." She flashed a smile as the crowd laughed. "Since this is a slow song, let's turn the lights down so all you couples out there can cuddle close."

As soon as she strummed the first chord, a content smile lit her face. Suddenly, Beckett realized that this wasn't an act. Starlet loved music. She loved playing it. She loved singing it. And she loved performing it. And whatever she'd done to get here, she had done it for this pure joy. For the first time, Beckett saw her as something more than a spoiled brat who had manipulated his brothers. He saw her as a determined woman who had done what she needed to do to achieve her dream.

The lights went down. Even in the dim lighting, Beckett knew that she was looking straight at him. She started to sing, and it was almost as if she had written the song just for him. Which made no sense. It was a song about a piano man, and Beckett had never played a piano in his life. Still, he couldn't stop the emotions the song pulled forth.

Without realizing it, he pushed his way through the crowd and moved closer to the stage. When Starlet finished the song and handed back the guitar to the deafening hoots and applause, he was there to help her down.

As she took his hand, she closed her eyes and smiled. Almost like touching him made her extremely happy. The funny thing about it was that it made Beckett happy too.

"Come on," he said. "I'll take you home."

She held back. "I need a piece of paper and something to write with."

He stared at her for only a second before he shook his head. "Songs really do hit you at random times." Then he led her through the crowd of starstruck townsfolk and over to the bar. He had just asked the bartender for a pen and paper when his cell phone rang. Since he still held Starlet's grocery bag, he had to release her hand to answer it.

"Where are you?" Billy asked. His brother sounded more than a little exasperated. Of course, lately, he always sounded exasperated.

"I'm at Bootlegger's. Why?"

"It's Jesse. He had a ten-o'clock curfew tonight, and he's still not home. I was wondering if you could stop by Sutter Springs on your way back to the house. A lot of kids like to party up there, and I want to make sure that Jesse isn't one of them."

"You know hunting him down isn't the answer, Billy," he said. "And what is up with a ten-o'clock curfew on a Saturday night?"

"He got an F on his geometry test. What was I supposed to do? Congratulate him?"

Beckett instantly felt guilty. Because of the craziness with Starlet and Jed, he hadn't had time to tutor the kid. "Okay. I'll check out Sutter Springs, but you really need to have a long talk with Daddy about raising wild boys." He hung up the phone just as the bartender arrived with the pen and paper. Starlet took them and started scribbling, but not before she grabbed Beckett's hand again.

"Look, I hate to interrupt your writing process," he said, "but I need to take you back to Elizabeth's house."

She glanced up. "Now?"

"Yeah, I need to go check on my nephew out at Sutter Springs and see if—"

Before he could finish, Starlet was pulling him toward the door. "I'll go with you. I've always wanted to see Sutter Springs."

Sutter Springs was only around fifteen minutes outside of town. But fifteen minutes seemed like a lifetime with Starlet glued to Beckett's side. After he'd helped her up on the passenger's side of Billy's monster truck, he'd walked around to the driver's side to find her sitting smack-dab in the middle of the bench seat. Not wanting to hurt her feelings, he'd kept his mouth shut. But after a good ten miles of brushing her breast every time he moved, he decided hurt feelings were better than blue balls.

"Do you think you could scoot over a little?" he asked.

She stopped writing and looked up. "Oh. Of course." She moved a mere millimeter before she started writing again.

Beckett tried to inch closer to his door, but his knee was already touching the handle. Things got even worse when he turned off the main highway and started up the bumpy dirt road. Every pothole had her thigh brushing his and the soft swell of her breast bouncing against his arm. By the time they finally reached Sutter Springs, he had a hard-on that felt like the size of the cottonwood tree he pulled next to. It was the only space left to park. The clearing in front of Sutter Springs was filled with cars and trucks.

Starlet finally stopped writing and glanced up. "So what is going on? Is someone having a party?"

"It would appear that way." Beckett wasted no time in opening the door and jumping down. When she started to follow, he held up a hand. "Look, why don't you stay here, and I'll go get Jesse? It shouldn't take me long, and you can finish your song."

"Actually, I'm done." Using his shoulders for balance, she jumped to the ground, her breasts jiggling just enough to keep Beckett hard as a stone.

He stepped away and tried to keep his mind on something other than the sweet scent of bananas that seemed to seep from her pores. "It only takes you that long to write a song?"

She smiled brightly as she reached back in the truck for the grocery sack. "When inspiration strikes, it strikes." She peered out into the darkness. "So where is this party?"

Realizing that he wasn't going to get away from her long enough to cool off, he took her hand. "Come on, and I'll show you."

The party turned out to be a typical high school summer shindig. A huge fire blazed from a pit dug in the sand, and bare-chested boys and bikinied girls danced around it. Or splashed in the spring that couldn't have been more than a few feet deep.

It was dark enough that the kids paid no attention to Beckett and Starlet's arrival. Or maybe they were drunk enough that they didn't care. Which gave Beckett plenty of time to look around for Jesse.

He found him by the beer keg, filling red Solo cups from the tap. When Beckett moved to the front of the line, Jesse handed him a cup without looking up.

"That will be three bucks. No freebies and no credit."

"Not even for relatives?" Beckett asked.

Jesse glanced up and dropped the tap. "Shit."

"After talking with your dad, I'd say that's exactly what you're in." Beckett rested his hands on his hips and released his breath. "So how do you want to handle this? You want me to take you home and explain what I found you doing? Or do you want to go home and tell your parents?"

Jesse looked at him as if he'd lost his mind. "Go home and leave all my profit? Are you kidding? I just tapped it and haven't sold near enough to cover the cost of the keg."

"That's your problem," Beckett said. "My problem is dealing with an angry big brother if I don't get you home by ten." He looked around. "Besides, I'm sure your friends have had enough."

"But ten is a stupid curfew! Especially when I did all my homework before I left."

Beckett cocked an eyebrow. "Which doesn't explain the F on your geometry test."

The kid's face grew even more belligerent. "What happened to you teaching me how to cheat?"

Beckett now understood how his brother felt. The kid could frustrate a saint. "We'll talk tomorrow. For now, the party is over." Releasing Starlet's hand, he walked over to a large rock and turned off the Bluetooth stereo that someone had set up.

"Hey," a teenage boy yelled, "what do you think you're doing?"

Beckett ignored him and spoke to the entire group. "You've got about three minutes to clear out before I call the sheriff." He looked at the burly kid standing next to him. "And Coach Calhoun."

"Crap," the boy said as he quickly collected his shirt and flip-flops. "I can't be kicked off the team for drinking—my daddy would kill me."

The boys that were obvious football players took flight first, but the other kids soon followed. Only Jesse remained. When he went to hoist up the keg, Beckett shook his head.

"Leave it."

"All right," Jesse grumbled, "but now you are officially my least favorite uncle—even beating out sourpuss Uncle Brant."

Chapter Nineteen

Starlet watched Jesse stomp off and couldn't help but laugh. "That kid is what my uncle Bernie would refer to as a firecracker."

"A firecracker that is going to kill himself or someone else if somebody doesn't turn him in the right direction," Beckett said.

"And you think you're the one to do it?" She walked over to a blanket one of the kids had left and sat down. She opened the grocery bag and pulled out the box of MoonPies.

"You carry those things with you?" Beckett took a seat next to her.

"Only when Kari's not around." She offered him one. He hesitated for only a second before accepting. "So if you're tutoring Jesse, I guess that means that you're not leaving tomorrow?"

He took a bite of MoonPie. "I guess not."

Since that fit right into her plans, Starlet almost rubbed her hands together and cackled with glee. Instead, she hid her joy behind a big bite of pie. While she savored the flavor, she studied him. He had left his cowboy hat in the truck, and a crumb of banana icing clung to the corner of his mouth. Starlet couldn't remember anything being so tempting. To keep herself from diving on him and licking it off, she pulled her gaze away. "You have to admit that it looked like fun."

"Don't tell me that you've never been to a wild teenage party before." He finished off the rest of the MoonPie in two bites, then wiped the icing from his mouth. Starlet felt deprived.

"I wasn't exactly what you would call popular. And how do you know about wild teenage parties? I thought you were a geek in high school."

Beckett bent his leg and tugged off a boot. "I got invited to parties because of my brothers. But you're right. Once there, I stuck out like a sore thumb. I guess bringing your laptop briefcase to a party is taboo."

She laughed. "I can just see you walking in like Sheldon from *The Big Bang Theory*, making everyone feel like idiots."

"I wasn't that bad." A grin tipped up the corners of his mouth. "But I was different enough from my gregarious brothers that people used to think I was adopted."

"I know what you mean." She finished the MoonPie and then tugged off her boots. "People couldn't believe that my thin, beautiful mama had such a fat, ugly daughter. Which was probably one of the reasons that she dropped me off at my uncle's after my daddy left. If I'd been pretty, my daddy might've stayed and she might've kept me." She didn't realize how pathetic she sounded until Beckett stopped in the middle of pulling off his socks and turned to her. She tried to backpedal, but it was hard to backpedal out of the truth. "I mean...it probably would've been harder to leave a cute baby."

There was a long, awkward pause before Beckett went back to peeling off his socks. "You do realize that your mama is screwed up, Starlet? She wouldn't have kept you no matter how cute a baby you were." He shot a glance at her. "And I figure that you were a pretty cute baby."

She snorted. "Don't start lying to me now. You've never thought that I was pretty. If you had, you would've taken me up on what I offered the night of my going-away party."

The words just sort of popped out. Once they were there, Starlet wanted to pinch herself. Why in the world would she bring up the most humiliating night of her life? Especially to the man who had made it so humiliating? Before she could get out of the mess she'd made, Beckett spoke.

"You honestly think my rejection had to do with your looks? You were drunk, Starlet. And I don't have sex with women who don't know exactly what they're doing—or with whom."

The revelation hit her right between the eyes like the rock Jed had thrown at her in grade school, leaving her twice as stunned. All these years, she had assumed Beckett had turned her down because she was fat and ugly. Now he was telling her that it had more to do with her being drunk.

"But you were drunk the other night at Miss Hattie's when you found me in the Jungle Room. Should I have turned you down?" She cringed and looked down at the box of MoonPies, wondering if banana and sugar worked like some kind of truth serum. It seemed likely when Beckett answered her.

"I wasn't drunk." Then, before she could get over her shock, he reached for his boots. "We better get going."

She stopped him by touching his arm. The music returned, but now it didn't consume her. What consumed her was the feel of his skin. The tightening of muscle. The heat that radiated to every part of her.

"I wasn't that drunk either," she said. "I knew exactly whose room I was sneaking into that night at Miss Hattie's."

He studied her, the pupils of his eyes reflecting the flickering flames of the fire. "But why?"

"Because you were the first boy who wanted to dance with me."

He shook his head. "Every man in the room danced with you that night—long before I did."

"But only because Minnie paid them. I knew right away that they were escorts. They laid on the compliments and flirtation too thick to be genuine. And then you showed up," she said, her voice barely above a whisper, "this skinny geek with a perpetual frown who had never lied to me, who had always told me exactly how he felt even if I didn't like it. When you asked me to dance, I believed it was the real thing. You gave me what Minnie's paid escorts couldn't. For one dance, you gave me prom night."

Beckett stared at her for a moment before he turned away. "Jesus." He smoothed the lock of hair back from his forehead. "Here I thought I was so damned smart—that I was the only one who had you figured out. The truth was that I didn't have you figured out at all. You really were that damned innocent. And I was just some asshole with low self-esteem who screwed up what should've been the best night of your life."

"But didn't you hear what I said? You didn't screw it up. I was the one who screwed it up by coming to—what are you doing? Are you calling someone?"

Beckett pulled his cell phone from his shirt pocket and tapped the screen until a Jason Aldean song came through the speaker. He set the phone down and got to his feet. "Come on, Miss Brubaker. I might've screwed up prom, but I can give you a high school summer party." He popped the snaps on his shirt and took it off. It was hard to think when staring at miles of sculpted muscle.

"This is crazy, Beckett," she said. Even though she didn't think it was crazy. She thought it was sweet and romantic. "You don't have to do this."

"I know I don't have to. I want to. You weren't the only one who missed out on having a good time at a high school party." He circled his arm over his head, and his shirt went sailing off into the darkness. "Well, what do you say, Starlet?" He held out a hand. "For one night, do you want to pretend that we're two wild and crazy popular kids?"

He did a little shuffle step, his bare feet kicking up sand on the blanket. He had nice feet. Long and narrow with toes that snuggled together at a perfect angle. She remembered those feet from that night. She remembered his feet and his bare chest when he had taken off his tuxedo shirt and covered her after she'd slipped off her dress. Back then, she had been humiliated and hated him all the more for it. But now she realized that even then Beckett had been a gentleman.

She pulled off her socks before taking his hand. "Why not."

The sand was too soft to two-step in. So Beckett pulled

her into more of an awkward country swing—guiding her under his arm before rocking her back and forth in a rock-step. After Jason Aldean, a Luke Bryan song came on, and she and Beckett separated and danced around the fire, gyrating and waving their arms like a couple of loons.

They danced for five songs before they took a break, and then, after sharing a cup of beer, they danced some more. Beckett gave up first, flopping down and falling back on the sand.

"You're not quitting now, are you?" She looked down at him, her gaze unable to resist the sweat-slick abs that stair-stepped down his stomach.

"I give." He rested the back of his arm over his eyes. "I feel worse than I did the first day of basic training." He scratched his chest, drawing her gaze to his hard pectoral muscles. "And itchier. In fact..." He rolled to his feet and unfastened his belt.

Starlet's eyes widened. "What are you doing?"

He grinned devilishly as he pushed his jeans down and stepped out of them. "Cooling off."

Starlet took a step back. "Oh, no. I'm not skinny-dipping with you, Becky."

Wearing nothing but an evil look and a pair of boxer briefs that left very little to the imagination, he took a step toward her. "Becky?"

"I mean Beckett," she quickly revised as she stumbled backward.

"Too late." He charged her. She barely had time to release a squeal before she was tossed over his shoulder and carried straight into Sutter Springs. "What's my name?" He dipped his knees.

"Don't you do it," she yelled. "Don't you dare—" The

rest of what she was going to say was cut off by the shock of cold water as he dumped her into the spring.

It wasn't very deep, but with the slippery rocks on the bottom, it took her three tries before she could stand. Her clothes were soaked, and her hair extensions covered her face in a thick, wet curtain. She parted the strands to find Beckett bent over with laughter.

"It's not funny!" she snapped. "This is a five-hundred-dollar silk shirt that you ruined. Not to mention the thousands I paid for these hair extensions."

He straightened. "You pay thousands for fake hair? That's crazy, especially when you had such beautiful hair."

Some of her anger dissolved. "You thought my hair was beautiful?"

"Yes, but don't get a big head about it."

Feeling all sappy inside, she smiled brightly before she pulled the shirt over her head and wiggled out of her jeans. It was his turn to look shocked.

"What are you doing?"

"I'm going skinny-dipping. Or at least panty and bra dipping." As soon as her jeans were off, she dove back into the water and straight for Beckett's legs. With the slippery bottom, it took very little to get him under, although his reflexes were much faster, and he snagged her before she could swim away. He dunked her, but she wrapped her legs around his hips and pulled him down with her. When he resurfaced, she came right along with him, her feet hooked behind his back. Their gasps for breath quickly turned to laughter.

"Taken down by a girl," Beckett said between chuckles. "My brothers would have a field day if they ever found out."

Starlet giggled and brushed the hair out of her face. "I guess all the time spent with the ThighMaster paid off."

"The ThighMaster?"

"Kari's idea to get rid of my fat thighs. And I must say that it worked." She smiled. "I took down Beckett Cates."

The smile slipped from his face to be replaced with a heated expression that took all the air out of her lungs. "That you did." He carried her back to the blanket, but once there, he didn't seem in any hurry to put her down. He just stood there with water dripping off the ends of his hair and the coals of the dwindling fire gleaming in his eyes. She had told him that it was their dance that had drawn her to his room. But now she had to wonder if it was something else. Some kind of invisible magnet that pulled her to him even when she fought against it.

Another song started playing from his phone. It was one of her songs. And not just any song, but "Good-bye Kiss." Usually she felt a pang of pain when she heard it, but tonight there was no pain. There was just Beckett.

She studied his mouth for a few moments before she lifted her gaze. "Why didn't you kiss me that night at Miss Hattie's? When the dance ended, I thought you were going to. But then you turned and walked away."

She watched his Adam's apple slide up and down his throat. "Maybe I didn't want to start something I couldn't finish."

"So what's stopping you now?"

His gaze lowered to her lips, and when he spoke, his voice was a husky whisper. "Nothing. Nothing at all."

His head lowered, and his lips brushed hers, hesitantly at first, then deeper. Since leaving the henhouse, she had kissed her fair share of men. Country singers, rodeo cowboys, a famous actor or two. But Beckett's lips erased all the kisses that had come before. He kissed like he seemed to do everything—with total concentration and dedication.

He released her legs, and she slid down wet, smooth muscle that already felt hot to the touch. Her hands curved over his shoulders and toyed with the curls at the back of his neck as he slanted his head and deepened the kiss even further, his tongue dipping into her mouth and doing a slow dance with hers.

She was so wrapped up in the kiss that she didn't realize he had unsnapped her bra until it popped open. His hand cupped her breast, his thumb sliding back and forth over her hardened nipple. A moan escaped her throat, and she pulled away from his lips to catch her breath, leaving Beckett enough space to slip off her bra. Her panties followed; then he took a step back, and his gaze ran over her until she blushed with embarrassment.

"I know," she said as she tried to angle her body away from the firelight. "I've put on a few pounds since I got here."

His eyes lifted. "You weren't made to be a skinny woman, Starlet. You were made to have curves." He reached out and caressed a breast with the back of his knuckles. "Sexy-as-hell curves." His hands curled over her hips, and he pulled her up against the hardness beneath his boxers. "Feel what your curves do to me?" He leaned down and took a nip of her bottom lip. "What they've always done to me. Especially when you got naked in my room."

Before she could do more than blush with happiness, he kissed her again and did a bump and grind that took all thoughts right out of her head. Save for one.

I want Beckett...now.

Pulling back from the kiss, she reached for the elastic of his boxers and pushed the wet material down his legs. Kneeling in front of him, she waited for him to step out of them. When he didn't, she looked up. The evidence of his desire was a little intimidating. It was also extremely hot. Or maybe what was hot was the way he stood there with his eyelids half-closed, just daring her to touch him.

Starlet didn't have a problem taking the dare. Without hesitation, she took him in hand and stroked up from the bottom of the shaft to the very tip. He moaned deep in his throat, and his hand slipped into her hair and pulled her closer.

"Kiss it," he rasped.

She leaned in and gave him a soft kiss before opening her mouth and taking him in deep. He sucked in his breath and cradled her head in his hands, allowing her to set the pace. She had just found a good rhythm that had his breath chugging and his muscles tightening when he stopped her.

"My turn." He knelt and eased her back to the blanket, his lips trailing sweet kisses over her breasts and down her stomach. He kissed her between the legs, softly at first, then deeper. Her toes curled into the sand and her hips lifted as his tongue flicked a beat that soon had her catapulting toward the star-filled sky.

But before she could reach those glittering stars, he stopped. No more than a second later, he had a condom on and was slipping deep inside her still-quivering body. He inhaled sharply and mumbled something that sounded a lot like "perfect" before he started to move. He didn't thrust as much as stroke. Deep, satisfying strokes that quickly had the fire inside her blazing out of control.

"Beckett!" she breathed as she climaxed. He followed right behind her. As she watched ecstasy consume him, the music returned—this time a sweet, mandolin melody that had her eyes closing and her lips humming.

"Please don't tell me that you need a pencil and paper."

She opened her eyes and found Beckett watching her with a desire-filled, heavy-lidded look that pretty much melted her like butter in a hot skillet.

"Nope." Starlet wrapped her arms around his neck. "Right now, I just need you, Becky."

Chapter Twenty

THEY FIT A LITTLE snug in the crotch, but they still looked good. Made of heavy cady—whatever that was—with a satin waistband, the black Latin competition trousers had cost Rye Pickett a pretty penny. As had the puff-sleeved dance shirt and lace-up leather shoes. After spending most of his life in cowboy boots, the flat-soled shoes had taken some getting used to.

Another thing that took some getting used to was seeing Rachel Dean's cousin Bear in a sequined dress that exposed most of his hairy chest and hugged the spare tire around his waist. Although Rye had to give it to him. Bear could sure dance in a pair of high heels. Of course, it was in his blood. His mama had been a West Texas Clogger whose lifelong dream had been to dance on the stage of the Grand Ole Opry. But her dream was lost forever when she pulled her Achilles tendon and had to stop clogging.

And maybe that was why Bear worked so hard. He wanted to achieve what his mama hadn't. Although Rye couldn't see the Latin salsa being performed on the stage at the Opry. Regardless of the fact that Bear kicked and shimmied better than any contestant on *Dancing with the Stars*.

After a good four months of Bear's dance lessons, Rye wasn't so bad himself.

At least, he thought so. Bear wasn't quite as appreciative.

"No. No. No." He pulled out of Rye's arms and clicked his way over to the boom box to turn it off. "In the cross-body lead, you need to do a quarter turn on counts two and three and, on counts four and five, lead me across in front of you with your hand firmly placed on my back." He demonstrated the move and then waited for Rye to copy him.

It took a few tries for Rye to get it. When he did, Bear nodded, pressed the play button on the boom box, and hurried back over to position himself between Rye and the floor-to-ceiling mirror. The mirror made no difference to Rye. Once Bear stood in front of him, all he could see was his friend's hairy chest.

The song started, and Bear counted off the dance steps. The counting sure helped. They went through the entire routine this time without one mistake, ending with Rye dipping Bear down into the splits. There was a moment of stunned silence before they both hooted with joy. Rye helped Bear to his feet, and they hugged and slapped each other on the back.

"Hot damn," Rye said. "We did it!"

"We sure did." Bear moved over to the mini-fridge. "I'd say that's cause for a celebration." He pulled out a couple beers, then slammed the fridge closed with his hip and came teetering back. "But it's a cryin' shame that no one gets to see how much work we've put in." He handed a bottle to Rye, who wasted no time twisting off the cap. "We've really gotten good in the last few months."

Rye guzzled down half his beer and wiped off his

mouth with the back of his hand. "That we have." He patted his stomach. "And this exercise has been better than Hydroxycut for tightenin' up the old abs. If I keep it up, I might get Dana Leigh to go out with me. Accordin' to her mama, she's turned into a real health nut since she got back from college." He took another drink and glanced over to see Bear studying the sparkly toes of his heels.

"Well, maybe she'd go out with you if she saw you do a sexy Latin dance."

Rye choked and spewed beer. "Have you lost your mind, Bear? I told you when I agreed to this craziness"—he waved a hand at Bear's dress—"that no one could know what we're doin' on Thursday nights."

Bear's expression turned mean. And when Bear turned mean, things could get ugly in a hurry. "So you think I'm crazy?"

The thought had crossed Rye's mind, but he figured this wasn't the time to bring it up. Especially when Bear's softball-sized fists were only one swing away from his nose.

He held up a hand. "Now, I wouldn't say you were crazy, Bear. All I'm sayin' is that folks in Bramble might not take too well to seein' a big bounty hunter doin' the cha-cha in high heels and sequins. Now, if we lived in New Orleans, that might be different."

Bear's face fell as his shoulders drooped. "You're right. I would fit in better there than I do here." He turned and walked over to the boom box and shut it off. "And this is craziness. Why would we practice every Thursday if no one is ever gonna see us dance?" He stared at himself in the mirror for a second before he headed for the door, his high heels clicking on the cement floor and his spare tire jiggling like low-hanging back boobs. "You can see yourself out, Rye."

"Now, wait a second, Bear." He started after him. "We don't have to stop dancin'. Hell, if you want someone to see us dance, we can go to my grandma's retirement home. Nana loves *Dancing with the Stars* and will forget all about the heels and crotch-huggin' pants five minutes after we leave."

Bear turned, the garage light reflecting off his shimmery blue eye shadow. "But that's the point, Rye. Maybe I don't want people to forget. Maybe I'm sick of hidin' who I am." He walked out in a swish of sequins, slamming the door behind him.

Once he was gone, there was nothing left for Rye to do but change out of his Latin dance clothes. As he folded them and put them back in his duffel bag, he glanced in the mirror. The plaid shirt and worn jeans didn't look half as cool as the lacy shirt and satin waist-banded pants. Or maybe what didn't look so cool was the man staring back at him. A man who had hurt his friend's feelings all because he was afraid of what other folks might think.

Slinging the bag over his shoulder, Rye shut off the light and headed out the door.

Bear lived in a trailer in the middle of nowhere. Which was another reason Rye had agreed to the dancing. Very few townsfolk came out this way. Bear had inherited the land from his and Rachel Dean's great-grandfather, who had purchased it after discovering a vein of silver in one of the ravines. Although some folks believed that he'd purchased the land not for the silver as much as its proximity to Miss Hattie's Henhouse. Especially when the vein hadn't produced more than a marble bag of silver. And plenty of descendants had tried.

Now all that was left was a ramshackle hole in the ground that had been closed for decades. Bear was in the process of putting up the cell bars he'd purchased from the town of Culver after their jail roof caved in, so that people couldn't go too deep into the mine and get themselves killed in a cave-in.

That was just the kind of person Bear was—always thinking of others. As a bounty hunter, he had tried to help Hope Lomax find a daddy for her unborn child and had brought Jenna Jay and Beau back home to Texas. As a citizen, he volunteered on the fire department and the city council. And as a friend, he had helped Rye build a man cave on the back of his house that rivaled all man caves.

Which was exactly how Rye had ended up being Bear's dance partner on Thursday nights. You couldn't really say no to a man who had built a room for your sixty-inch flat-screen and not asked for a dime in payment. Once Rye got over his shock of Bear in sequins, he had to admit that he enjoyed the ballroom dancing.

At least, he did in the privacy of Bear's shed.

But sometimes being a friend meant doing something that might embarrass the hell out of you. And Rye figured that if he was going to be embarrassed anyway, he might as well do it up right. By the time he contacted Darla and got her help, New Orleans would have nothing on Bramble.

He had just reached for his cell phone when he noticed the headlights coming down the dirt road. Curious as to who would be out there at nine o'clock on a Thursday night, he waited for the car to pass.

It turned out that it wasn't a car, but a beat-up truck. One that had been parked in Jones's Garage for more than a few days while it was getting fixed. Rye lifted his hand in greeting, but it was too dark to tell if the man inside reciprocated. He watched as the truck headed down the road, the two-by-fours in the back bouncing against the tailgate.

As Rye pulled out his cell phone, he shook his head.

Talk about good men. That Cowboy was one hard-working sonofagun.

Chapter Twenty-one

THE RUNDOWN TRAILER STILL belonged to Billy and Shirlene. Although why his brother hadn't had it torn down and turned into scrap metal, Beckett didn't know. The siding was peeling, most of the windows were cracked, and a string of Christmas lights dangled from the rusted gutters. Christmas lights he'd helped Billy put up for his wedding reception. That probably explained why the trailer was still there. Women were extremely sentimental about the silliest things.

Take Starlet for example.

Why would a woman offer herself to a man just because he asked her to dance? It made absolutely no sense whatsoever. Luckily, you didn't have to understand women to enjoy them. And Beckett had sure enjoyed Starlet. Not just the sex. But the conversation. The MoonPies. The skinny-dipping. Hell, he'd even enjoyed the dancing. Beckett had always hated dancing because it made him feel awkward and clumsy. But for some reason, dancing with Starlet hadn't made him feel awkward or clumsy. It had just made him feel right.

What didn't feel right was hunting down a delinquent

kid that wasn't even his own. But Beckett had no choice, seeing as how he'd stuck his nose where it didn't belong. Jesse was supposed to meet him an hour ago at the guest-house so they could start their tutoring. Beckett might've let it slide if Jesse hadn't also failed to tell his parents about the keg party. The kid was really pushing it, and Beckett didn't know how Billy had kept from skinning him alive.

The set of stairs looked as rickety as the trailer, but they held as Beckett stepped up to the door. Since he didn't expect Jesse to answer, he didn't waste time knocking. Unfortunately, the door was locked tight, which seemed suspicious since no one in Bramble locked their doors. Walking around to the back, he found a bedroom window with a busted screen. He jimmied with the frame until he got it open.

Once inside, he had to wonder if Jesse's brother Brody had given him correct information or just swindled his uncle out of a movie-sized candy bar. The inside of the trailer looked more like a bachelor pad than a teenager's hideout. An expensive leather sectional sat in front of an entertainment center that housed a huge flat-screen televi-sion, a Blu-ray DVD player, and Bose speakers.

Beckett had just started for the door when he glanced down at the coffee table and noticed the envelope with Starlet's name on it. He didn't hesitate to open it and pull out the piece of paper and DVD. The paper had letters cut out of a magazine and glued to it. *If you don't loan me $150,000 dollars, I'll send a copy to the press.*

Beckett stared at the sentence. *Loan?* And a copy of what? He walked over to the player and popped in the DVD. Then he sat down on the couch and pushed the play button. It was a video of the night of Starlet's going-away party. Not the party, but what had happened in Miss Hattie's room after the party. Half-naked women gyrated around Brianne and Dusty while Reverend Josiah Jessup, who had orchestrated the entire thing for a reality television show, preached about the evils of Miss Hattie's Henhouse. In the midst of it all, Starlet walked in, wearing nothing but Beckett's tuxedo shirt. If this DVD got in the wrong hands, it could spell disaster for Starlet's career—

"Why, that little blackmailing shit," Beckett muttered as he clicked off the television and jumped to his feet.

Once he took the DVD out of the player and locked it in the glove box of his truck, he pulled the truck around back and waited for Jesse to arrive. It didn't take long. Beckett had no more than poured out the bottles of beer he'd found in the refrigerator when he heard the key fit into the lock. Figuring that the kid would make a run for it, he waited for Jesse to step inside and close the door before he made his presence known.

"Hey, Jess."

"Jesus!" Jesse whirled toward him. "How the hell did you get in here? You know there's a law against breaking and entering."

Beckett moved in front of the door. "Sorta like the laws about underage drinking and blackmail."

Jesse's gaze shot over to the opened envelope on the coffee table. "You went through my stuff?"

"Your stuff? Seeing as how this is Billy and Shirlene's trailer, I'd say it was their stuff. Although I don't know if they want to be included in your blackmail scheme."

The look of belligerence dimmed slightly. "It's not a blackmail scheme. I was just going to borrow the money from Starlet to start up my Internet business. Once I made it big, I planned on paying her back with interest."

"So where did you steal the tape?"

"I didn't steal it! I found the digital camcorder on the ground at Miss Hattie's."

Beckett crossed his arms over his chest. "Which brings up another good question—what were you doing out at the henhouse that night?"

Instead of answering, Jesse glared at him. Figuring that it was time to cut to the chase, Beckett walked over to the briefcase he'd gotten out of Billy's truck and took out his laptop. "Here's how this is going to work. You're going to tell your parents about the keg party and take whatever punishment they give you without one grumble. Then every day after summer school, you're going to meet me here so you can ace geometry."

"Ace? I ain't never gonna ace that class."

Beckett shrugged. "If you'd rather spend the rest of the summer and your senior year in the Lubbock Juvenile Detention Center, that's your choice." He started to put his laptop away when Jesse stopped him.

"You'd turn your own nephew over to the cops?"

Beckett thought for a second. "No. You're right. I probably couldn't do that." When Jesse's shoulders relaxed, he added, "But I would tell Starlet, and I'm sure that she'd have no problem telling the cops about your blackmail scheme." He glanced around. "Especially when it looks like you've already fleeced her for some money."

Jesse clenched his fists. "She didn't send me any money. I wheeled and dealed for this stuff. And I'd already changed my mind about sendin' the letter."

"Something I'm sure Judge Seeley will believe,"

Beckett said dryly. "Now, what's it going to be? Jail or school?"

"Fine!" Jesse flopped down in a kitchen chair. "But I'm not smart enough to get A's, so you'll have to settle for B's."

Beckett pulled out a kitchen chair. "I guess we'll have to see."

It turned out that, once Jesse had the right kind of motivation, he was a good student with a sharp mind. Of course, the breakthrough came when Beckett changed all the math equations to money problems. By the time he took Jesse home, he was feeling pretty good about the kid's chances of graduating from high school.

That was if his father didn't kill him first.

"You what!" Billy's voice boomed off the ceiling in his study.

Jesse sat in the chair in front of his father's desk and stared at the toes of his scuffed cowboy boots. "I had a keg party out at Sutter Springs and charged everyone for beer."

Billy's mouth flapped a couple times as he struggled to find words. He looked at Beckett, who only shrugged.

"He promised me that he was going to tell you."

Billy sat down in his chair and released his breath. "I don't know what to do with you, Jesse. I've tried lectures, restrictions, and taking your phone, computer, and driving privileges away, and nothing seems to get through to you." He lifted his hands. "I give up."

Jesse stared at him with more than a little shock. "You're giving up on me?"

"I'll never give up on you, son, but I'm not going to fight you anymore."

"So you aren't going to punish me?"

Billy shook his head. "No. If you want to break the law,

you'll deal with the consequences of your actions. But your mama and I won't be coming to bail you out of jail. You get there, you'll stay there. And if you want to drop out of school, I guess you'll have to live with that choice too."

It took a moment for Jesse to digest the information that his father wasn't going to punish him. When he finally did, he didn't look too happy about it. "Well, maybe I don't want to quit school." His chin got a stubborn tilt to it. "In fact"—he got to his feet—"I think I'm going to go study right now."

Once he was gone, Billy released a long sigh. "That kid is going to be the death of me."

"Doubtful," Beckett said. "Dads are tougher than you think. Just look at ours. Besides, I think Jesse might've turned over a new leaf." He picked up a magazine off the end table, the same magazine that he'd picked up a week earlier. Except this time, the picture of Starlet with the cowboy annoyed him even more. So much so that he tore off the cover, wadded it up, and tossed it at the trash can by the desk. It missed by a mile.

"What's going on, Beck?" Billy asked as he retrieved the crumpled paper and hit the trash can dead center. "Do you know something about Jesse you're not telling me?"

Beckett flipped down the coverless magazine. "Sometimes it's best if you leave things alone, Billy. And if anyone should know that, you should. As of now, Jesse has agreed to let me tutor him and to stay in school. Does the why or how matter?"

It took a while for his brother to answer. "I guess not." He glanced over at Beckett. "So what changed your mind about staying and tutoring Jesse? And don't tell me that it was the kid's sparkling personality."

Beckett got to his feet. "Maybe I just missed hanging out with my big brother. Now, if you'll excuse me, I—"

Before Beckett even made it to the door, Billy had him in a headlock. "Aww, ain't that sweet. In fact, you brought tears to my eyes. But I think it has more to do with the crush you have on a certain country singer." He gave him a noggin rub that brought tears to Beckett's eyes. He knew he could get out of the headlock, but for some reason, he chose not to. Maybe because he no longer had anything to prove to his brothers. Or maybe he had finally accepted the fact that a little brother's lot in life was to be tortured by his big brothers.

After another noogie, Billy released him and grinned. "Now, how about a game of pool before supper?"

As it turned out, Beckett beat Billy five games in a row before Shirlene arrived and rescued her husband.

"So who's winnin'?" she asked as she leaned over and gave Billy a kiss on the cheek. The pig that followed behind her lifted his snout as if to get his own kiss. Instead, Billy scratched his ears as he continued to scowl at the placement of the balls. Shirlene flopped down in a chair. "Hopefully, you two had more fun than I had at the Fourth of July celebration plannin' meetin'."

"Did you get everything figured out, sugar buns?" Billy asked without taking his eyes off the table.

"The only thing I got figured out is that the folks of Bramble are plumb crazy. There are so many people on the mayor's ballot that if something isn't done, everyone will just be voting for themselves."

Billy glanced at her. "Did you try getting ahold of Hope again?"

"Yes, but I haven't heard a thing back from her or

Faith. I guess those mountains in New Mexico can jumble up reception somethin' fierce." Her expression turned sad. "I just can't believe that Hope would keep news like twins from her best friend." She glanced over as Brody came into the room. "Is that chocolate on your mouth, Brody? You know that you're not supposed to be eatin' candy after you had three cavities at your last dental visit."

Brody looked over at Beckett, who decided that it was time to leave.

"I think I'll stop by and say hi to Beau and Jenna Jay," he said as he replaced his pool cue in the rack.

"Oh, no, you don't," Billy said. "The game's not over yet. Besides, we both know that you're not going over to Beau's. You're headed to Elizabeth's old house."

"Elizabeth's old house?" Shirlene looked confused. "Now, why would Beckett be going—" She paused, and her eyes lit up. "Starlet?"

Billy leaned on his pool cue and grinned. "It seems that Beckett has a little crush on Miss Star Bentley."

His brother's teasing hit a raw nerve. "I don't have a crush," Beckett said. To prove it, he grabbed the pool cue and resumed the game. "And I had no intention of going over to see her at Elizabeth's house." It was an out-and-out lie. One that cost him when Shirlene waited for him to take his shot before smiling sweetly.

"Well, in that case, honey, you won't mind babysitting the kids so Billy can take me out on a date."

Instead of spending the evening with a hot country singer, Beckett spent it with two kids and a belligerent teenager. Although Jesse appeared only for dinner before he went back to his room to study. Which left Beckett to entertain his niece and nephew by himself. After a cannonball contest in the swimming pool, a Disney movie, and a Nerf gunfight that left a floor lamp casualty, he settled them down in bed—first Adeline and then Brody.

"So did you find Jesse at Mama's trailer?" Brody asked as Beckett waited for him to climb into bed so he could turn out the light.

"Yes, and thanks for the tip. Did you brush your teeth good?"

"Yep." The kid plumped up his pillow before lying down. "So what would you give me if I had a real good secret?"

"No more candy." He turned off the light. "Besides, I don't think I'll have to hunt down Jesse again." He started to close the door when Brody spoke.

"This secret ain't about Jesse. It's about Aunt Starlet."

Beckett slowly turned to the bed. "Starlet? What do you know about Starlet?"

"Milk Duds," he said. "Two boxes."

Obviously, some of Jesse's blackmailing techniques had rubbed off on his little brother, and any good uncle would point that out and tell the kid to take a hike. And if the secret hadn't been about Starlet, Beckett might've been able to do it.

"One box, not movie-sized."

Brody sat up. "It's okay if you have a crush on Starlet, Uncle Beck, because I was listening in on Mama's conversation with Jenna Jay the other day, and I guess Starlet has a crush too. And has ever since she lived at the henhouse." He flopped back on the pillow. "Night, Uncle Beck."

Beckett stepped out in the hallway and closed the door. Starlet had a crush on him? At first it was hard to believe, but once he started thinking, it made perfect sense. A crush would explain a lot of her actions—the way she'd always left the room when he walked in, the nickname, the night of her going-away party. She had never hated him. She had actually liked him all along.

And standing there in the hallway of his brother's house, with a stupid smile on his face and his heart thumping overtime, Beckett realized that he'd never hated Starlet either.

Chapter Twenty-two

"AFTER THE FOURTH!" KARI'S voice rang through the receiver so loudly that Starlet had to pull the phone away from her ear. "What do you mean that you're not coming back until after the Fourth of July? Are you crazy? I have a full schedule for you that weekend, including a special surprise appearance with Toby Keith."

Starlet stared down at the bacon crackling in the skillet. Was she crazy? It seemed pretty crazy that she would rather spend the holiday standing on a float in a small-town parade than perform with Toby Keith. But she couldn't leave Bramble now. Or maybe it wasn't Bramble she couldn't leave as much as Beckett.

Beckett who gave her music and three orgasms under the stars.

And three orgasms rated right up there with Toby.

"I'm sure you can reschedule," she said as she flipped the bacon. "And I promise I will be back in Nashville..." She let the sentence drift off.

"I didn't catch that," Kari said. "When will you be back?"

"Soon." Then, before Kari could start ranting again, Starlet grabbed up the *Bramble Gazette* that had been delivered that morning and crumpled it next to the phone. "Sorry, but I think we've got a bad—" She hung up and then turned to find her uncle standing in the doorway of the kitchen, grinning.

"I always knew there was a steel magnolia beneath the fragile daisy." He took the newspaper from her hand and walked over to the table and sat down.

"I wouldn't say that." Starlet removed the bacon from the pan. "A steel magnolia would've fired Kari a long time ago."

"Now, don't throw out the baby with the bathwater," he said. "Kari might have a few bad qualities that need corrallin', but don't we all. Look at me. I have more than a few. Luckily, I've finally found a woman who knows how to corral me."

Starlet pulled the carton of eggs from the refrigerator. "So how are things going with Olive?"

"Slow." He tucked a napkin in the collar of his pale blue western shirt. "It seems that a few kisses is all the woman is going to give me until I get a job that doesn't include moochin' off you."

Starlet laughed as she cracked the eggs in the hot bacon grease. "Olive said that?"

"Her exact words." He paused. "And I guess she's right. I have been moochin'. And so have Jed and Jaydeen."

"It's not mooching when you're family, Uncle Bernie." Starlet slipped the sunny-side-up eggs onto the plates with the bacon and toast. But when she turned to carry the plates to the table, she noticed that Uncle Bernie was sitting there with not a hint of a smile on his face.

"Yes, it is," he said sadly. "Family should help family, but family should also never take advantage of family. And that's exactly what we've been doin' to you. We've been takin' advantage of your goodness and kindness without givin' anything in return."

Starlet set the plates down on the table and took a seat across from him. "But you raised me, Uncle Bernie."

"No, Star Baby, you raised yourself. And damned if you didn't do a better job than Maybelline and I did with Jed. You're much tougher than Jed or Maybelline. They never would've survived your childhood or fought for their dreams as hard as you fought for yours." His eyes welled with tears. "But as strong as your life made you, I'm still sorry. Sorry I was too drunk to realize the gem Jaydeen had given us."

In all the time she'd known him, she'd never seen her uncle apologize to anyone. The sincerity and sadness in his eyes had her reaching for his hand. "We can't go back. We can only go forward. Isn't that what you've always told me, Uncle Bernie?"

His smile slid back into place. "I guess I did." He squeezed her hand. "After my drunkenness and neglect, I probably don't have the right to say this, but I'm as proud as a daddy could be of who you are and what you've accomplished."

Starlet couldn't help the tears that ran down her cheeks. They caused Uncle Bernie to pat her hand before he changed the subject. "Now, I didn't mean to start the mornin' with a bunch of crying." He picked up his fork. "What say we eat this fine breakfast that God has seen fit to bless us with—and you've seen fit to prepare so nicely—and try to decide what job I'm going to get?" He took a bite of eggs before glancing down at the newspaper and the mayoral headline. "What do you think about politics?"

"Oh, no," she said as she picked up her fork. "Everyone in town seems to be in that election. You don't need to be too."

He nodded. "You're probably right." He thought for a moment before his eyes lit up. "But with all those candidates, they might need some promotional items. Like maybe a few hats and T-shirts with their pictures on them."

Starlet couldn't help but giggle.

Once Uncle Bernie left for town, Starlet cleaned up the dishes. She had just taken the broom out of the pantry to sweep the floor when a car pulled into the driveway. Dropping the broom, she hurried over to the window. Unfortunately, it wasn't Beckett's big monster truck, but a red pickup with a bent front fender. The passenger door opened, and her mama got out. With the reflection of the morning sun on the windshield, Starlet couldn't see who was driving. But it must've been a man by the way her mama wiggled her way around the front of the truck and waggled her fingers.

"Thanks for the lift, sugar!" she called. "You sure you don't want to come inside for a little...coffee?"

If the man answered, Starlet couldn't hear him. Although she figured it was no when the truck backed up and pulled away. A few minutes later, her mama came into the kitchen, looking like she'd been run through the wringer and hung out to dry in a stiff wind.

"Coffee," she mumbled as she flopped down in a chair. Starlet poured her a cup and took it over to her. "So I'm going to assume that you snuck out to Bootlegger's last night after I went to bed."

Her mama took a sip of coffee and sighed. "You would assume correctly. Although I didn't have to sneak. You were dead to the world."

Starlet had slept well. After Beckett dropped her off, she had written nonstop until the music left. Once it was gone, she'd made herself a ham sandwich with the groceries Uncle Bernie had purchased and crashed on the sofa.

"So who was that in the truck?" She picked up the broom and started sweeping.

"Some cowboy named Cowboy." Her mama laughed, but it quickly turned into a smoker's cough similar to Miss Minnie's before she'd quit. Her mama took another sip of coffee to stop it. "He works at Bootlegger's and reminds me of that Julio Iglesias guy, except with really scary eyes. You know the kind I'm talking about? Dark ones that look bottomless."

Starlet stopped sweeping. "You're not going to bring strangers back here, Mama. There's barely enough room for the three of us as is. We don't need someone else living with us."

Her mama lowered her cup and stared at her. "Living with us? What do you mean living with us? We aren't living here. We're only staying here until you finish writing your songs." She looked around the kitchen. "And why you chose this hellhole to inspire you is beyond me." She snorted. "You're just like your daddy. He never did know how to live right. Hell, he didn't even die right. I heard he lingered on for months with that lung cancer. If you're gonna die, then die—"

Before Starlet could stop herself, she dropped the

broom and slapped her mama hard across the face. As she stood there staring into her mama's bloodshot, shocked eyes, she had to wonder if Uncle Bernie wasn't right. Maybe she was a steel magnolia. There was certainly steel in her voice when she spoke.

"Don't talk about my daddy. And if you don't like where we're living, you can leave anytime." She grabbed her purse and walked out.

Halfway into town, Starlet thought about going back and apologizing to her mother, but then realized that she had nothing to apologize for. Her mama was wrong-headed and would always be wrongheaded. While Starlet couldn't change the fact, she could no longer allow her mother to get away with being cruel.

The realization brought with it a certain inner peace. On her way past Duds 'N Such, she saw the pretty blue prom dress and stopped in her tracks. No more than five minutes later, she stood in front of the full-length mirror in the dressing room. The blue confection of a gown wasn't as tight as her other dresses had been, but for the first time in a long time, she felt like herself. Not just a famous country singer, but also a small-town girl from east Texas. Suddenly, she realized that she didn't have to be one or the other. She was both Starlet Brubaker and Star Bentley.

Once she bought the dress, she headed over to the pharmacy and purchased a bottle of brown hair dye. It would've been easier to go to Twyla's salon, but she'd heard the rumors about Twyla. And with Brianne still on maternity leave, she wasn't willing to chance it. Besides, she had watched Baby use home dye enough to know how to do it.

She'd expected her mama to be sleeping when she got home. But she wasn't. She still sat at the kitchen table, exactly where Starlet had left her. The guilt returned, but Starlet shoved the feeling down and headed for the bathroom. Surprisingly, she had no more than sat down on the toilet and started reading the dye instructions on the box when her mama came in.

"So I guess you finally decided to go back to that mousy brown."

Starlet pulled her eyes away from the handprint on her mother's cheek and took out the dye tube and bottle of developer. "Yes, ma'am. I've never been much of a blonde." She would've started mixing the two right then and there if her mama hadn't stopped her.

"Oh, for Pete's sake." She walked over and took the items from Starlet. "You're gonna stain your clothes. Go grab that old T-shirt from my suitcase and get back in here. We can't have the sweetheart of country music runnin' around with purple hair, now, can we?"

Starlet smiled. "No, I guess we can't."

Her mama turned out to be pretty good at dying hair. She even cut off the extensions, leaving Starlet's locks to fall just below her shoulders.

Jaydeen spent the entire time complaining about the allowance Kari gave her, and she reeked of alcohol and smoke, but for some reason, Starlet enjoyed the time with her mother. Of course, once Starlet's hair was finished, her mama threw up in the toilet and then passed out on the bed.

Starlet had just covered her with a light blanket when a loud rumbling drew her attention to the window and the street beyond. It was strange how just the sight of the monster truck with the flapping flags could make her heart beat in overtime. She hurried to the front door and opened it as the truck pulled up in front of the house. Her heart thumped even faster when a handsome cowboy in faded jeans and a pressed western shirt jumped down from the driver's side.

The passenger door opened as well, but Starlet only had eyes for Beckett as he walked around to the back of the truck. He started to pull down the tailgate when his cowboy hat tipped in her direction.

His hands stilled. "Hey."

She didn't know why the one word made her smile. Or maybe it wasn't the word as much as the way he said it—deep and breathy, like he had just woken up from a nice dream.

Starlet moved to the top of the porch steps and hooked an arm around the post to help balance her suddenly unbalanced world. "Hey."

"Yeah. Yeah. Hay is for horses." Jesse Cates moved next to Beckett and, reaching into the bed of the truck, pulled a lawn mower to the edge of the tailgate. "Can we get on with the mowing so I have a little time to spend with my friends?"

"Think again," Beckett said as he helped Jesse pull the lawn mower from the truck. "Once you finish mowing and trimming here, I volunteered your services to the mayor, who says that he needs help getting the Fourth of July decorations down from the town hall attic."

Jesse scowled and grabbed the handle of the lawn mower, pushing it toward the gate. "You really suck."

Beckett laughed. "So I've heard." He followed Jesse inside the gate with a lawn trimmer. Once he had leaned it against the fence, he headed up the steps, stopping on the one just below Starlet. Beneath the shadow of his hat, his eyes looked blue and piercing.

"Your hair." He reached up and smoothed a strand off her forehead, sending a tingle of heat cascading from his fingertips. While she struggled not to grab his hand and press her lips into his palm, he smiled. "Better. Much better."

The lawn mower started, cutting off any reply her giddy mind might've come up with. Beckett glanced back at Jesse for only a second before he took her hand and led her down the path to his truck. He opened the driver's door and helped her up.

"Are you kidnapping me, Mr. Beckett Cates?" she teased.

"Yes, ma'am." He climbed up beside her and reached for the key in the ignition. His arm brushed her breast and heat sizzled all the way down to her toes. "Do you have a problem with that, Miss Starlet Brubaker?"

She studied his handsome, familiar features and tried to act like she wasn't busting at the seams with happiness. "No, no problem at all."

Chapter Twenty-three

"WHY DON'T YOU JUST give it up, Kenny Gene," Rye Pickett said. "If you were so jealous of Twyla dancin' with all the guys at Bootlegger's the other night, just marry the girl and make her your own."

Kenny Gene stared down at his half-eaten dinner and felt even more depressed. He was so upset about Twyla flirting with every man in town that he couldn't even finish Josephine's chicken-fried steak. And he loved Josephine's chicken-fried steak.

"I couldn't agree more, Rye." Rachel Dean topped off Rye's coffee and heaped even more guilt on Kenny. "I'm tired of watchin' that poor girl fight for the bouquet at every weddin' and come up empty-handed."

Rossie Owens set down his coffee cup with a loud clatter. "Well, maybe if you were the next bride, you could just hand it to her."

"Rachel Dean the next bride?" Cindy Lynn pushed her way up to the counter and took a stool next to Kenny, dropping her bag of campaign bumper stickers on the floor. "Now, who in the world would Rachel Dean marry?"

Rachel's brows lowered, and Kenny figured that Cindy Lynn was about to get put in her place. Instead, Rossie jumped in again.

"I think there are plenty of men who would love to be with Rachel. In fact, I—"

"Need a refill of coffee," Rachel cut him off and hurried down to pour him a cup. Although Rossie didn't appear to be happy about it. Of course, the owner of the only bar in town probably preferred beer to coffee. Kenny could use a beer himself. Especially when his life was headed straight down an outhouse commode.

"So what are you working so hard on, Rye?" Rachel asked. "You've been scribblin' on that napkin ever since you sat down." She leaned closer. "Is that a float for the parade?"

Rye folded the napkin and tucked it into his shirt pocket. "Just a little surprise I'm workin' on with Darla."

Cindy leaned around Kenny. "Don't you be takin' my float designer, Rye Pickett. Darla is supposed to make me the biggest and best float in the parade, seein' as how I'm going to be the next mayor."

"Not likely," Rachel said with a smug smile. "Once Rossie wins the election, he'll be on the best float."

That started quite a ruckus from the other candidates that were present. Kenny had never been as good as Sheriff Hicks at keeping the peace. He was much better at handing out tickets and keeping an eye out for suspicious criminals. But since Dusty was still on new-daddy duty, it was up to Kenny to keep things calm in Bramble. And depressed about his woman or not, he had to do his job.

He lifted his hands. "Now, simmer down, folks. I'm sure everyone is gonna have a great float in the parade—although it won't be quite as good as startin' the parade in a car with flashin' lights and a si-reen. And I don't see why you need Darla to design your float, Cindy Lynn, when Ed is the best carpenter in Bramble."

It was strange, but as all eyes in the diner turned to her, Cindy seemed to lose her words. Which Kenny had never seen happen in all his born days.

"I better get back to campaignin'," she said. "Remember 'Cindy Lynn is Like Your Next of Kin.'" She hurried to the door, sidestepping when it opened. "Sorry, Twyla. No time to talk."

Just the name of his one true love had Kenny's chicken-fried steak wanting to make a second appearance. He swallowed it back down and tried not to act like his heart was breakin' when she completely ignored him and sat down next to Rossie Owens.

"Hey, Rossie," she said in that cute little way that made Kenny's heart race as fast as Scooby-Doo when he was after a Scooby Snack. "I was wonderin' if maybe you'd like to sit on my blanket at the Fourth of July picnic. I've heard that older men really know how to—what the...!" She jumped up from her stool and swiped at the coffee Rachel had just spilled on her.

"I'm sorry, honey," Rachel said. "I guess I just wasn't payin' attention."

Rossie chuckled as he got to his feet. "I think I'll head out before someone gets hurt."

"You do that," Rachel said.

He pointed a finger at her. "When I win..."

Rachel blushed redder than a McIntosh apple in late September. Kenny had to admit that, for a woman with hands the size of dinner plates, she was kinda pretty.

Although not near as pretty as his Twyla. His gaze locked with hers, and the sadness he saw in her eyes was worse than getting kicked by a Brahma bull. Mostly because he knew that he had put that look there. He was the one making her flirt with every man around. The one who couldn't say the words she desperately wanted him to say—even if they were the words he wanted to say with all his heart.

Before he made a mistake that would take away his job and get him tossed in jail, he hopped up and headed for the door. "See y'all later."

Once outside, he bypassed his patrol car and ambled across the street, greeting folks as he went. That was the great thing about Bramble. He knew he wasn't the sharpest tool in the shed, but the folks here didn't seem to care that he wasn't a genius. From the moment he stepped into town, they'd accepted him for who he was. And he still couldn't believe that the prettiest girl in the world had accepted him the most.

Twyla made him feel ten feet tall. She was the one who gave him the courage to fight for his dream of becoming a deputy. The one who had nursed him back to health when Alejandro had shot him. The one who was willing to spend the rest of her life with him. But Kenny knew she had reached the end of her rope. And he couldn't very well blame her. A woman couldn't wait forever.

Once inside the post office, he didn't waste any time heading to his post office box and opening it. When he peeked inside, he expected to see nothing but empty space just like he'd seen for the last few months. Instead, there was a letter.

With new hope springing to life, he pulled it out and ripped it open, searching the sheet of paper for an address or phone number. If either were there, Kenny wouldn't have known. The person who had written the letter had the worst handwriting he'd ever seen. Thinking it might have something to do with the lighting in the post office, he carried it outside. It didn't help. It all looked like gibberish to him.

His shoulders slumped as he released a defeated sigh.

"I guess it's hard work takin' over for Sheriff Hicks while he's at home with that new youngin'."

Kenny glanced up from the letter. Moses Tate sat on the bench in front of the post office, his crumpled cowboy hat pulled low over his face. "Hey, Mose, why ain't you sittin' in front of the pharmacy?"

"After I was almost killed by Starlet Brubaker, I thought it was God tellin' me to change my ways." Moses pushed up his hat. "So you gonna explain your long face? You look like a man who has the weight of the world on his shoulders."

"Maybe I do." Kenny walked over and sat down on the bench.

Moses pulled a plastic cup out of his shirt pocket and spit a stream of tobacco juice into it, then took his time putting it back before he finally spoke. "Well, I've had the weight of the world on my shoulders a time or two. And all it took to get it off was to share the weight with a friend."

Kenny squinted his eyes in thought. "You mean tell you my secret?" He slapped a hand over his mouth, but Moses didn't seem shocked that Kenny had a secret. He only stared out at the street and shrugged his bony shoulders.

"Every man has secrets, Kenny." He glanced over. "Some are big, and some are small. Some you'll go to your grave with, and some you'll share with folks you trust."

Kenny looked into Moses's faded blue eyes and figured that if a man could trust anyone with their secret, it would be Moses.

"I'm married," he blurted out.

Moses didn't even blink. "To Twyla? Well, with the way the town's been after you two to tie the knot, I can't say as I blame you for runnin' off and gettin' hitched." He reached for the cup again, but his hand froze when Kenny continued.

"But that's the thing, Mose. I ain't married to Twyla." He hurried on before his courage could desert him. "It happened when I was first rodeoin'—before I ever came to Bramble. I was in Austin for some bronco ridin' and met this cute little Mexican gal named Rosarita. She was real nice to me. And no woman had ever been that nice to me before—not even my mama—so I guess I lost my head. Before I knew it, I was standin' before a judge gettin' married. Of course, it didn't work out. It turns out that Rosarita was only usin' me to stay in the country."

"So why don't you just get a divorce?" Moses asked.

"It took me a little while to figure out that she hadn't just gone to visit her mama in Mexico. After she didn't come back for a year, I figured she'd up and left me." Moses choked on something as Kenny continued. "I didn't even think about a divorce until I got to Bramble and met Twyla. That's when I went to a lawyer in Austin. But by then, I couldn't do what the lawyer wanted me to do."

"What was that?"

"Put an ad in the newspapers summonin' Rosarita to court. I mean I can't put an ad in the Austin newspaper lookin' for my wife. Not when half of Twyla's family lives there. Why, if word got back to Twyla that I had been datin' her while I was married, she'd drop me like a hot flapjack. And I can't live without that woman." He shook his head. "No. I need to find Rosarita and give her the divorce papers to sign without anyone findin' out."

Moses nodded down at the letter in Kenny's hand. "Is that what that letter is about?"

"I had Cora Lee help me locate Rosarita's parents— told her it was some criminal I was needin' information on. She got me an address, and I wrote them. This is their reply." He handed the letter to Moses. "Not that it's gonna do me any good. Her folks must be backward because I can't make out a word they wrote."

Moses studied the letter. "That's because it's in Spanish."

"Spanish? No kiddin'?" He leaned closer so he could look at the letter. "Now, why would Rosarita's Mexican family speak Spanish?" Kenny glanced down the street. Cowboy was just coming out of the Feed and Seed, his hat pulled down almost as low as Moses's when he napped. Kenny hadn't spent a lot of time talking with Cowboy— he'd been too wrapped up in his own misery—and suddenly that just didn't seem right. Especially when it was Kenny's job to make people feel welcome in Bramble.

"Well, it appears to me that you got your—" Moses started. But before he could finish, Kenny jerked the letter from his hand.

"I need to be goin', Mose." He folded the letter and placed it in his front pocket. "But thanks for listenin' to my troubles." He got to his feet. "And I shore hope that you keep this under your hat." Without waiting for a reply, he hurried down the street.

He caught up with Cowboy just as he was getting in his truck.

"Hold up there, Cowboy," he hollered.

Cowboy froze and dropped the sack he carried. Kenny didn't hesitate to hurry over and pick up the things scattered on the ground.

"Didn't mean to startle you," he said as he picked up the flashlight and batteries and put them in the sack. "Sorry about that." He reached for the coil of rope, but Cowboy beat him to it.

"No need to worry about it." He grabbed the bag from Kenny and climbed in the truck.

"Now, don't hurry off," Kenny said. "I was hopin' we could set a date to go fishin'."

"I don't fish." Cowboy kept his eyes lowered and his hat tipped. Obviously, the man was shy. Which made Kenny feel even worse about not talking to him sooner.

Kenny might've continued to throw out suggestions of things they could do if Twyla hadn't stepped out the door of Josephine's. The wind was whistling today, but not a hair on her head shifted. That was how good the woman fixed hair. She was chattering up a storm to Rye Pickett, no doubt telling him an amusing story. Twyla could tell some mighty amusing stories.

She crossed the street and waved at someone in the pharmacy. But when she noticed Kenny, her hand dropped, and she continued on her way without a word. She disappeared around the corner, and by the time Kenny turned back to Cowboy, the man was already backing his truck out of the parking space. Kenny sighed and pulled the letter out of his pocket.

How long would it take him to learn Spanish?

Chapter Twenty-four

THE LITTLE GIRL LOOKED up at Beckett with the biggest brown eyes he'd ever seen. No, he took that back. Starlet had eyes just as big and just as brown. And maybe that's why he hesitated a moment. A moment that made him realize that the little girl sitting in the alleyway was injured. Blood oozed from a deep cut on her cheek and trickled down the side of her face to be absorbed in the red Afghan head scarf she wore.

He glanced at his recon unit, who were edging down the street, checking out doorways with rifles at the ready, then back at the little girl. It took him only a second to make his decision. Hooking his M4 rifle over his shoulder, he moved down the alley and squatted in front of the child.

"It's okay," he said, even though it was unlikely that the little girl spoke English. "I'm not going to hurt you."

Her eyes widened, but she remained perfectly still as he examined the cut. It wasn't as deep as he had thought at first, but it still needed attention. He had just pulled down the mouthpiece of his radio headset so he could call for the medic when Sully's voice came through the receiver.

"Beck! Where the hell are—"

An explosion rocked the ground, causing Beckett to fall back on his ass and the little girl to leap to her feet and race off down the alley as a daisy chain of explosions followed. Once on his feet, Beckett raced toward the billows of dust and debris. When he finally rounded the corner of the building, he froze in his tracks and stared at the carnage.

"Beckett?"

His eyes scanned the rubble and bodies until they landed on the one survivor. The one living monument to his shame and guilt. He would never forget the look in Sully's eyes. Never forget the confusion and pain. Beckett should've raced over to his friend. Instead, he stood frozen. He didn't know how long he stood there before a bloody hand reached up from the rubble and grabbed on to his leg.

"Beckett." The whisper of the dead echoed through his heart as more hands joined the first. Grabbing. Clinging. Shaking. "I mean it. Wake up, Becky!"

A sharp slap had him opening his eyes. Starlet straddled him, her brown gaze filled with concern.

"Are you okay?" she asked.

It took him a moment to realize where he was. Billy and Shirlene's guesthouse. He released his breath and rubbed the sleep from his eyes. "Yeah. It was just a dream."

"A dream?" she said incredulously. "The way you were thrashing and moaning, it sounded more like a nightmare."

He attempted a smile. "It was nothing. Although I could've done without the slap." He rubbed his cheek. "For a skinny little thing, you have one wicked wallop."

"It was the only way to wake you up. And I'm far from

skinny." She rolled off of him and reached for the sheet, suddenly making him aware of plump, moonlit breasts and sweet rose-colored nipples. The last of the dream melted away, replaced by happier images.

Starlet sitting next to him in Billy's truck with her dark hair flying in the breeze. Starlet fishing at Sutter Springs in her tight T-shirt, cutoff shorts, and bare feet. Starlet enjoying a chocolate-dipped cone from the Dairy Treat like it was the best thing she'd ever had. Starlet sitting across from him at Josephine's Diner signing autographs and chatting with the townsfolk like they were her closest friends.

Starlet in his bed all naked and willing.

He sat up and took the sheet from her. "Oh, I think there's another way to wake me up." His hand slid over her breast. The feel of the soft warmth against his palm turned him hard as a stone. He leaned over and kissed the nipple, lightly flicking his tongue until it pebbled. She hummed deep in the back of her throat, the sound musical and sexy as hell. But when he started to ease her down to the mattress, she stopped him by cradling his cheek in her hand.

"Tell me about it, Becky. Tell me what happened."

"It doesn't matter." He tried to distract her by going straight to the sweetness between her legs, but she caught his hand and held it against the inside of her thigh.

"Is that why you left the marines? Because of what happened?"

If her gaze had held pity, he would've made up a lie. But there was no pity in her soft brown eyes. Just sincere compassion that gave him the strength he needed to finally face his demons.

Falling back to the pillow, he rested an arm over his eyes and tried to come up with the right words. "I didn't leave the marines," he said, his voice holding all the pain of the last few months. "I was honorably discharged." He snorted. "Ironic, since what I did was so dishonorable. A marine never leaves his platoon—never. But I did."

Once he started, the words spilled out like playground marbles from a bag. He didn't tell her just about the little girl and the IEDs. He told her about the shock and confusion he'd felt when he discovered the bodies.

"I didn't even call for help. I just stood there trying to make sense of the senseless." He swallowed hard. "Then I started looking for survivors—digging through the rubble with my hands, praying to find a pulse. I found one."

He blinked back the tears. "Brian Sullivan was my best buddy. We were both the youngest of a big family. Both trying to prove that we weren't just snot-nosed kids who needed their older siblings to watch out for them." He smiled. "At first we pretty much hated each other. We competed on just about everything—from the obstacle course to who could eat the most food at the mess hall. Sully won that one. He can eat like nobody's business." His smile faded. "At least, he used to. I heard that he only weighed eighty-five pounds when he left the hospital to go home. Of course, if you don't have any legs..."

"Oh, Becky." Starlet didn't touch him. It was almost like she knew that if she did, he wouldn't be able to get the rest of the poison out. But the way she said the nickname gave him the strength to go on.

"Did you know that I went to talk to the family of every marine who died that day?" He continued in a hollow voice. "I told them how sorry I was and gave them money.

But I didn't have enough guts to talk with the one survivor. No apology. Nothing but a blank check with my signature."

He waited for Starlet to move away from the gutless wonder he was. Instead, she pressed her lips against his shoulder and pulled him closer. That was all she did. She didn't tell him that he needed to let it go, or talk with a therapist, or go see Sully. She didn't tell him anything. She just held him.

After a few silent moments, she started to sing. It was a song he hadn't heard before. A song about guilt, pain, and forgiveness. A song that seemed to mirror the emotions that swirled around inside his gut.

Before she finished, he fell asleep.

A deep, dreamless sleep.

When Beckett woke in the morning, Starlet was still there, curled against his body as the sun spilled in through the window. For the first time since Afghanistan, he felt whole. Like all his empty places had been filled.

Pressing his nose to the back of her neck, he kissed the baby-fine hair that grew there until she fidgeted in her sleep and rolled to her back. He propped his head in his hand and looked at her.

Gone was the country singer Star Bentley, and in her place was this dark-haired beauty. A dark-haired beauty who had taken his breath away the first moment he saw her. Like it was yesterday, Beckett could remember walking into the henhouse and seeing Starlet coming down the long *Gone with the Wind* staircase. Even in the ill-fitting prom dress, he had thought that she looked as beautiful as Scarlett O'Hara. In fact, the name had even popped out of his mouth when Beau had introduced them.

"It's nice to meet you, Scarlet," he'd said.

She flashed a smile. "The pleasure is mine, Becky."

Now he realized that she had been teasing him. But to an awkward young man who was uncomfortable around women, it had seemed like she was making him the brunt of her joke. So he'd hidden his attraction behind a wall of arrogance and some snide remark about her dress. Thus their dislike for each other had begun.

He picked up her hand and kissed the tiny nail on her pinkie. At one time, he was jealous of the way she'd wrapped his brothers around this little finger. Now he wouldn't mind being wrapped. In fact, if the warm feeling in the pit of his stomach was any indication, he already was.

"What are you doing?"

He glanced from her hand to find Starlet watching him.

"I'm giving you a pinkie kiss." He kissed the nail again before sucking the tip into his mouth and nibbling on it.

She giggled—something she had done a lot of in the last twenty-four hours. He liked the girly sound. It reminded him of the trickling brook that ran through his parents' farm. The memory caused a thought to pop into his head.

"Do you know what?" he said. "I think I'm going to take you to Dogwood today and show you around the farm. When I talked with my daddy yesterday, he was complaining that he didn't get to visit with you very much at the hospital. He rates you right up there with Loretta Lynn and Tammy Wynette."

Pulling her hand from his, she held the sheet against her chest and looked uncomfortable. "Umm...I don't know, Beckett. I mean, I probably should write."

He wondered what had caused her reaction for only a

second before the truth dawned on him, and he laughed. "I'm not taking you home to meet my parents, Starlet. You already know them." He tipped his head and continued to smile. "And don't tell me that you've never been taken home to meet the parents."

"Actually, I haven't." She shot him a glance. "Have you?"

"Once when I was in college, and I must say it wasn't a whole lot of fun. I'm not much of a conversationalist." He inched the sheet out of her hands. "I'm better at nonverbal languages."

"Did you love her?"

He lifted his eyes from the beautiful breasts he'd just exposed. "I thought I did, but it turned out that it's easy to fall in love with the first woman you have sex with."

"And is that what this is, Beckett? Just sex?"

It was weird how her big brown eyes could get the truth out of him. "No. It's not just sex, Starlet. At least, it's not for—"

"Me either." She cut him off, then blushed a pretty pink and bit her bottom lip, bringing his attention to the mole at the top corner of her mouth. "But if it's not just sex, what is it?"

"Hmm?" He leaned over and kissed the mole, tracing the shape with his tongue. "I'll have to think on that."

He slid his hand through her hair and cradled her head, giving her a deep, thorough kiss. A kiss she quickly took control of. Her tongue tangled with his in a heated dance that left him light-headed. While her mouth seduced him, her hand traced over his shoulder and down to his biceps. There was something about the way her hand cupped his muscle that made Beckett feel like the strongest man on the face of the earth, and he couldn't help but flex. And when she finally reached between them and clasped his main muscle, it was already flexed.

Rolling to his side, he reached for the box of condoms on the nightstand. It took him a moment to suit up, and when he turned back around, she was waiting to guide him into her heat.

The fit was tight and perfect. He started to move, and she quickly picked up his rhythm like he was one of the musical instruments she played. More than likely a fiddle.

It took sheer, teeth-clenching willpower to hold back his orgasm until hers hit. When she arched her hips and hummed deep in her throat, he released and sailed over the edge. He came back to earth to find his face snuggled against her shoulder and neck. He breathed in the scent of lilacs before he lifted his head. He wasn't the least bit shocked by the words that spilled from his mouth.

"I love you."

Starlet's face registered surprise, and then something that looked a lot like fear. Her gaze skittered away from him, and she swallowed hard. "I need to go to the bathroom." She pushed at his shoulders until he rolled off her, then scampered to the bathroom and slammed the door.

Most men might've been hurt by the fact that the words hadn't come as easily to her as they had to him. But Beckett figured that he had broadsided her with his declaration. She needed some time to get over her shock and realize that he cared for her like she had always cared for him. The thought of her crush had him tucking his hands behind his head and smiling at the ceiling.

He must've dozed off. When he woke up, he discovered Starlet had climbed back in bed and was watching him sleep. She no longer looked scared, but she did look pensive. He reached over and smoothed the wrinkle out of her forehead.

"It's okay. If you're not ready, you're not ready."

She shook her head. "It's not okay. And I need you to understand why it's so difficult for me." She took a deep breath. "I didn't grow up like you, Beckett. I didn't have people telling me that they love me every day of my life. In fact, I don't think anyone ever said it to me until your family. So I'm not used to it, and when people say it…" She shrugged. "I guess it freaks me out."

He smoothed her hair behind her ear. "Then I guess we'll just have to get you used to hearing it, won't we?" He leaned over and kissed her forehead. "I love you, Starlet." He kissed her nose. "I love you, Starlet." Her breath released as he kissed her earlobe. "I love you, Star—"

A pounding cut him off.

"Beckett!" Billy's voice boomed through the front door of the guesthouse. "Open up."

Muttering an oath, Beckett got to his feet and grabbed a pair of jeans. "Don't go anywhere," he said as he walked out of the room, closing the door behind him.

He unlocked the dead bolt of the front door, prepared to tell Billy to take a hike. But when he saw his brother's face, the words died on his tongue.

"What happened?" he asked.

"It's Jenna Jay," Billy said. "She's missing."

Chapter Twenty-five

STARLET SAT IN THE back corner of Billy's study, surrounded by a sea of male testosterone, and tried not to panic. She wasn't responsible for Jenna Jay's disappearance. It was all just a freaky coincidence that it happened right after the model Starlet had hired left town. It was too bad that Sheriff Dusty Hicks didn't agree.

"So this cowboy that Twyla said showed up at her shop," Dusty said. "You say that Jenna never mentioned running into him?"

"No." Beau's eyes narrowed on Dusty. Starlet had never seen him look so angry—or so lost—in all her life. "I know what you're getting at. And I'd watch my step if I were you, Sheriff. Jenna didn't run off with any cowboy."

Starlet crossed her fingers and prayed that Beau was right. Which probably had God snorting in disgust. After all, Jenna running off with a cowboy had been Starlet's plan from the get-go. Now here she was praying that Jenna Jay had just taken a little road trip and forgotten to tell anyone. What a hypocrite!

"Settle down, Beauregard," Brant said. "The sheriff is only trying to figure out what happened."

Brant's wife, Elizabeth, hooked her arm through his. "Was Jenna upset about anything, Beau? I know how hard it was on her to lose the baby, and how much she wanted another one."

Just the mention of Jenna losing the baby made Scarlet slump farther down in her chair. What kind of a person would want to take a grieving woman away from the man she loved?

A bad person.

A bad, bad person.

"Jenna was over that." Beau looked down at his boots. "Or at least, she'd moved on."

"Are you sure, Beau?" Shirlene said. "You have to admit that she has been acting a little strange lately, honey. I mean, why would she go and cut off all that beautiful hair?"

Beau turned on Shirlene. "Jenna has always been different, Shirl. That's what makes her so special. And I like her short hair."

"Okay," Dusty said as he flipped through his notepad. "Let's go over this again, Beau. The last time you saw her was the morning before you left for Houston. And the last time you spoke with her was that night when you got to the hotel room."

Beau nodded. "She said she had spent the day in Odessa, and that she had a surprise for me when I got back. She sounded more excited than she'd been in years, which is why I decided to cut my trip short."

His words had Starlet heaving a silent sigh of relief. Certainly Jenna wouldn't consider leaving town with a male model a surprise she'd want to share with her husband.

"When I arrived home late last night," Beau continued, "her truck was gone and she wasn't there. That's when I called you." His eyes hardened. "But so far, you haven't done shit to find her."

"That's not true, Beau," Bri defended her husband. "Dusty has been working all night to locate her." Bryson started to cry, and she gently jostled him back to sleep. "He has interviewed almost the entire town, has notified law enforcement in every county in the state, and has checked the hospitals and the airlines—"

"She didn't leave me!" Beau threw the cell phone he clutched in his hand. It hit the wall and shattered, causing Starlet to almost jump out of the chair and start confessing. The occupants in the room seemed as shocked by his actions as she was. They exchanged looks while Beau collapsed in a chair and covered his face with his hands.

As Starlet looked at him, it finally hit her. Beau loved Jenna Jay and had always loved Jenna Jay. She hadn't bullied him into marriage. That was just a fantasy Starlet's wayward imagination had conjured. Beau had given his love freely to the woman he'd wanted to give it to.

Starlet glanced at Beckett, who stood guard over his brother as if he could somehow protect him from the pain. Pain that Starlet suddenly understood. She would be lost if Beckett disappeared out of her life. The knowledge made her realize that somewhere along the way she *had* fallen in love with a Cates brother. Just not the one she'd first thought.

"Of course she didn't leave you." Beckett placed a hand on his brother's shoulder. "In fact, I bet she's just pulling together the surprise she told you about. What time did you tell her that you'd be back from Houston?"

Beau lifted his head. "Today at four."

Beckett glanced at the clock on the bookshelf. Four o'clock was less than an hour away. "Then you need to get home." He moved out from behind Beau's chair. "Bri, why don't you and Billy head over to the house with Beau. The rest of us will stay here and contact you if we find out anything."

It took a moment for Beau to get to his feet. Then he slowly walked to the door as if he struggled to carry the burden of his pain. Bri and Billy followed him out. Once they were gone, both Dusty and Brant got on their phones while Elizabeth and Shirlene left the room to check on the kids.

Beckett came over and sat down in the chair across from the chess table. "Are you all right? You look a little pale."

"I'm fine," Starlet said. "I'm just worried about Jenna."

He took her hand, pulling her out of her chair and onto his lap, completely oblivious to the surprised looks on Dusty's and Brant's faces. "Me too," he said as he nuzzled her neck. "Hopefully, she's just planning a surprise."

"Hopefully," Starlet choked out.

Unfortunately, that wasn't the case. Not more than thirty minutes later, Dusty got a phone call. When he hung up, his face looked grim.

"They found Jenna Jay's car."

"Where?" Beckett asked.

"Just off the main highway between here and the henhouse." He grabbed his hat. "I'm going to check it out now, but it doesn't look good. They found her purse inside and signs of a struggle."

"What kind of signs?" Brant asked.

Dusty glanced over at Starlet before answering. "A broken window and blood."

"Damn it." Brant ran his hand through his hair. "As if Beau hasn't had enough to deal with in his life." He picked up his hat from the desk and turned to the door. "I'll go break the news."

Beckett lifted Starlet off his lap and got to his feet. "I think we need to look into the cowboy Twyla mentioned."

"I agree," Dusty said. "There has to be someone in town who got his name."

Starlet hesitated for only a second. "Vance. His name is Vance Vinson. But I don't think that he's the one responsible for Jenna Jay's disappearance. He's a model from LA, and he left town a few days ago."

Beckett looked at her. "He's the same cowboy who was with you at Bootlegger's?"

Starlet nodded as Dusty pulled out his notepad. "So how do you know him?"

Starlet cleared her throat. "I hired him."

Dusty lifted his head. "Hired him? He's an escort?"

It was hard to answer with Beckett's blue eyes drilling a hole through her. "Sort of. Except I didn't hire him for me. I hired him for Jenna Jay."

"Jenna wanted you to hire her an escort?" Beckett looked thoroughly confused.

Starlet took a quivery breath. "Jenna didn't know about it. I hired him to take her away from Beau." Once the words were out of her mouth, they sounded as awful as she had always thought they would. Still, she tried to justify her actions. "I know how it must sound." She started to wring her hands. "But it all had to do with me thinking that I was in love with Beau. And it didn't dawn on me how crazy the entire plan was until just a few days ago. Then I fired him—"

"Beau?" Beckett took her arm and spun her around. "You love Beau?"

"No." She shook her head. "It was just a schoolgirl crush. Something that I blew completely out of proportion."

Suddenly, Beckett looked like he could strangle her with his bare hands. He stared at her for only a moment before he turned and headed for the door.

"I'll be at Beau's," he said to Dusty. "Call me after you talk to the escort."

"Beckett!" Starlet hurried after him, catching up with him at the front door. "Please let me explain," she said as she grabbed his arm.

He shook her off. "Explain? There's no need to explain. You're exactly who I thought you were—a manipulative brat who wants every man to fall at her feet. And you got your wish. I fell hard, didn't I?" He jerked the door open. "But it will be a cold day in hell before I ever grovel at the feet of the great Star Bentley again."

He walked out and headed for the monster truck. Starlet stood in the doorway, her sobs muffled by the rumbling engine and the spray of gravel as he pulled from the driveway. When he was gone, Dusty came up behind her.

"I'll take you back to town," he said solemnly.

On the way, he asked her one question after the other about Vance and the rodeo cowboys she'd hired. She answered as thoroughly as she could. When they reached town, he got another phone call. Not wanting to hold him up from the search any longer, she had him drop her off in front of the pharmacy. But before she got out, he asked her one last question. A question that cut her to the quick.

"Do you know where Jenna Jay is, Starlet?"

She took her hand off the door handle and turned to him. "You think that I have something to do with her disappearance?"

Looking out the windshield, he shook his head. "No. But it's part of my job to leave no stone unturned." He looked back at her. "Another part of my job is making sure you don't leave town until this is all figured out. This is serious, Starlet. And even though I don't think you're a suspect, other people will once the word gets out about you hiring those men. Which means we have to dot all the i's and cross all the t's. Do you understand?"

She nodded before she pulled open the door and got out. The last time she'd been in Bramble, Main Street had been filled with people handing out campaign flyers. Now the street was empty, the only flyers were the ones blowing down the sidewalks in the stiff west Texas wind.

"They all went lookin' for some woman named Jenny something-or-other."

Starlet turned to see her mama sitting on the bench Moses normally slept on. For once, she looked sober. And not happy about it.

"The idiots closed down the entire town," she grumbled. "I couldn't even buy a six-pack at the grocery store. Now, what kind of town closes down just because somebody went missing?"

Starlet sat down on the bench. "I guess the right kind of town."

"A crazy kind of town," her mama said. "And what has you looking like you lost your best friend? Don't tell me that you knew this Jenny."

"Jenna Jay."

"Yeah, that's it. Jenna Jay." She fluffed her hair. "I should've remembered the name. Cowboy mentioned it enough the night he drove me home. I mean, any man should know that you're not gonna get lucky if you keep bringing up another woman."

Starlet looked at her. "What cowboy are you talking about, Mama?"

"Not a cowboy, Starlet. Cowboy. The new man in town who works at Bootlegger's and the gas station. The one who drove me home the other night." She got to her feet. "In fact, speaking of Cowboy, I wonder if the man has a couple beers stashed in the soda machine at the garage." She started down the street. "Don't wait up for me."

Starlet hurried after her. "Vance is still in town?"

"I don't know about any Vance." Her mama adjusted her breasts in her bra until her cleavage pushed up over the neckline.

"Dark eyes and a bad haircut?"

"Dark eyes is right, but I don't know about the haircut. I haven't ever seen Cowboy without his hat on." She tipped her head in thought. "Which does make me wonder. You think he leaves it on during sex?"

Starlet didn't answer. Her mind was filled with too many questions: Why was Vance still in town? What was he doing working at Bootlegger's and the gas station? And why was he asking questions about Jenna Jay? The answer pointed to one conclusion: Vance was responsible for Jenna's disappearance. And somehow Starlet didn't think it had to do with a love connection. Not with the blood in Jenna's car.

"Listen, Mama," she said, "why don't you go home and fix yourself some supper."

"I ain't hungry as much as thirsty." She kept walking.

"Fine." Starlet grabbed her arm and stopped her. "If you really need something to drink, I found one of your bottles of whiskey the other day and tossed it in the trash. I'm sure it's still there."

A strange expression settled over her mother's pretty features. "So you're just gonna let me drink myself to death?"

"Do I have another choice?"

Her mama opened her mouth to say something, but instead closed it again. Taking the opportunity, Starlet made her excuses. "I'll be home in a minute. I want to see if the mayor is in his office so I can go over the songs I plan to sing in the parade." Without waiting for a reply, she hurried toward the town hall and ducked behind the statue of William Cates. She waited for a full five minutes before she peeked around the bent fishing pole.

Her mama was just rounding the corner of their street. Once she had disappeared, Starlet headed for the gas station. It looked as closed as the rest of the businesses. Standing on her tiptoes, Starlet peeked in the high glass windows of the garage doors. There were stacks of tires, rows of tools, and a car jacked up on a lift. But no one appeared to be working on the car.

Starlet had just started to turn away when a movement to the left had her leaning closer. The office door was open, and a man stood behind the counter. A man wearing a cowboy hat that looked nothing like the one Vance had worn. Although that didn't mean anything. Vance could've discovered how stupid he looked and gotten a new hat.

As Starlet watched, he pulled money out of the cash

register and stuffed it in his pocket. She was so angry that she considered beating on the garage door and reading him the riot act. The only thing that kept her from it was the thought of Jenna Jay's blood.

Vance wasn't an airheaded escort. He was a criminal. And if he was responsible for Jenna's disappearance, a dangerous criminal. She ducked down below the window and reached for her cell phone.

Unfortunately, she had just started to push Brianne's contact number when the phone rang. Not a little ring, but the loud ringtone that Kari had programmed in. Starlet answered quickly, but not quickly enough. She hadn't even gotten a word out when the front door of the gas station opened. She didn't hesitate to jump to her feet and take off. As she ran, she whispered in the receiver.

"Call Dusty. It was Vance. He's the one who—" Her cell phone went flying as she was tackled from behind. She hit the ground with a grunt. The last time she'd found herself in the arms of an assailant, she'd been too terrified to do more than whimper. She wasn't terrified now as much as pissed. She rolled over and started swinging. But the only thing she succeeded in doing was knocking off his cowboy hat. Once it was off, she couldn't do anything but stare in horror at the evil face that looked down at her.

Chapter Twenty-six

THERE WAS NO WAY to keep Beau from Jenna's truck once Brant broke the news to him. And since his brother wasn't in any shape to drive, Beckett volunteered to drive him out to the isolated spot just off the highway. A spot that was already taped off.

From what Dusty had said, Beckett expected Jenna's pickup to have a broken window and blood on the front seat. But the truck didn't have one broken window or one spot of blood. In fact, it looked as if Jenna had just pulled over to the side of the road and gone for a walk. It wasn't until Beckett slipped under the crime-scene tape and walked a few feet in front of the truck that he saw the broken glass and blood on the ground.

Beau saw it at the same time as he did.

"No," he hissed from between his teeth before he turned away from the sight and started yelling. "Jenna! Jenna Jay!" He stumbled down the ditch that ran next to the highway. "Answer me, damn it!"

Beckett caught up with him and grabbed his arm. "Calm down, Beau. We're going to find her."

He jerked away. "Jenna! Where are you?" His voice cracked as he tripped over some low-growing mesquite and went down on one knee.

Beckett helped him up but didn't release him. Numerous people had lost it in Afghanistan, and he knew that tough love was sometimes the only way to bring them back to reality. He grabbed a fistful of his brother's shirt and pulled him close.

"Look at me, Beau. We don't know that the blood is Jenna's. And knowing your wife, it could very easily be someone else's."

It took a moment and a slight shake before Beau's eyes cleared. "But who, Beck? Who in Bramble would do this?"

"I don't know. But we're going to find out." He released the front of his shirt. "First, you have to hold it together. You can't help Jenna if you lose it."

Beau stared back at him and swallowed hard. "I can't live without her. I can't do it."

"We're not going to think about that now. The only thing we're going to think about is finding her."

After a few seconds, Beau nodded. Beckett hooked an arm over his shoulders and walked him back to where Dusty was taking pictures of the blood. He glanced up when they approached.

"Maybe you should take Beau to the house. I'm almost finished up here, and Tyler is on his way with the tow truck."

"I'm not going back to the house!" Beau snapped. "Not without Jenna."

Dusty glanced at Beckett before he nodded. "Fine, but if you get in my way, you're out of here." He aimed the camera down at the tire tracks to the right of the broken glass and snapped off a couple of pictures.

Beckett examined the tracks. "So the glass is from another vehicle?"

"A truck by the size of the treads." He moved around the tracks and took some shots from a different angle. "Since there were no signs of struggle by Jenna's truck, I'd say that she approached whoever was in this vehicle of her own free will."

"But why would she do that?" Beckett asked.

Dusty lowered the camera and glanced at Beau. "You want to answer that?"

Beau didn't hesitate. "Jenna Jay likes helping people. She would stop if she thought someone was in trouble."

"Or at least someone was acting like they were in trouble," Dusty added. "But Jenna also isn't stupid. Which means that she knew the person."

"Cowboy," Beckett said.

Until then he had pushed down any thoughts of Starlet so he could focus on his brother. Now they all came swarming back. Betrayal seemed too mild a word to describe his feelings. Broadsided was more fitting. He felt like he'd been T-boned by a freight train, his emotions scattered in a million pieces along the tracks.

Starlet loved Beau. She had never loved Beckett. Why would she fall in love with a skinny nerd when there was a handsome rodeo cowboy around? Everything fell into place. Her preoccupation with cowboys. Her reaction that day in Bramble when she saw Beau. And now the crazy scheme she had concocted to break up Jenna and Beau's marriage. A scheme that could very well cost Jenna her life.

Dusty broke into his thoughts. "I don't think it's Cowboy. I called the escort service and got Vance Vinson's home number in LA. He answered on the second ring."

"Maybe he took Jenna with him?" Beau stood with his fists clenched and his jaw tight, and Beckett figured that, if Vance had been there, he would've strangled him with his bare hands.

"I considered that," Dusty said, "but the timeline doesn't add up. The escort service said that he has worked two jobs for them since he got back—last night and the night before, which was the last time Beau talked with Jenna. Unless Vance has access to a private jet, I can't see him getting from LA to here and back in that time."

"So what do we do now?" Beau asked.

"We question everyone in town again and organize a search." He looked at the setting sun. "First thing tomorrow."

"Now," Beau said. "I want you searching now."

Dusty rested his hands on his belt. "I get it, Beau. I would feel the same way if it were Brianne missing. But we have to keep our heads and do this right. If we have people racing all over the place looking for Jenna, they could destroy important evidence of her whereabouts." An approaching vehicle had him glancing at the highway. "Here's Tyler."

As Dusty moved away, Beau started to go after him, but Beckett stopped him by placing a hand on his shoulder. "He's right. For Jenna's sake, let Dusty do his job."

Beau turned to him. "But I can't just sit by and do nothing, Beck."

Since it was hard to ignore the desperation in his brother's eyes, he conceded. "Fine. While Dusty is interviewing people in town, it probably wouldn't hurt for us to get with her family and try to figure out what she was doing in Odessa. Maybe the guy followed her from there."

Beau nodded. "I'll try to get ahold of Hope and Faith.

If Jenna confided in anyone, it would be those two." He pulled his cell phone out of his pocket and walked back to Billy's truck.

While he was calling, Beckett joined Dusty and Tyler, who seemed to be in deep conversation over something other than how to hook the tow cable to the bumper of Jenna's truck.

". . . I'm tellin' you, Sheriff," Tyler said, "I think someone is dipping into the till."

"Were there any signs of a break-in?" Dusty asked as he pulled out his notepad. Beckett figured it had gotten more use in one day than it had in the last five years.

"Nope, but the front door was unlocked. And I remembered locking up when I heard the news about Jenna Jay." He glanced back at the truck. "Do you have any clues about what happened to her, Sheriff?"

"We're getting there." Dusty tapped the end of the pencil on the pad. "Does anyone else have a key to the station?"

Beckett instantly thought of Jesse. He didn't want to believe that the kid would out-and-out steal, but he hadn't thought he would try to blackmail someone either. He was relieved when Tyler shook his head.

"I took Jesse's key when his daddy made him quit. Cowboy is the only one with a key now."

Dusty's head came up. "Cowboy? Cowboy worked at your station, Ty?"

"Works," Tyler said. "But you don't have to worry about him, Sheriff. He's too much of good ol' boy to steal."

Beckett couldn't help but jump in. "When did you see him last?"

"Night before last. When I left, he was organizing all the tires by sizes. He would've finished last night if his truck hadn't broke down again, and he couldn't get in to work."

Dusty and Beckett exchanged glances before Dusty asked, "So what did this Cowboy look like, Ty?"

Tyler thought for a moment. "You know, I really couldn't tell you. He likes to keep his hat on most of the time. Even when he's inside. But he has dark skin and told me he was Italian."

Dusty slipped his notepad in his back pocket and pulled out his cell phone. Within seconds, he lifted it up to show Tyler the picture on the screen. Beckett leaned closer. It was the same picture he'd seen on Starlet's nightstand of Vance Vinson.

"Is this the man you hired?" Dusty asked.

Tyler shook his head. "No, sir. But that guy stopped by the gas station a couple times. He had the worst fake Texas accent I've ever heard."

Dusty released his breath and unclipped his radio from his belt. "I'll need the description of Cowboy's truck and his license plate number if you remember it." Once Tyler gave him both, he stepped away and radioed Cora Lee to give her the information.

"I've always admired Dusty's law-enforcement skills," Tyler said as he hooked up Jenna's truck. "But I think he's way off on this one. I mean, why would Cowboy steal from me now? If he was after money, why would he wait so long before he took it?"

It was a good question. One that had a bad feeling settling in the pit of Beckett's stomach. "Is there anything else about the man that you remember?" he asked. "Any birth marks, tattoos, or distinguishing mannerisms?"

Before Tyler could answer, Beau called out to him.

"Beckett!"

Beckett turned to find his brother hurrying toward him. "I just talked with Shirlene. I guess Hope and Faith are back from their camping trip. Shirlene told them about Jenna, and she says that Hope has some information on why Jenna was in Odessa."

The bad feeling intensified. "What did she say?" Beckett asked.

"Hope wouldn't tell Shirlene. She wants to talk to me first." Beau turned back to the truck. "So let's go. She's over at her parents' house."

Beckett glanced at Dusty. "Give me a minute. I'll be right there."

When he walked up behind Dusty, the sheriff was just finishing his conversation with Cora Lee.

"And we need this ASAP," he said.

"As if I didn't know that," Cora Lee answered. "The entire town is worried sick about that little gal. I'll get right on it."

Dusty hooked the radio on his belt and turned to Beckett. "This isn't good. The blood and glass might've been explained by a roadside accident that Jenna came upon. But a stranger in town and the robbery at Tyler's doesn't bode well. Damn." He took off his hat and smoothed back his hair. "I shouldn't have left Kenny Gene in charge of Bramble. He means well, but he just can't seem to stay focused on what is important. He never once mentioned any strangers in town. He was too wrapped up in getting to drive the squad car in the parade."

"We don't know for sure that this Cowboy is responsible for Jenna," Beckett said. "He might just be some petty thief passing through."

Dusty looked at him. "What's your gut telling you? Because mine is telling me that they're connected."

Before Beckett could answer, the radio crackled, and Cora Lee's voice came through the receiver. "Dusty?"

He unclipped the radio and pressed the button on the side. "You already have the plates?"

"No. Before I could find who they belonged to, I got a call from Agent Riley at the FBI." There was a long pause. "It seems that their informant in Panama just checked in. Alejandro left town more than a month ago. His girlfriend said that he mentioned something about coming to the States to kill some chickens."

"Shit!" Dusty started for his car, but Tyler stopped him.

"Hold up, Sheriff. There was something weird about Cowboy. He claimed to be Italian, but one day he was out in the garage and dropped a wrench on his toe and started hopping around and cussing a blue streak. Now, I might only speak English, but I know the difference between Italian and Spanish."

Chapter Twenty-seven

"*¿Dónde estas, chica?*"

At first Starlet thought Alejandro was talking to her in Spanish—not that she could answer with the bandana tied around her mouth—but then he spoke in English, and she realized he was talking to someone else.

"*Chica?* Where are you?" he said. "Don't you want to come out and say hi to your *amiga?*"

Starlet twisted and tried to see around the back of Alejandro's legs. But all she saw was the occasional flash of rock wall in the beam of his flashlight.

They were in some kind of a cave. Having spent the duration of the trip from the gas station hog-tied on the floor of a truck, she didn't know where the cave was. She only knew that it had taken a while to get there on a bumpy road that jarred her with every rut.

"*Chica?*" Alejandro spoke again. "I know that you're planning an ambush, but I have your sister chicken here. And you do one thing to me, I'm going to hurt her real bad." He stopped and fished something out of his pocket.

Then there was a click, followed by the rattle of a chain and the squeal of hinges. "You understand?"

He set Starlet on the ground. She thought she had been cold before. Without Alejandro's body heat, she was freezing. But she forgot about the temperature when he twisted a piece of her hair around his hand and swept the flashlight beam over the walls of the small, enclosed area. It caught the glimmer of two eyes and then flashed back to the woman crouched in the corner holding a sharp-looking rock.

Relief washed over Starlet. Not because Jenna Jay had been abducted by a crazy Mexican madman, but because she hadn't been abducted by the escort that Starlet had hired. Of course, they both would've been better off with metrosexual Vance. Jenna could've easily kicked his ass.

Alejandro's hand tightened as he laughed a sinister laugh that echoed off the stone walls. "Ahh, there you are, my feisty puma. For a second I thought you'd run off."

"And leave this dank paradise? Not hardly." Jenna shielded her eyes from the direct light. "So who did you bring? Is it Minnie?" Her face hardened. "So help me God, Alejandro, if you hurt one hair on that little old woman's head, I'll kill you with my bare hands."

"Oh, I plan on hurting that little old woman. I plan on slowly killing her right before your eyes."

Jenna took a step closer. "You'll never get away with it."

"Really? Because I just abducted the sweetheart of country music in broad daylight and not a soul stopped me." He jerked Starlet's hair until she stood up and then shined the light on her. She squinted and mumbled against the bandana as Jenna moved closer.

"Starlet!"

Alejandro released her and pulled out a gun, pointing both it and the flashlight back at Jenna.

"I hope you don't plan on taking the joy of your slow death away from me, *chica*," he said. "I would be very disappointed if you did." He stepped back and slammed what appeared to be some kind of jail cell door before he adjusted the chain and clicked the padlock closed. "After all the months of planning my revenge, it seems only fair that I should get to implement it."

"Fuck you, Alejandro." Jenna walked over and knelt down next to Starlet and removed the gag. As soon as it was off, Starlet croaked out the words she'd wanted to say since being abducted.

"I'll pay you back, Alejandro. I'll pay back every cent of the money and more. I'll give you whatever you want to release us."

"Don't waste your breath, Starlet." Jenna untied her hands. "This isn't about the money."

"Yes, it is," Starlet said. "That's exactly why he came back. He knows that I stole his money from the hens to pay for my mama's rehab. I told him when he caught me in Miss Hattie's garden." She turned to the beam of light. "Tell her, Alejandro. Tell her that it's all about the money."

There was a long stretch of eerie silence before he spoke. "At one time, it was about the money, little mouse. And if you had given it back to me then, instead of to the Feds, we wouldn't be here right now. But in the last few months, I've realized that money is nice, but revenge is sweeter. You got me exiled from my country and family, and for that, you must pay with your life."

Jenna snorted. "You screwed up your connection to

the cartel yourself, Alejandro, by coming to the henhouse in the first place. You should've paid back the money out of your own pocket and kept your mouth shut."

There was a click of a gun hammer being pulled back. "I would watch what you say, *chica*. Perhaps I can live without torturing you and end your life now."

"That's doubtful," Jenna said as she rubbed the feeling back into Starlet's wrists. "You wouldn't get any enjoyment out of that."

He laughed, and the hammer clicked back in place. "You're right. Besides"—he flashed the light up at the ceiling of stone—"I wouldn't want to die in a cave-in." Gravel crunched beneath his boots as he turned. "I'll be back soon, my little chickens. I saved the easiest hen for last."

The beam of light disappeared down the tunnel. Once it was gone, a thick blackness closed in on Starlet. And if it weren't for the warm hands holding her wrists, she might've panicked. But if Starlet had learned anything over the years, it was that panicking wouldn't help the situation. So she tried to channel her uncle Bernie's good humor.

"I wanted to take some time out of the spotlight, but this is ridiculous."

Jenna laughed and released her wrists to untie the rope around her feet. "I certainly wouldn't wish this on anyone, but I can't help being glad for the company. I was starting to go a little stir-crazy. You wouldn't happen to have some food, would you?"

Starlet wiggled the feeling back into her feet. "I'm afraid not."

There was the crunch of gravel as Jenna stood and moved away. She came back a moment later with a bottle of water and handed it to Starlet. "I wouldn't drink a lot; he only left one. I guess he figures, without water, we won't survive long enough for his fun." She sat down next to her. "I also figure that once Minnie gets here, our time is up. Which is why we need to ambush him as soon as he gets back."

Suddenly feeling sick to her stomach, Starlet recapped the bottle of water without taking a drink. "How do you do it? How do you stay so calm? Aren't you terrified?"

"Yes." Jenna leaned back on the wall. "But we can't go down without a fight. Especially when no one knows we're here. My family is off on a camping trip, and Beau won't be home until late tonight. Which means they won't start a search until tomorrow morning. Alejandro knows this, which is why we'll be dead long before then, giving him plenty of time to leave town without anyone being the wiser."

"But Beau already came back," Starlet said. "And Dusty has started a search."

Jenna sat up and grabbed Starlet's arm. "Are you sure? They know I'm missing?"

She started to nod and then realized that Jenna couldn't see it. "Yes, I'm sure. I was there with all the Cates brothers and Dusty when they were trying to figure out where you'd gone. They even found your truck."

Jenna released a squeal—something Starlet could never remember her doing—and hugged her. "Maybe we have a chance. Maybe Dusty and Beau can put two and two together."

It was a long shot. Especially when they were headed in the wrong direction. They were on the trail of a metrosexual escort. Not a bloodthirsty criminal. But Starlet wasn't about to burst Jenna's bubble.

"Of course they will. Dusty is the finest lawman

in Texas. And Beau won't rest until he finds you." She reached out and found Jenna's hand. "He loves you. I didn't realize how much until today."

Jenna squeezed back. "So does this mean that you're going to stop sending the hot cowboys to try to break up my marriage?"

"You knew?"

"It wasn't that hard to figure out, Starlet. Bramble is a small town with very few visitors. Suddenly, one cowboy after another starts showing up—all of whom are sexually interested in me. Now, I realize that I'm not bad-looking, but I've never attracted so much attention. Of course, I didn't know for sure until I got it out of one of them."

"Rowdy?"

"That would be the one." There was a smile in Jenna's voice. "Although he hung in there pretty good. It was the scissor hold that finally made him confess like a kid to a principal."

Tears burned Starlet's eyes. "I'm so sorry, Jenna. I wish I had some good excuse, but I don't—besides sheer stupidity."

"I don't know about that. Being in love is a pretty good excuse for acting stupid. Lord only knows that I've had my fair share of stupid moments because of it."

"But you never would've done what I did. Especially to a sister hen."

"I wish I could say I wouldn't. But if you had gotten Beau instead of me, I would've done anything to get him away from you—even send a horde of hot cowboys. Where did you find all those guys?"

"Most were rodeo cowboys I met, but the last was from an escort service."

Jenna laughed. "No wonder he had trouble taking no for an answer." When Starlet didn't laugh, she squeezed her hand. "Beau and I never meant to hurt you. In fact, Beau has been devastated that you two couldn't remain friends."

"I guess he knew why?"

"Yes. Although I kept the cowboys a secret. It never hurts for a man to think that he's got a little competition."

Starlet sighed. "Can you ever forgive me?"

"Only if you can get over Beau and move on with your life," Jenna said.

In the total darkness, sitting hip to hip and hand in hand with his wife, Starlet realized that she had gotten over Beau. Now when she thought of him, it was with a deep affection for being the first man who had tried to make her feel beautiful. But there was only one man who had succeeded. One man who gave her music, and with it, the confidence to love herself. Not the innocent, blond image thought up by Kari, but the true Starlet—a simple, brown-eyed girl from east Texas who was a successful songwriter and country singer.

Suddenly, she didn't feel scared anymore. In fact, she felt stronger than she'd ever felt. Maybe it had to do with confessing to Jenna. Or maybe it had to do with Jenna's forgiveness. Whatever the reason, a calm washed over her. A calm that allowed her to voice her truth.

"I love Beckett." The words were followed with such joy that she laughed. It echoed off the walls and came right back at her like a beam of sunlight.

"What?" Jenna released her hand and shifted toward her. "Are we talking Beckett Cates? The man you used to call Geeky Becky?"

"That's the one."

"So I guess those marine muscles changed your mind."

An image of Beckett reclining back in bed popped into Starlet's head. And she had to admit that marine muscles did look mighty fine washed in moonlight. But it wasn't the muscles that she loved as much as the man beneath.

"I know it sounds weird, especially after the way that I treated him," she said. "But there was something that drew me to Beckett from the first moment he walked into Miss Hattie's. If he had been nicer, I probably would've realized my feelings for him much sooner. But it's hard to confess to liking someone who doesn't appear to like you."

"I take it that he likes you now."

Starlet slumped back against the wall. "He used to— before he found out about my crush on Beau and hiring the cowboys to break you two up. Now he hates me. And I don't blame him a bit."

There was a long stretch of silence before Jenna spoke. "Well, I can see where that could cause some problems. But I don't think Beckett hates you. He's just hurt and needs some time to get over it."

"And you think he will?"

"He really doesn't have much choice, now, does he? Considering everything you did to get a man you only had a crush on, the man you truly love won't stand a chance." She scooted away. "And speaking of chances, if we want to have one against Alejandro, we need to get our weapons ready. Feel around for anything that we can use—a rock, a bottle we can break, anything that is sharp and deadly."

Starlet got to her hands and knees and carefully ran

a hand over the ground. "Do you really think we have a chance, Jenna?"

"Are you kidding?" she said. "Of course we have a chance. We're sister hens, remember. And hens don't ever give up." She paused. "Especially nesting hens."

Starlet sat back. "Nesting hens?" Before Jenna could answer, the truth dawned on her. "Oh my God, you're pregnant?"

"Not just pregnant. Pregnant with twins."

"You *and* Hope?"

"Hope isn't pregnant, and where the crazy town got that idea, I'll never know. I couldn't tell them the truth, because I haven't told Beau yet. I know—talk about love being stupid. I just didn't want him devastated if something went wrong, so I wanted to wait to tell him until I was further along in my pregnancy. And now..." Her voice trailed off. When she spoke again, for the first time, she sounded as scared as Starlet. "And now I might not ever be able to tell him."

Realizing that it was her turn to be strong, Starlet reached out and hooked an arm around Jenna. "You'll be able to tell him, Jenna, because we're going to survive this. In fact, we're going to kick Alejandro's ass from one end of this cave to another." She held up her fist and shook it. "Sister hens rule!"

Jenna laughed. "Dammit straight, they do!"

Chapter Twenty-eight

"STARLET!" BECKETT BEAT ON the front door, not caring that the pounding and his loud voice caused porch lights to come on all over the neighborhood. He wanted Starlet to open the door. Then, once he saw that she was fine, people could go back to sleep and he could go back to hating her. But Starlet didn't open the door. Her mother did. For once, the woman looked sober.

"What do you want?" she asked.

"Where's Starlet?" He pushed past her and looked in the living room and kitchen before heading for the bedroom.

"Now, wait just one damn minute." Jaydeen followed behind him. "You can't come bustin' into someone's house without an invitation. It's bad enough that you busted into our lives and changed my daughter from a sweet, little gal to a real pain in my ass."

When he didn't find Starlet in either bedroom, he turned to Jaydeen. "Just answer the goddamned question. Where is your daughter?"

Jaydeen took a step back. "How the hell would I

know? After being around you, she comes and goes as she pleases."

He grabbed her by the arms, and it took a strong will not to give her a good shake. "Did you see her today?"

His desperation must've gotten through to her because some of her sass drained out. "Yes," she said. "I saw her today. What happened?"

"When?" He did give her a little shake. "When did you see her?"

"In town, a few hours ago. She was going to talk with the mayor about the parade. What happened? Where's Starlet?"

He dropped his hands. "There's a chance that Starlet might be in trouble."

"Another one of Jed's crazy plans?"

"No. Real trouble this time." He headed for the door. "I want you to lock this and don't let anyone in unless you know them." He turned back around. "Especially not Cowboy."

Jaydeen stared at him for only a second before her shoulders relaxed. "What is with you and Starlet being so concerned about Cowboy?"

"Starlet knew Cowboy?"

Jaydeen nodded. "I guess so. She seemed real upset when she found out that he worked at the gas station."

Without another word, Beckett headed for the door. It didn't take him long to get to Jones's Garage. Since Tyler was on his way to the crime lab in Lubbock with Jenna's truck, it was closed up tight for the night. Beckett was about to turn around and head back to his truck when he heard Starlet singing "The Good-bye Kiss." The song caused his heart to seize up for a second before he realized that it was recorded. He followed it to the cell phone lying under a bush on the side of the building. He picked it up and stared at the crack that ran through the picture on the screen.

It was a picture of him fishing at Sutter Springs the day he'd taken Starlet there for a picnic.

"What in the hell is going on, Star?" Kari yelled as soon as he pressed the talk button. "I've been trying to get ahold of you for the last three hours, after that crazy conversation we had. What happened? Have you been drinking with your mother? Because alcohol has almost as many calories as those MoonPies you love—"

"This is Beckett," he said. "Starlet is missing. Now, tell me everything she said to you."

"Missing? What do you mean she's miss—"

Beckett cut her off. "What did she say?"

There was a pause before she spoke. "She was babbling something about cowboys and a guy named Vance. But I didn't take it seriously. I thought she was drunk. Then I heard her gasp some other name—Alfredo. No, Alejandro."

Without another word, he hung up the phone and exchanged it for the one in his pocket. He punched the number Dusty had given him and waited for his brother-in-law to pick up.

"What's up, Beckett?" Dusty said. "Did you find Starlet?"

"Alejandro has her." The words felt like dust in his mouth. "She must've stopped by the gas station, and he abducted her here. I found her cell phone on the ground."

"Damn it," Dusty said. "He must have a plan for the hens. By the time I got to the henhouse, Minnie was missing."

Beckett climbed up in the truck and started the engine. "So where do we go from here?"

"I'm going to stay at the henhouse until backup gets here—just in case he decides to come back for the other hens. I want you to question people in town and find out everything you can about what Alejandro did while he was here."

"What about Brianne and Elizabeth?" Beckett pulled onto Main Street.

"I just talked with Billy and Brant, and I think they've got things handled on that end. Being an outdoorsman, it sounds like your big brother has an arsenal at his disposal and isn't afraid to use it." He paused for a moment. "Although I think Alejandro has the hens he's interested in. They were the ones who caused him the most harm."

"But wasn't Beau the one who helped capture him?"

"It's doubtful that Alejandro will go up against a man without his posse of cartel thugs. Besides, he knows he can get back at Beau by hurting Jenna Jay."

"How long do you think we have?" Beckett finally asked the question that had been eating at him since leaving the gas station.

There was a long pause before Dusty answered. "Not long. That's why we need to find them. Listen, the Feds are here. I'll finish up with them and meet you in town. And see if you can find Kenny Gene. Cora Lee and I have been trying to radio him about Alejandro, but he's not answering. No doubt he's on the wrong frequency again."

Once he hung up, Beckett couldn't stop the cold chill that seemed to permeate every bone in his body. Death had been his constant companion in Afghanistan, so he should be used to the feeling. But the images of Minnie,

Jenna, and Starlet being tortured or killed were almost more than he could handle. Before joining the marines, he had never been much for prayer. But war had a way of forcing you to get in touch with your spiritual side. Now, as he drove down Main Street, he took a moment to ask for God's help.

He figured that the only bar in town would be the best place to find the townspeople. He was right. The parking lot of Bootlegger's was jam-packed with trucks, SUVs, and dinged-up American-made cars. He had just parked Billy's truck in the space by the front door when Beau pulled into the lot, followed by two trucks and two SUVs. Hope and Colt hopped out of one of the SUVs. Slate and Faith out of another. Jenna Jay's brother, Dallas, and sister, Tessa, got out of a truck. As did their parents, Burl and Jenna Senior.

"Have you heard anything?" Beau strode up, looking even worse than he had when Beckett had dropped him off at Jenna Jay's parents' house. His hat was missing and his hair messed, and his eyes held a desperation that Beckett understood completely. He felt just as desperate.

"He has Minnie and Starlet," he said.

"Sonofabitch." Beau hissed through his teeth as Hope and Faith walked over. Hope had a mean look on her face similar to the one her sister, Jenna Jay, got when she was ticked off about something. Faith's identical face was sad but determined.

"We'll find them, Beau," she said in her soft voice.

"Of course we will, Faith," Hope said. "But not if we're standing around here jawing. We need to start searching every place in town."

"You don't need to do anything." Colt came up. "This

isn't some petty criminal we're talking about, Hope. We need to let Sheriff Hicks and the FBI handle it."

"Sheriff Hicks is only one man, Colt. He can't look everywhere. And the Feds probably won't start their investigation until the morning. By that time, it could be too late."

Colt glanced over at Beau before he conceded. "Fine. We can take the southern part of town." He looked at Dallas and Tessa. "You two can take the northern."

Burl Scroggs came up, cradling a shotgun in his arms. "Mama and I can check out the eastern side."

"That leaves us the western." Slate took Faith's hand. "Everyone have their cell phones so we can keep in touch?" There was a murmur of agreement before Beckett spoke up.

"I realize that you're all worried about Jenna Jay. But Colt is right. Alejandro will be armed and dangerous. If you find his truck or see anything suspicious, you need to call Dusty. I'm going to stay here and interview people to see what they remember."

"Why don't you stay and help your brother, Beau?" Hope said. "You still look a little shook up by the news." She waved everyone to their vehicles before hopping into the SUV with Colt.

Beckett thought the news that Hope was talking about was Jenna being kidnapped by Alejandro. But once everyone had pulled out of the parking lot, Beau dropped another bombshell on him.

"Twins," he whispered in a voice raw with emotion. "Hope told me that the surprise Jenna had for me was she's pregnant with twins." He stared up at the star-filled sky. "So help me God, if he hurts one hair on her head, I'll…"

Beckett had never believed in promising something that he might not be able to deliver, but this time he didn't hesitate. Not only to ease the fear in his brother's eyes, but also to ease the fear that ate at his own insides. "I promise you. We'll find them before he has a chance to hurt them."

As soon as they stepped into the bar, Beckett was assailed with memories from the last time he'd been there. But tonight the mood of the bar wasn't as jovial. There was no band, and the jukebox had been turned down so it was easy to hear the conversation coming from the townsfolk who clustered around the bar.

"Maybe she went back to New York City," Rossie said. "She went there once with her rocker boyfriend. Maybe she ran off there again."

"Or maybe Beau left her first." Cindy Lynn downed a shot of tequila and released a sigh. "It can happen—" She cut off when she glanced up and saw Beau.

"I didn't leave, Jenna," Beau stated as he pushed his way to the bar. "Cowboy abducted her."

Mayor Sutter thumped a hand on Beau's shoulder. "Now, I realize that you're mighty upset about Jenna's disappearance, son. But let's not lose our heads and start pointin' fingers. Especially at a fine member of our community who wouldn't hurt a flea."

"Cowboy is Alejandro Perea." Beckett moved up next to Beau. "The same man who terrorized the hens out at the henhouse and almost killed Beau and Jenna Jay."

"That can't be," Rachel Dean said. "I held a gun on that man when Beau brought him out of the henhouse barn. And he was one mean-lookin' villain with hair as black as his soul. Cowboy has lighter hair and a friendly smile." She glanced over at Rossie. "Tell him, Rossie. In fact, why don't you just go get Cowboy? Isn't he sweepin' up in the back?"

"He was supposed to be, but he didn't show up for work tonight." Rossie looked between Beau and Beckett. "You think he would go to all the trouble of trying to become part of the town for a chance at revenge?"

"I know he would," Beau said.

Beckett waited for the people of the town to digest the information before he spoke. "We need you to tell us everything you remember about Cowboy. What he ate. What he liked to do. Where he went."

The townsfolk looked at one another before the mayor spoke up.

"He didn't do much but work."

"Harley's right," Rachel Dean said. "He never even came into the diner once. When I asked him about it, he said that he liked to cook at home. Of course, now that I think about it, does anyone know where he was stayin'?"

Everyone exchanged looks and shook their heads in bewilderment. Then Rye Pickett pushed his way through the group. Instead of his usual plaid western shirt, he wore a black satiny-looking shirt with an open collar. "Maybe he was campin' out on Miner Road. That might explain what he was doin' out there the other night."

Beckett leaned around Mayor Sutter. "You saw him on Miner Road, Rye? What direction was he headed in?"

"South. Toward the old mine."

Chapter Twenty-nine

"*CHICAS*." ALEJANDRO'S VOICE ECHOED down the tunnel, followed by a flash of light that cut through the thick darkness. "My quest is complete. I've got your head chicken."

Starlet tried to still the shaking of her knees, but it was impossible. She had never been so scared in her life. The jagged rock she held in her hand had caused a slick pool of sweat to collect in her palm. Somewhere on the other side of the tunnel, Jenna Jay waited with a jagged rock of her own. But two jagged rocks were nothing when compared to a gun. And Alejandro knew it. He didn't hesitate to unlock the jail cell door. The light lowered as he leaned down, and Starlet heard a moan that no doubt belonged to Minnie.

"Now!" Jenna yelled, and Starlet raced toward the light, making sure to slash high like Jenna had told her so she wouldn't accidentally hit Minnie. There was a clang of metal, and when she reached the light, she realized that no one was holding it. It was propped against the huddled form on the ground.

Starlet grabbed it and flashed it over the cave, stopping

on Alejandro, who stood on the other side of the bars with Jenna in his grasp. He had a hand over her mouth and a knife held to her throat.

He squinted his eyes in the light and laughed deviously. "What a pathetic effort. I expected more from the infamous hens."

"Go to hell," Starlet said, although her voice shook as much as her hand when she noticed the blood dripping down Jenna's throat into the neckline of her shirt.

"Ahh, the frightened chicken has finally found her courage," Alejandro said. "But a little too late."

Minnie moaned again, and Starlet knelt down and removed the gag. "Are you okay, Minnie?" she asked.

"Well," the old woman rasped, "I've had better days." She raised her voice. "So, Alejandro, if you're plannin' on killin' us, you might as well start with the head hen. And that sure as hell ain't Jenna."

Jenna mumbled against Alejandro's hand as Starlet spoke up. "She's right. Jenna is only an honorary hen. I'm the head hen."

"Not until I'm dead," Minnie said before she leaned in and whispered something in Starlet's ear that sounded like "Let's pock him."

While she tried to figure out what Minnie was trying to tell her, Alejandro chuckled. "Such loyalty. And you're right; it was a hard decision to figure out who needs to suffer the most. Jenna for getting me captured. Minnie for stealing my money. Or Starlet for giving it back to the Feds." He kicked open the cell door with his boot and released Jenna, shoving her inside before slamming the door closed. "But I've decided that I'm going to let fate make the choice." He locked the padlock with a loud click. "With less than one bottle of water, I figure it will only take you a few days to die." He pointed the knife at Minnie. "I would've said that the old one would go first, but now I think it might be the weakest one." He pointed the knife at Starlet and then looked at Jenna. "Which means that you will get to watch your friends slowly die and breathe your last breath all alone. And since you were the one who started it all, it seems fitting. Wouldn't you say?"

"I'd say that you can go fuck—" Jenna started, but Minnie cut her off.

"Now, Jenna, there's no need to get so nasty with the man. He does have a point. We did take his money." She nudged Starlet with her shoulder. "And the truth is that not all of it went to the FBI. Some of it is still in the lockbox at the henhouse. In fact, I have the key right here in my left pocket. Could you get it, Starlet? Perhaps we can negotiate with Mr. Alejandro."

Since the money had never been in a lockbox that needed a key, Starlet was confused until she slipped her hand in the pocket of Minnie's peignoir and felt the derringer. She should've been happy about the discovery. Instead, she just felt scared. While Minnie was a crack shot, Starlet had never shot a gun in her life. She got to her feet in hopes that she could somehow pass it off to Jenna, but before she could, a flash of light came from the opposite direction, followed by a voice that was easily recognizable.

"There you are, Cowboy." Kenny Gene stepped into the light. "When I followed you from town, I never thought you'd come all the way out here. You thinkin' to make a little extra money by minin' silver? 'Cause I gotta tell you that I tried it once, and it ain't near as easy as you think." He flashed the dim beam up at the ceiling of the tunnel. "Lucky for me, I brought my trusty Scooby-Doo flashlight with me, or I might never have found you. So if you don't want to go fishin', how about quail huntin'—"

Alejandro dropped the knife and pulled out his gun. But before he could shoot Kenny Gene, Starlet lifted the derringer and fired off one shot right after the other. When the smoke cleared, Alejandro lay crumpled on the floor.

"Holy shit!" Kenny Gene shined his Scooby-Doo flashlight down at Alejandro. "You just kilted Cowboy, Star Bentley. Which puts me in a bit of a pickle. I mean, how do I arrest my fav-o-rite country music singer?"

Before Starlet could explain who Cowboy was, a strange rumbling sound came from overhead.

"Oh my God," Jenna said. "The tunnel is caving in." She hurried over to the bars and reached through and got the key out of Alejandro's pocket. "Get Minnie, Kenny," she said as she unlocked the padlock. When he only stood there shining his light on Alejandro, she yelled, "Now!"

It seemed to take forever for them to get down the tunnel. They could've taken their time. The dust was just settling as they came around the corner and found tons of rock covering the entrance.

Jenna groaned in frustration, while Kenny Gene set Minnie down.

"Well, this ain't good." He tapped something against his leg. "I think my Scooby-Doo flashlight just ran out of batteries."

"Your radio, Kenny." Jenna sat down on the ground. Since Jenna rarely sat down, Starlet flashed the light over to her. She was holding her shirt to her throat, blood already soaking through the material.

"Jenna!" Starlet handed the flashlight off to Minnie and hurried over. Unfortunately, unlike Beckett, she wasn't good in emergency situations. The only thing she knew to do was strip off her shirt and press it against Jenna's neck.

"Good Lord," Kenny Gene breathed. "Am I dreamin'?"

Minnie snorted and flashed the light over to Kenny. "Quit gawkin' at Starlet and get on that damned radio and get us some help." She moved the beam of light back over to Jenna. "How is she, Starlet?"

"I'm fine," Jenna answered. "I'm not weak from the loss of blood as much as the loss of food."

With the warmth seeping through her fingers, Starlet didn't believe her for a second. But she kept her mouth shut and applied more pressure. It seemed to take forever for Kenny to figure out the radio frequency. He tried different ones until Dusty's voice finally came through the speaker.

"Kenny? Where are you?"

"I'm right here, Sheriff," Kenny said. "But things aren't lookin' good. Cowboy is dead. Jenna is bleedin' to death. And my Scooby-Doo flashlight is broke."

"Jesus!" came through the speaker loud and clear before Dusty collected himself. "Give me your location?"

"We're stuck in the old mine shaft. You know the one I'm talkin' about. The one out on—"

"I know the one you're talking about, and help is already on the way."

There was another creak of rock, followed by dust filtering down. Kenny glanced up, his dark eyes fearful.

"Okay, Sheriff, but you better hurry. I don't know how long before the entire tunnel caves in." He started to lower the radio, but then pulled it back to his mouth. "And, Sheriff, tell Twyla that I love her. And that if things were different, I'd marry her as fast as greased lightning."

Dusty didn't hesitate to answer. "You can tell her yourself when you get out."

Kenny grinned from ear to ear, as if Dusty saying it made it so. But Starlet had her doubts. The dust filtering down from the ceiling was getting heavier. For a second, Starlet thought about grabbing the radio from Kenny and giving Dusty her own message. Instead, she just pressed on Jenna's throat and chanted the words in her head.

I love you, Beckett. And I'm sorry, so sorry, that I didn't figure things out sooner.

"Starlet." Minnie coughed, and the light jostled. "Why don't you sing a calming song? Not too loud, mind you. We don't want to shake anything else loose."

"Sing my favorite, Miss Bentley," Kenny chimed in. " 'The Good-bye Kiss.' "

Starlet didn't feel much like singing. She felt more like sobbing. Still, she cleared her throat and sang in a soft voice. But this time she didn't sing the song for Beau. This time she sang it for Beckett.

"Can you hear my heartbeat asking you to stay? Can you see my lips asking for a taste? I'm thinkin' this might just be the last... but hoping it's the first. If you say this isn't love... tell me, why does good-bye hurt?"

The pile of rocks that covered the door seemed to shift, and a few broke loose and tumbled to the bottom, but Starlet ignored them and the blood that seeped through her fingers as she sang.

"Don't walk away. Don't let this pass. Just hold me close. Can't we make it last? Don't turn to go, saying I'll be missed. Just take me in your arms, and give me our first good-bye kiss—"

"Now, isn't that sweet."

The chilling voice had Minnie flashing the light at the tunnel. Alejandro stood there, blood soaking his shirt and dripping from the hand that held the gun. If he was in pain, he didn't show it. Not in the evil smile. Not in the way he moved closer.

"Makes me almost feel sad for your unrequited love." He pointed the gun at Starlet. "You've moved up on my list, little chicken. Now you'll be the one to watch your friends die." The barrel of the gun moved a couple inches over to Jenna.

"No!" Starlet shoved Jenna back and charged Alejandro, but before she could reach him, there was a loud, resounding gunshot. She stopped, expecting to feel pain. Instead, she felt nothing. Nothing except Alejandro's body brushing hers as he dropped to the ground.

Starlet's gaze followed Minnie's flashlight over to Kenny Gene, who stood there with a gun in hand and a Scooby-Doo flashlight in the other. He looked as surprised as Starlet felt.

Then, before anyone could say a word, the loose wall of rocks started tumbling down. At that point, there was nothing to do but pray that the end would be quick. But instead of the overhead rock caving in, the only rocks that moved were the ones at the very top of the pile. Starlet stared in disbelief when tiny beams of light trickled through.

"Jenna!" Beau's voice came through the growing opening.

"Beau!" Jenna struggled to her feet, and Starlet went over and helped her.

"We're going to get you of there," Beau said. "So don't you"—his voice hitched—"or my babies go anywhere. You understand me?"

"Stop being so darned bossy," Jenna said before she released a sob.

Starlet hugged her close. "It's okay, Jenna." She smiled. "Your hero is here to rescue you."

It didn't take Beau long to get through the opening. He climbed down the mountain of rocks, his flashlight briefly touching on Alejandro's crumpled form before landing on Jenna and Starlet. The only indication that he saw the blood was a slight intake of breath, and then he had Jenna in his arms.

"Shh, love. I'm here." He flashed the light at Kenny. "Kenny, climb up halfway and I'll hand her off to you," he instructed. "Beckett's waiting right on the other side."

The name left Starlet feeling relieved and thankful. She knew Beckett wasn't there for her, but it was enough that he was there.

Minnie went next. And finally it was Starlet's turn. When Beau noticed that she didn't have on a shirt, he took his off and helped her put it on before bending to lift her into his arms.

She pulled back. "I'm good, Beau. You need to be with Jenna."

He studied her for a moment before he nodded, then quickly scaled the rocks and disappeared through the opening.

On shaking legs, Starlet started to climb to Kenny, who reached out and helped her the rest of the way. When she reached the top, hands appeared through the opening. She had held on to a secret hope that Beckett would be waiting for her. That he would pull her into his arms and erase the horrors of the last few hours. But it wasn't Beckett who was waiting at the top. It was Brant. Brant who helped her out, then examined her in the headlights from all the vehicles parked in front of the mine.

"Are you okay?" he asked. "Did he hurt you?" Emotion welled up in her throat, and all she could do was shake her head as a tiny sob escaped. He pulled her close. "It's okay. Everything is going to be okay." After a few minutes, he released her and passed her along to Billy, who gave her another tight hug before leading her through the townsfolk, who all looked as stunned as Starlet felt. On the way to Billy's SUV, they walked past the big monster truck. Beau sat in the bed of the truck with Jenna's head elevated on his chest while Beckett worked to stop the bleeding.

"Is she going to be okay?" Starlet couldn't help but ask.

Beckett glanced back at her for only a brief second before returning to Jenna. But that was all Starlet needed to read the truth in his eyes. There would be no forgiveness. She had killed any love he might've had for her.

Beau answered the question. "She's going to be fine."

"And the babies?" Jenna asked. "They're going to be fine too. Right, Beck?"

"The babies are going to be just fine." Beckett secured the gauze Beau held on Jenna's throat with tape. "Brant's helicopter is on the way, and we're going to get you and Minnie to the hospital." Starlet had just closed her eyes in a prayer of thanks when he added, "Billy, find Starlet somewhere to sit down and keep her warm."

Starlet might've read something into the words if they hadn't come from a man who took care of everyone.

"Come on, Starlet." Billy led her away. He had just gotten her seated in his SUV and turned on the heater when Dusty came to a dust-spitting halt in front of the mine. He jumped out of the cruiser and took in the scene. But before he could start asking questions, Kenny Gene finished climbing down from the pile of rocks and held out his hands.

"Go ahead and arrest me, Sheriff. You told me not to use bullets, and you was right. Now I've gone and kilt Cowboy."

Chapter Thirty

BECKETT TOOK ANOTHER SIP of his third cup of coffee as he stared out the window of Josephine's Diner. He wasn't really looking at anything. His mind was too busy going over the events of the previous night. A night that had been the longest of his life. Of course, fear had a way of slowing time down. It seemed to take forever for him and Beau to get to the mine and much longer to dig through the rubble with their bare hands. And his fear had only intensified when he saw the blood covering Jenna Jay. But as concerned as he was about his sister-in-law, he'd been even more concerned about Starlet. The entire time he'd been administering first aid to Jenna, his gaze had kept going back to the mine. When Starlet finally appeared, he'd been able to breathe again, although he had still wanted her to go with Minnie and Jenna to the hospital in Austin.

She had stubbornly refused. Which explained what he was doing sitting in the back booth at Josephine's Diner, sipping on his third cup of coffee. He was hoping that Starlet would show up in town. Once he knew for certain that she was fine, he could go back to Billy and Shirlene's and get some sleep.

"Let me top that off for you, Beckett."

He glanced away from the window and up at Rachel Dean. As she refilled his cup, she sent him a sympathetic smile. "You sure had yourself a hard night, didn't you, honey? All of us saw what good care you took of Jenna Jay. If you hadn't been there, we could've lost her." There was a murmuring of agreement from the townsfolk sitting around before Mayor Sutter spoke up.

"I still can't hardly believe it." He swiveled around on his bar stool. "Cowboy seemed like such a kind, hard-workin' soul. He shore didn't seem like the type of person who would want to hurt anyone—especially a woman."

"Those are the worst kind." Cindy Lynn sat alone at a table, her hair flat and her eyes red-rimmed. Being that it was Election Day, Beckett was surprised she wasn't campaigning. Instead, she looked as drained as he felt. "You think you know a man," she continued, "and the truth is that you don't know him at all."

Rachel Dean walked back over to the counter. "Now, I wouldn't say that, Cindy." She poured Rossie another cup of coffee. "Sometimes a man is exactly as good as you think he is."

A look came over Rossie's face that could only be described as pissed. He got up from his stool and tossed down his napkin. "And sometimes a woman can be too stubborn for her own good." He turned and strode out of the diner, sidestepping Hope Lomax and Sherman the Pig, who had just walked in the door.

"What's wrong with Rossie?" Hope asked as she took Sherman's leash off.

"I think we're all a little stressed over what happened last night," Mayor Sutter said. "Not to mention the stress of finding a new mayor." He shook his head. "I wish I'd never brought up retirement."

"And I wish I had a college education and small hands," Rachel said, her voice cracking as she turned around and placed the carafe of coffee back in the machine.

"And I wish Kenny Gene would marry me." Twyla started to sob.

"Good Lord, Twyla," Cindy Lynn said. "Does everything always have to come back to Kenny Gene?"

Twyla turned on her. "You can't blame a woman for wanting to talk about the man she loves. You, on the other hand, don't ever talk about Ed, which might explain why he's always off huntin' or fishin'."

Cindy Lynn jumped to her feet. "At least Ed married me. We all know that Kenny Gene is never gonna—"

Hope Lomax opened her mouth and released a sound that caused the hairs on Beckett's neck to stand at attention. The entire room quieted, and Sherman trotted over and sat at her feet.

"What's going on here?" Hope said. "I realize that everyone is upset about what happened last night, but that is no reason to turn on your neighbor."

Everyone glanced around guiltily before Twyla spoke up. "You're right, Hope. And I'm sorry, Cindy Lynn. You and Ed have a great marriage. I'm just jealous, is all. My sisters are married, so I guess I thought I should be too. But the truth is that I'm good at findin' men, but not so good at keepin' them."

Cindy Lynn shook her head. "I'm the one who should apologize. Ed isn't fishin'. He's livin' in Houston." She looked down at her pile of campaign flyers. "He wants a divorce."

"Oh, honey." Twyla hurried over and hugged her. "Don't you worry. After three divorces, I'm an expert on gettin' through them."

Without warning, Rachel blurted out, "I love Rossie Owens!"

Followed by the mayor's declaration. "I hate fishin'."

"I love fishin'," Rye said. "And the Paso Doble."

"The Paso what?" Darla asked as she continued to knit.

"I think it's a Mexican food," Tyler Jones said. "Which reminds me, I want to apologize for givin' Cowboy a job. I should've never welcomed that boy with open arms."

"You aren't the only one to blame," Cindy Lynn said. "None of us should have welcomed a stranger like we did. Obviously, we shouldn't be so trustin'."

Hope stepped up to the counter as her gaze scanned the crowd. "What are you talking about? Trust and friendship is what this town was founded on. Wasn't it two friends, Joseph Sutter and Wade Lowell, who started this town? Didn't they welcome immigrants, oilmen, and farmers with open arms to be part of the community they built?" Beckett couldn't be sure, but it looked like Sherman nodded his head in agreement. "Okay, so you misjudged someone," Hope continued. "But at least you misjudged them with good intentions instead of bad. You gave Cowboy the benefit of the doubt. You gave him a job. You called him your friend. As far as I'm concerned, you did nothing wrong."

Mayor Sutter got to his feet. "Hope is right. You should never regret making a friend—even if that friend turns out to be the enemy." He looked at Hope. "You were born to be a leader, Hope Lomax. It's shore a shame that you ain't runnin' for mayor."

Hope looked confused. "Not running? What makes you think that I'm not running?"

"Because you're pregnant with twins," Rachel said.

"Who in the world told you that?"

All eyes turned to Cindy Lynn, who pointed a finger at Hope. "But I heard you. You were in the bathroom talking to Faith, and you said you were thinking about not runnin' because—"

Hope cut Cindy off. "Jenna Jay is pregnant with twins, and I wanted to be there for her." There was a collective gasp, and Beckett couldn't help but smile. Only the folks of Bramble could turn a simple misunderstanding into a crazy mayoral mess.

"But I've changed my mind," Hope continued. "I figure I can be a good mayor and help my sister with her twins." She glanced at Mayor Sutter. "If you'll stick around and help me, Uncle Har—"

"I'll do it!" Mayor Sutter hopped up. He lifted his hands like he was shooing a flock of chickens. "Well, what are we waiting for? Let's get to the polls and elect our new mayor."

The diner cleared out. And within seconds, Beckett found himself alone. At least, he thought he was alone until a voice broke the silence.

"They're a flighty bunch, but their hearts are in the right place."

Beckett turned to find Moses Tate sitting in the booth behind him. He lifted an age-spotted hand and pushed back his cowboy hat, displaying a weathered face with piercing blue eyes.

"I sure appreciate you lookin' after Minnie last night," he said. "I would've traveled to Austin to be with her at the hospital, but my drivin' skills ain't what they used to be, and my nephew Elmer can't take me until after his AA meetin'."

Rather than crane his neck, Beckett picked up his cup and moved to Moses's booth. "I wouldn't worry about it. Despite a few scrapes and bruises, she seemed to be fine, and Brant said that she will be back at the henhouse by this evening."

"She told me about your doctorin' skills." Moses took out the plastic Solo cup from his pocket and spit a stream of tobacco in it. "And I saw it firsthand when Starlet took that joyride through town." He studied Beckett with his penetrating eyes. "Doc Mathers has been talkin' about retirin'. 'Course, he'll never do it unless he has someone good enough to replace him."

Beckett shook his head. "I don't have the medical education to be a doctor." He took a sip of coffee, and when he lowered the cup, he found Moses watching him with a smile on his wrinkled lips.

"Bein' a good doc ain't about education as much as carin' for folks. Medical stuff you can learn. Carin' has to come from within. And from the sounds of things, I'd say that you care quite a bit." He spit another stream of tobacco before placing the squashed cup back in his pocket. "Which makes me wonder why you're sittin' in an empty diner. Since you ain't an old goat with drivin' issues, I would've thought that you'd be with Starlet."

Beckett stared down at his coffee. Too tired to think up a good excuse, he told the truth. "I'm not the Cates brother she wants."

There was a long pause before Moses spoke. "I guess you're referrin' to the crush she had on Beau." When Beckett's gaze snapped up to him, he shrugged. "I sleep a lot, but that don't mean I don't pay attention."

"So then you understand why I'm not with her." Suddenly realizing what an idiot he was to be sitting there waiting for Starlet, he got up and pulled out his wallet to pay for his coffee.

Moses slowly got to his feet. "I had me a crush once. Mrs. McMurray had this pile of red hair and the prettiest blue eyes you ever saw. I would sit in class and daydream about that woman all day, completely ignoring the fact that she was married, had three kids, and was a good thirty years older than I was. I might've kept it up for years if my first wife hadn't caught my eye. After that, I forgot all about Mrs. McMurray." He shuffled to the door and waited for Beckett to open it before stepping outside. "But I guess that's how crushes work. They're just innocent practice until the real thing comes along." He glanced across the street. "And speakin' of the real thing…"

Beckett followed his gaze. Kenny Gene was coming out of the post office and was so busy looking at the large manila envelope he carried that he ran smack-dab into the flagpole and knocked off his hat.

Moses snorted. "I guess I'd best get over there and help the boy. I'd hate to have gone to all the trouble to locate his wife and get her to sign the papers Judge Seeley drew up only to have Kenny lose them." He shook his head as he ambled to the door. "Sometimes this town is more trouble than it's worth."

Beckett barely registered the information about Kenny

being married. His mind was too consumed with the story Moses had told him about his high school crush. The story reminded Beckett of his own crush. Not on a teacher, but on Madonna. He could remember watching her music videos and thinking she was the hottest woman alive. At one point, he'd even conjured up a scheme to kidnap the singer in Brant's private jet and take her to Mexico. Looking back, it seemed silly. But to a sixteen-year-old nerdy kid, it had been a viable plan. Which was just as crazy as Starlet's plan to get Beau.

Suddenly, the crack in Beckett's heart didn't feel quite as big. Moses was right. A crush was just innocent practice while you were waiting for the real thing to come along. But that still left one question. One question that kept Beckett's heart from completely healing.

Was he Starlet's real thing?

A loud whoop startled Beckett out of his thoughts. Kenny Gene raced down the street waving the envelope over his head.

"I'm free!" he yelled. "I'm free!"

Chapter Thirty-one

IT WAS A BEAUTIFUL day for a parade. The west Texas sky was as blue and clear as the Cates brothers' eyes. Or at least Beckett's. Starlet couldn't remember the exact color of his brothers' eyes. But she knew that Beckett's were a soft sapphire blue on the edges and a deeper cobalt blue right next to his pupils. And she knew that he squinted them when he didn't have his reading glasses and rubbed them when he was tired. Held them steady and intent when he was trying to figure something out and crinkled them when he smiled.

She also knew that she would miss them. Miss them more than she would miss the hens, Billy, and Brant. Much more than she had ever missed Beau.

"I see that you're all packed up." Uncle Bernie stepped out the screen door, pulling Starlet's attention away from the sky.

Brushing at her eyes, she turned to her uncle, who was all spiffed up in a blue western suit. She reached out and adjusted the American flag pin on his lapel. "Mama and I plan on leaving right after the Fourth of July parade." She patted his chest and smiled. "I'll miss you."

"I'll miss you too, Star Baby." He wrapped his skinny arms around her and pulled her close, thumping her awkwardly on the back. "But you know you'll always have a home here in Texas. Especially now that I've got me a job selling henhouse paraphernalia on the Internet." He pulled back and winked. "Authorized by the head hen herself. I thought I'd start out with T-shirts and caps quoting the henhouse rules and move on to snow globes and feather fans. I only get a percentage, but with room and board, I can't complain."

Starlet lifted her eyebrows. "Not to mention being close to the love of your life."

Uncle Bernie actually blushed, making him look even more like a Keebler Elf. "That too. Olive's still holdin' out. I figure it will take some time to prove my worth."

"In your case, Bernie"—Starlet's mama pushed open the screen door and waltzed out—"that could take a lifetime."

Uncle Bernie only grinned. "I've got nothin' but time, Jaydeen."

Her mama reached down and picked up Hero, who had been snoozing on the porch. "Don't we all. Since I decided to see what the world looks like outside of a bottle, time seems to move like molasses in Alaska."

Starlet still couldn't believe that her mama was on the wagon. Uncle Bernie thought that his sister had been scared straight by Alejandro kidnapping and almost killing Starlet. It didn't seem likely. But whatever the reason, it was nice to see her mother clear-eyed and functioning for a change.

Not that it had changed her disposition that much.

"Well, what are we waiting for?" her mama snapped.

"Let's get to this crazy parade so we can get out of this Podunk town and back to civilization."

Her words turned out to be prophetic. The parade was the craziest thing Starlet had ever seen. And that was before it even started. When she arrived at the parking lot behind the town hall, she found complete chaos. Decorated semitrailers and flatbed trucks were surrounded by excited high school band members, flustered prom queens, manic clowns, and gussied-up horses, sheep, and dogs.

"Stop twirling and get to your positions!" Cindy Lynn yelled at a group of little-girl baton twirlers who paid her no attention whatsoever and kept right on high-stepping and twirling around Sherman, who was dressed up in a red, white, and blue Uncle Sam costume. When Cindy saw that the girls weren't going to listen, she turned to the senior citizens with their tennis-balled walkers. "Old Coots with Scoots!" She looked at her clipboard. "You'll go after the Feed and Seed's 'Love Your Livestock' float, but before the First Baptist's 'Come to Jesus' float. You got it?" When the senior citizens just looked confused, Cindy threw up a hand in exasperation and stormed away.

A motorized buzz like Minnie's wheelchair had Starlet glancing behind her. But it wasn't Minnie who stopped inches from the toes of her cowboy boots. It was Mayor Harley Sutter in a little motorized kid's truck. The mayor was dressed up like a cowboy clown with a huge foam cowboy hat.

"Don't you worry, Miss Bentley," he said, his voice sounding nasally because of the red rubber nose. "I know it looks a little chaotic right now, but Cindy will have everyone whipped into shape before the parade starts.

And the way I figure it, this parade is the best thing for that little gal right now. Especially since she didn't win the election."

Having spent the last few days nursing a broken heart, Starlet had forgotten all about the election. "Who won?"

The mayor's handlebar mustache, the only thing not covered in white face paint, twitched with a smile. "The one who should've." He pointed a white-gloved finger at Hope Lomax, who was helping the patriotic pig into a red convertible Cadillac. The mayor shook his head. "Things always work out in the wash." He looked at Starlet. "We thought about having you ride with our new mayor, but Miss Minnie insisted that you be on the henhouse float."

Starlet hadn't known that the hens were going to be in the parade. She glanced around until her gaze landed on the large float at the back of the lot. It took her only a second to recognize the two-story miniature house surrounded by lilac bushes. Miss Minnie looked right at home sitting in the rocker on Miss Hattie's wraparound porch.

Starlet laughed. Only the hens.

"Minnie says that she has your costume all ready." Harley pulled off his red nose and scratched beneath it before putting it back on. "And you can use the town hall bathroom to change."

Starlet hadn't planned on wearing a costume. Her plan had been to quickly honor her commitment before heading to the airfield, where the helicopter she'd ordered should be waiting—hopefully, after it had taken care of some other business for her. Unfortunately, she had learned how to deal with Kari and her mother, but she hadn't learned how to deal with one very determined old hen.

"Of course you're gonna wear a costume," Minnie said as she rocked in the chair. "Costumes are what make a parade worth watchin'." She nodded at the float next to them. "I haven't been able to take my eyes off those two since they started dancin'."

Starlet glanced over at the float and did a double take. Not because of the bull that stomped and snorted in the pen that had been constructed on the float, but because of the two dancers who whirled around on the elevated stage above the bull—one in a matador costume and one in a sequined gown that showed off hairy legs, beefy shoulders, and a beer belly that rivaled Mayor Sutter's.

"Now, that's a great costume," Minnie said. "I've always loved a man who could dance."

Unable to pull her gaze away, Starlet continued to watch until the matador ended the dance by swirling the hairy guy into the splits. The people standing around watching applauded, which caused both men to grin broadly and slap each other on the back like two football players after scoring a touchdown.

Starlet blinked to clear her vision before she turned back to Minnie. "Okay, so those are some good costumes. But what about you? You're not wearing a costume."

Minnie lifted a plastic headband with two sparkly blue stars bouncing on wire springs and put it on her head. "What do you call this?" Without another word, she reached down and grabbed a paper sack and held it out to Starlet.

Releasing a sigh, Starlet took the bag. But when she looked inside, she pulled back in horror. "Are you kidding me?"

Minnie sent her a pointed look. "Now, have you ever known me to kid?"

"My dad said that you weren't comin' to the parade."

Beckett opened his eyes to see Jesse standing in the doorway of the guest bedroom. Like any true cowboy, even in the heat of summer, the kid wore a western shirt, jeans, and his cowboy hat and boots.

Beckett rolled to his back and rubbed a hand over his face. This business of two hours of sleep a night was killing him. He'd stayed up most of the night thinking about Starlet. She was leaving today. And he was going to let her. Not because he wanted to, but because he didn't know how to stop her. Or maybe he just wanted her to fight for him like she'd fought for Beau.

"I thought I'd head to Dogwood today," he said.

"Why would you do that?" Jesse moved into the room. "Grandpa and Grandma Cates arrived this mornin' and are already headed to the parade with Mama and Daddy."

Well, shit. There goes my excuse.

"I've never much cared for parades." He sat up and stuffed a pillow behind his back. "I'll catch up with you at the picnic and fireworks." *After Starlet is long gone.*

"Yeah. The fireworks are the best part anyway." Jesse shifted from one foot to the other. "Well, I guess I'll let you get back to sleep." He turned, but Beckett stopped him.

"Wait a minute. Why didn't you go with your parents to the parade? And what do you have in your hand?"

Jesse turned back around. "Since Grandpa's Suburban was full, Daddy said that I could take his monster truck." He looked down at the sheet of paper he held. "And this

is nothin'. I just thought that you might want to see—"
He shrugged. "It's not a big deal."

Beckett held out his hand. "Hand it over." When Jesse
didn't comply, he gave him the meanest marine look
he could muster. "Don't make me get up and give you the
Russian Noggin Rub."

"As if," Jesse said, although a smile played on his
mouth as he walked over and handed the paper to Beau. It
took only a glance to figure out what it was.

"Hmm?" It was hard to keep his pride and happiness
from showing. "I thought you said you were too stupid to
get an A."

Jesse blushed and shuffled his feet. "Well, maybe I
was wrong."

Beckett swung his legs over the side of the bed. "That
makes two of us. Because if I learned anything from my
brothers, it's that an A always deserves a noggin rub."
Jumping to his feet, he hooked an arm around Jesse's neck.

After only a few minutes of horsing around with the
kid, Beckett discovered what his brothers had always
known. It was kind of fun to torture a younger Cates. He
also discovered that he couldn't let Jesse go to the parade
by himself. Not after he'd aced his math test and gotten
his driving privileges back.

That, and Beckett didn't want Jesse making any stupid
detours and screwing things up.

By the time he showered and they got to town, Beckett
expected the parade to be in full swing. But Billy's monster truck was the only vehicle driving down Main Street.
You would've thought they were part of the parade by the
whistles and exuberant hand waves from the folks who
lined the street.

"I swear people love this truck," Beckett said.

"Yeah, it's a cool truck." Jesse kept his hands on the steering wheel and his eyes on the road. "But I don't think they're whistling at the truck as much as paying tribute to the man who saved my aunt Jenna Jay." He flashed a smile over at Beckett. "And got me an A on my geometry test."

Since all the parking spaces on the street were taken, Jesse pulled into Josephine's parking lot. It took him a while to maneuver the big truck into a space. Beckett was just about to congratulate him on a job well done when the crowd lining the street separated and a man in a wheelchair appeared.

Beckett's heart rose up to his throat. He wanted to tell Jesse to back up and get the hell out of there, but since the man was staring straight at him, Beckett accepted his fate and climbed out of the truck. Although it was hard to talk when all the oxygen seemed to be sucked out of the air. He did get one word out.

"Sully."

"Beck." Sully stretched out a hand. His handshake was firm and strong, and for some reason, Beckett had trouble letting go. Or maybe it was Sully who didn't let go. They stood there gripping hands for several minutes before Jesse spoke and broke them apart.

"I'm going to find my folks, Uncle Beckett. You comin'?"

"I'll catch up with you later," he said, his gaze still on his friend. Once Jesse was gone, he asked, "What are you doing here, Sully?"

"I've always loved a parade." He patted the golden Lab that Beckett hadn't noticed until then. "Although Jasper here would probably like to get out of the hot sun."

Beckett nodded at the diner. "Since most of the town is watching or in the parade, we probably won't be able to get a cold drink, but we can have a seat." He cringed when he realized what he'd said, but Sully only laughed.

"Thanks, man, but this lucky bastard already has one."

"Ryan Sullivan!" A pretty woman in a sundress came up behind the wheelchair. "Watch your mouth. There are children around."

Sully reached back and took her hand. "Yes, ma'am." His eyes sparkled with mischief. The same mischief that had gotten Beckett in more than a few fights. "Beck, I'd like you to meet my fiancée, Susie."

The woman smiled at Beckett. "It's nice to meet you, Beckett. Ryan has told me so much about you."

"All bad," Sully teased as Susie pushed him toward the door of Josephine's.

As predicted, there was not a soul in the diner. Which was probably for the best. If Sully were there for more money, Beckett didn't exactly want the gossiping townsfolk to know about it. He chose a table close to the front windows and pulled out a chair so Susie could push Sully in close. He went to pull out a chair for her, but she shook her head.

"I'm going to leave you two to talk." With one brief kiss on Sully's cheek, she walked out.

"I didn't know you had a fiancée waiting for you at home." Beckett took the chair across from Sully.

"I met Susie at the rehab hospital. She was my physical therapist. I figured any girl who could put up with the shit I dish out was a girl worth living for."

Beckett swallowed. "I'm happy for you, Sull."

Sully studied him. "It's funny, but you don't look happy, Beck. You look like shit."

"Thanks." He took off his cowboy hat and rubbed a hand over his face. "I haven't been sleeping very well."

"PTSD?"

"Some."

"Yeah, me too. But it gets better every day." Applause and whistles had them both looking out the window. The parade had started. Kenny Gene led it in his cruiser with lights flashing and siren blaring and a big banner on the grill that read HOMETOWN HERO. After what he'd done out at the mine, Beckett figured he more than deserved the title. In the front seat next to him, Twyla beamed and held her hand out the window, waving and flashing her diamond engagement ring.

Beckett turned back to Sully and cut to the chase. "I guess you need more money."

Sully studied him for a few minutes before speaking. "Always." He pulled a folded envelope from his front shirt pocket. The same envelope that Beckett had sent him when he first got back to the States. "Just not guilt money from my best marine buddy." He held out the envelope, but Beckett refused to take it.

"I want you to have it." He held up a hand. "I need you to have it."

Sully slammed the envelope down on the table. "What you need, Beck, is to pull your head out of your ass! Money can't change what happened. It can't give me back my legs. It can't give our friends back their lives."

Beckett jumped to his feet. "Don't you think I know that! It's something I'll have to live with for the rest of my life."

The dog that had been lying down next to Sully's chair sprang up and growled. Sully calmed him by reaching out and stroking his head. "Did you know that scientists believe that dogs have no more than a twenty-second memory. That's it. If it hasn't happened in the last twenty seconds, it's just not fuckin' important to them. It doesn't matter." He shook his head. "Unfortunately, humans have much longer memories. And that works out okay if we only remember the happy times. But we like to hang on to everything. The hurtful name some kid called us in elementary school, the broken heart some girl gave us in high school, and the tragic things that happen to us in war." He looked up at Beckett. "And what happened was tragic, Beck. People we don't even know built and set up some explosive devices that took my legs and all those lives. And even if you had been with us, you couldn't have stopped it."

Air rushed into Beckett's lungs, allowing him to speak the truth that he'd hidden for so long. "But if I had been there, I wouldn't have to remember."

"But you weren't there, Beck. For some reason that we'll probably never figure out, you and I were meant to live. And I'll be damned if I'm going to spend the rest of my life living in the past."

Living in the past. Sully's words resounded in Beckett's heart like a church bell, ringing with clarity and truth. Beckett *had* been living in the past. And not just since Afghanistan. He'd always had trouble letting things go. Which was one of the reasons he'd joined the marines. He couldn't let go of the feeling of inferiority he had about not being as tough or as strong as his brothers. But now, confronted by a man who had lost his legs and was still able to move on, Beckett could no longer excuse his behavior.

As if reading his mind, Sully smiled. "Twenty seconds, man. What do you want to do in the next twenty seconds? Because I sure as hell don't want to sit here talking about war and death when I could be enjoying a Fourth of July parade." He looked back at the window. "Especially one with a stripper who looks an awful lot like Star Bentley with dark hair."

Beckett's gaze followed Sully's, and his eyes widened in shock. "Starlet?"

"Starlet?" Sully repeated. "Is this the same Starlet who called me and demanded that I attend today's parade so I could talk with you?" He laughed as his gaze went back to the window. "I should've known that somber Beckett Cates would find himself a firecracker who doesn't mind dancing down Main Street in nothing but two feather fans."

Chapter Thirty-two

STARLET WASN'T DANCING. SHE stood like a statue with one fan spread in front of her and the other spread in back. Of course, that didn't stop the stiff west Texas wind from ruffling her feathers. Fortunately, she wore a skin-toned leotard beneath. Something the men in the crowd didn't seem to be aware of. The whistles were getting louder and louder, and Starlet didn't think that the men's enthusiasm was entirely due to her singing.

Not when the sound system kept going in and out.

Starlet might've tried to adjust the microphone, but she wasn't willing to let go of the feather fans for a second. A leotard had to be the least flattering article of clothing a woman could wear, and Starlet wasn't about to end up plastered on the cover of some rag mag with the headline "Star Bentley's MoonPie Demise." So she just kept right on singing as the hens tossed out candy below her.

From the second-story balcony of the miniature hen-house, Starlet could see most of the parade up ahead. She could see the flashing lights of Kenny's squad car, the marching band, the row of floats, and parade clowns, Mayor Sutter and Rachel Dean, as they weaved in and out of the floats—the mayor in his mini truck and Rachel on her unicycle.

For a large woman, Rachel was amazing on the one-tire bike. She jigged and jagged around baton twirlers, horses, and walkers with surprising agility. She had just cycled around the front corner of the semi that pulled the bull and the *Dancing with the Stars* guys when something caused her to freeze in midpedal.

Starlet looked up ahead and immediately saw what had stopped her. It was hard not to see the big sign in front of Bootlegger's Bar. It usually announced happy hour or drink specials. Today it announced something else entirely.

ROSSIE OWENS LOVES RACHEL DEAN

It was about the sweetest thing Starlet had ever seen. Rachel must've thought so too because she lost her balance and fell backward off the unicycle, landing in the pathway of the oncoming semi. The truck braked just in time, but the sudden stop started a chain reaction.

In a split second, Starlet saw it all:

The hairy dancer being torn from his partner's arms and falling backward off the stage to crash through the boards of the bullpen. The bull jumping to freedom and scattering high school band members, baton twirlers, and Old Coots with Scoots like dogs released from a kennel. One little baton twirler raced in front of Mayor Sutter's mini truck, sending him veering out of the way and straight into the path of the henhouse float.

There was another screech of tires before Starlet went sailing over the railing of the balcony. Modesty was forgotten as she dropped the fans and grabbed on to the rungs of the railing. She didn't know how long she hung there with her heart in her throat and her leotard up her butt crack. It seemed like hours before a deep voice spoke from below her.

"Let go."

Starlet's heart dropped back down into her chest with a thump. As the pain of the last few days came spiraling back, she couldn't find her voice. All she could do was dangle there and hope that Beckett would go away. Instead, he stepped closer. Close enough for her to see the toes of his boots amid the tissue-paper lilacs hot glued to the float.

"Let go, Starlet," he said. "I'll catch you."

Tears welled in her eyes. "Go away, Beckett."

For a long moment, all she heard were the excited voices of the townsfolk as chaos continued to ensue; then Beckett spoke. "I can't."

She wanted the words to hold another meaning, but if she had learned anything since coming back to Texas, it was to pull her head out of the clouds and accept things at face value.

"Yes, you can," she said. "You walked away easily enough at Billy and Shirlene's."

"For the love of Pete, woman, just let go!"

"No." She tightened her grip, even though the muscles in her arms had started to cramp. "I don't trust you as far as I can throw you."

"Trust me?" He snorted. "Let's talk about trust. I trusted you to be truthful with me. And you never once mentioned the fact that you had a crush on my brother—or that you were trying to break up his marriage by hiring cowboys to seduce his wife."

The smart thing to do would be to let Beckett get her down and then get the heck out of Dodge. But for some reason, she couldn't bring herself to give him the satisfaction of rescuing her.

"Fine," she said. "You want the truth? I'll give you the truth. I'm a devious manipulator who loves your brother Beau. There. How's that for the truth? Now, run along and find someone to get me down from here."

"Like hell you love Beau! If you loved him so much, why did you show up in my room that night at the hen-house? Why didn't you say no that night in the Jungle Room? And why did you invite Sully here?"

Along with the throbbing muscles in her arms, a lump formed in her throat. A lump that made her voice sound choked when she answered. "Because you tricked me into believing that you were my hero."

When he didn't reply, she thought that he'd left. All she could hear was the sound of Cindy Lynn yelling and trying to get the parade back on track. But before she could panic, strong hands encircled her waist from above and lifted her back over the railing. With the brim of his cowboy hat shading his eyes, she couldn't read Beckett's expression, but his voice held a mixture of anger and conviction.

"I'm not a hero, Starlet." He gave her a little shake to emphasize the words. "And I'm tired of trying to prove that I am. I'm just an imperfect man who likes computers, reading, and noncontact sports. An imperfect man who has made a lot of mistakes and will no doubt make a lot more in his lifetime. One of the biggest is not letting you know how I felt from the first moment I stepped into Miss Hattie's and saw you standing on the stairs in that pretty prom dress."

"Pretty? You thought my dress was pretty?"

"Yes, but not even close to as pretty as the young woman who wore it." He released her arms and stepped back. "I love you, Starlet. And I want to marry you and spend the rest of my life loving you. But I won't compete with anyone—my brother included—for your love. You'll either give it freely, or not at all."

Before she could get a word out, he disappeared through the fake balcony doors, and she was left standing there trying to absorb the fact that Beckett still loved her. After everything she'd done—all the mistakes she'd made—he still loved her. And he wasn't going to leave her because she wasn't perfect. He was going to leave her because she wasn't willing to stop him.

"Well, don't just stand there," Minnie called up from the porch. "Henhouse rule number fifty-one states: Never let a good cowboy get away."

Minnie's words snapped her out of her daze, and uncaring that she wore nothing but a skin-colored leotard, Starlet followed Beckett through the fake balcony doors and down the ladder that led to the lower level of the float. When she came out on the porch, Minnie grinned broadly and pointed her finger.

"He went that way."

It wasn't easy finding Beckett in the chaos of horses, senior citizens, and clowns. Mayor Sutter almost ran over her with his mini truck as he raced in the opposite direction. In fact, everyone seemed to be running in the opposite direction. If Starlet hadn't been on a mission, she might've wondered why. Instead, she pushed against the stream until she spotted a tall cowboy in a plaid shirt picking up a little baton twirler and swinging her up into the bed of a pickup truck.

"Beckett Cates!" Starlet yelled at the top of her lungs.

He stopped in his tracks and slowly turned. With his gaze pinned on her, it was a little more difficult to be brave. In fact, it took a couple times of clearing her throat before she could speak.

"I've always had a hard time expressing my emotions," she said. "I guess that's why I love music as much as I do. I can express my feelings in a song much better than I can express them with just words." She stepped closer. "I love you, Beckett. I don't know when it happened. All I know is that when you touch me, I hear music. Sweet, beautiful music that makes my world brighter than it has ever been before." The lump in Starlet's throat dissolved into about a hundred tears. Tears that raced down her cheeks, over her chin, and down to her leotard. "And the thought of living without that music breaks my heart."

She expected him to say something, just not what he ended up saying.

"Sonofabitch!" He ran toward her and swept her up in his arms. Not in a romantic way, but like a sack of potatoes. She lifted her head and started to complain when she saw the bull. A bull heading straight for them, with wild red eyes and two very pointy horns. But before it reached them, Beckett lifted Starlet and threw her. She landed in a pile of hay and had barely gotten her bearings before Beckett joined her in the back of the 4-H trailer. There was a loud thump as bullhorns hit the tailgate. Then there was nothing but silence.

Starlet looked at Beckett. His hat had come off, his hair was messed, and his eyes held nothing but concern as he leaned over her.

"Are you all right?"

A smile sprang up from deep inside her as she hooked her arms around his neck. "I am now. And you're wrong, you know." She pulled him closer, her lips brushing his as she whispered, "You are my hero."

Epilogue

JOSEPHINE BUCKLEY SAT IN one corner of the reception hall right next to Sherman the Pig. Having never been much of a partier, or a talker for that matter, she was content to sit and watch as the newlyweds waltzed to Star Bentley's newest hit. What made it even more special was that the song didn't come from a DJ's booth, but rather from Star Bentley herself. The country singer stood on the small stage in a pretty blue prom dress, strumming her guitar and singing so sweetly that it brought tears to Josephine's eyes.

Or maybe what brought tears to her eyes wasn't the singing as much as the way Starlet was looking at her husband of three months—sorta like he hung the moon. Beckett stood just to the left of the stage, his Cates-blue eyes filled with pride and abundant happiness. And Josephine figured he had a right to both emotions. Starlet had just taken home five Grammies for her new album *Coming Home Again*. Beckett had gone back to college to become a doctor—hopefully, Bramble's next doctor. And they were expecting their first child.

Life couldn't get any more prideful or happy than that.

Josephine had catered the Cateses' wedding only months earlier. Being a healthy eater, Starlet had ordered most of Josephine's specialties: Chicken-fried steak, chicken and dumplin's, meat loaf, frog legs, biscuits and gravy, and enough Texas red chili to fill Sutter Springs during drought season. The only thing Starlet hadn't ordered was Josephine's Raspberry Jamboree Cake. Instead, she had wanted Josephine to come up with a new recipe—Banana Moon Cake. Which had turned out to be quite a success and something Josephine was considering putting on the menu.

Of course, if she'd learned anything over the years, it was not to mess with perfection. And her menu was pretty perfect as is. Some folks might think that was egotistical. But if there was something Josephine knew, it was good food. Having grown up with a bad stutter, food was how she had chosen to communicate with folks. Spending most of her time in the kitchen suited her just fine. Although she did have a special place in her heart for weddings. Which was a good thing, seeing as how she'd catered three in the last four months.

Including her best friend's.

"Good Lord." Rachel Dean flopped down next to her. "I've forgotten how painful pretty shoes are. If Rossie didn't think they were so hot, I'd chuck them right in the trash." She slipped off a pump and rubbed her foot. "I swear my bunions are killin' me." She glanced over to the opposite corner of the reception hall and shook her head. "I don't know how Bear can stand those high heels he's wearing."

Josephine's gaze slipped over to the big man in the

sequined gown and stilettos who, with Rye Pickett's help, was trying to teach Cindy Lynn how to follow her husband Ed's lead. It was a monumental task, considering Cindy's controlling personality. But if anyone could do it, the two gentle giants could.

Noticing the slice of Jamboree Cake Sherman was eyeballing, Josephine reached across the table and slid it in front of him. He snorted a thank-you before he dove in. And not a crumble of cake or glob of raspberry filling ended up on the black tie around his pudgy neck. That was just the kind of pig he was.

"It was shore a pur-dee wedding, wasn't it?" Rachel said. "It was everything a weddin' should be. From Twyla's rhinestone-studded cowboy boots to the bright purple, hot-glued flower bouquets that Darla whipped up. And wasn't it the cutest thing when Jenna Jay and Beau's twin baby girls let out simultaneous screams when Pastor Robbins finally pronounced Kenny and Twyla husband and wife? I gotta tell you that I felt like joining in. For a while there, I wondered if these two would ever tie the knot." She smiled at the dancing couple and released a long, satisfied sigh. "'Course, how could I have doubted it when Bramble is the perfect place for happily-ever-afters?"

Before Josephine could comment, Rossie walked up. "What are you doin' sittin' in a corner, woman?" He pulled Rachel to her feet and gave her a big smack of a kiss on the lips. "You don't have time to be sittin' when they're playin' our song, Mrs. Owens." Rachel giggled and allowed her husband to whisk her away, her high heels lying forgotten beneath the chair.

When they were gone, Josephine settled back and watched the dance floor fill up with couples. Couples who had been married for decades and some who had been married for just hours. Couples who had lived in Bramble for all of their lives and some who had just started calling the town their home.

As she looked around at Slate and Faith Calhoun, Colt and Hope Lomax, Ethan and Samantha Miller, Billy and Shirlene Cates, Brant and Elizabeth Cates, Beau and Jenna Jay Cates, Dusty and Brianne Hicks, Beckett and Starlet Cates, and all the townsfolk, Josephine had to agree with Rachel Dean.

Bramble was a happily-ever-after kind of place.

A place where hearts healed.

A place where dreams came true.

A perfect place to call home.

With tears in her eyes, she looked over at Sherman. He had finished his cake and stared back at her with eyes that reflected the same contentment she felt.

"You want to know a secret, Sherman?" She leaned over and kissed his head. "Bramble is the best place in the world."

The pig smiled.

**Psychologist Ellie Simpson is
about to get a healthy dose of
sex therapy...**

Please see the next page
for an excerpt from

Ring in the Holidays

by Katie Lane

"WOULD YA LOOK AT THAT? Shi-i-it, I love Vegas."

Matthew McPherson glanced up from the label he was methodically peeling off his bottle of beer and followed his friend's gaze down to the lower level of the club. It only took a second to spot what Tubs was referring to. Standing at the bar were the two women Tubs had pointed out earlier. One of the women was fondling another woman's breast. Not her friend's, but a different woman's. A petite, big-busted woman with really ugly hair.

While his other two friends joined Tubs and leaned over the railing of the VIP section, Matthew went back to peeling. At the moment, the job of pulling the beer label off in one perfect piece was more important than a little lesbian action. Which probably should concern Matthew, but didn't. He had grown weary of girls going wild. These days, everywhere you looked women were kissing or fondling women. At clubs, strip joints, and spring break beaches around the world, the opposite sex had figured out exactly what two women kissing and rubbing around on each other did to men.

Made men go wild.

And, at one time, he was no different from Tubs or his

other buddies who were transfixed by the women's entertainment for the evening. But not anymore. Now it just bored him. Of course, lately, everything bored him. The condo he lived in, the women he dated, the car he drove, and the job he worked at. All of it was boring. Which made no sense whatsoever. He could understand it if he was an Average Joe who drove a Honda Civic, worked as an accountant, and was married to his high school sweetheart who had put on a few extra pounds after the birth of their third child. If he were that guy, it would make perfect sense. But he wasn't.

No, he was the youngest son of Big Al McPherson who owned M&M Construction, a multimillion-dollar company. The same company where Matthew worked as a top corporate lawyer and had a huge office with a panoramic view of downtown Denver. An office only miles away from his trendy condo where a Range Rover and brand-spanking-new Porsche Carrera GT sat in his double garage.

What more could he possibly want? He was young, single, and wealthy with the uncanny ability to make women fall at his feet and money collect in his bank account. How could a man be bored with that?

Yet, he was.

Bored and completely out of his mind.

Matthew stopped peeling when he remembered another McPherson who had gone Looney Tunes. Poor Uncle Rudy had become bored with life and had given away all his money to live on the streets. After he was caught in a Chicago park wearing nothing but his birthday suit while roasting a squirrel for supper, the family slapped his ass straight into a mental ward. Every year at Christmas, his aunt Marsha still received a death threat written on three squares of toilet paper.

Matthew preferred stationery. Nice, clean, expensive stationery with the company letterhead printed across the top. Besides, it wasn't his friends' fault that he was bored with life. They had come with him to Vegas on New Year's Eve expecting to party, not peel labels off beer bottles and ruminate with him about not having any adventure in his life.

"So you think those are real?" Stan asked.

Trying to appear interested, Matthew looked down at the women who stood at the bar. "What ones are we talking about?"

"The petite blonde's that just got felt up."

He examined the breasts in question. He had to admit they were impressive. Impressive, but about as genuine as his last girlfriend's. "Fake."

Always a sarcastic drunk, Mitch turned to him. "And just how can you tell that from this far away, O Great One?"

"Simple. Very few petite women have real breasts that big."

"What about Ronda Letterman?" Stan asked.

Matthew shook his head. "The only thing Ronda had in common with this woman is height. The bone structure is completely different."

Tubs laughed. "Bone structure? Only you, Mattie, would notice some woman's bone structure."

It was true. Matthew did notice more about women than their obvious physical traits. To him, women were like works of art. In order to enjoy the piece, you first needed to study every nuance: The butterfly sweep of a hand. The musical pitch of laughter. The gentle slope of a naked shoulder. These were all part of the entire package. A package that, when appreciated, could offer a man hours of enjoyment.

"Who cares about her bone structure"—Stan rested

his arms on the railing—"I just want to get my hands on those sweet chest puppies."

Matthew shook his head at such ignorance. "Which is exactly why you never will. And why most men strike out. They don't take the time to really study a woman before they approach her." He nodded at the bar. "Take her for example. You've been watching her for a while now. So what can you tell me about her—besides the sweet chest puppies?"

Stan seemed befuddled by the question, but Tubs chimed in. "For being so short, she has nice legs. And her face doesn't look too bad. Although her hair looks like mine after I went to SuperChop. With the way she's downing that drink, I'd say she's out for a good time. Of course, letting her friends fondle her breasts is a dead giveaway on that count."

Matthew took a moment to study the woman. "As far as pickup lines go, you need to throw out the boobs and legs," he said. "But you're on the right track with the hair. Her haircut is flat-out ugly. Which leads me to believe that she's more concerned with what's inside a person than what's outside. An intelligent woman who isn't interested in what people think . . . or in men who are after only one thing."

Which made him wonder why she let her friend feel her up. She didn't dress like a tease. In fact, the simple black dress she wore could just as easily work for a funeral. It said the exact opposite of the tall brunette's tight, short dress. One shouted, "I'm ready for a night of hot sex," while the other whispered, "Get ready to work for it."

Tubs laughed. "You kill me, Mattie."

Matthew pulled his gaze away from the woman and smiled. "It's a gift."

"A gift of bullshit," Mitch said. "So now tell us how this information will get that woman in bed?"

Matthew shrugged. "Information is a building block. Once you have it, you have to know how to use it. Take law for example. A court attorney can have all the information about a case in the world, but if he doesn't know how to present it, it becomes nothing but a pile of notes. In this case"—he nodded down at the bar—"I would appeal to her intellect. Ask what she does for a living—where she went to college."

"What if she doesn't work or go to college?"

He studied the woman in question. "Doubtful. But, in that case, I would have to rely on my charm."

"Fuckin' Prince Charming," Mitch grumbled.

Matthew grinned. "Most women believe in the fairy tale. Which is exactly what I give them. They want a man who looks at them as more than just a pretty face and a nice body. A man who cares about their feelings and emotions and really listens when they talk. A man who fits into their illusion of a happily-ever-after."

"A man full of shit?"

"Aren't we all, Mitch? Especially in the hunt for the prize." Matthew's cell phone rang, and he pulled it out of his pocket and glanced at the number. "Excuse me." He got up from the table and moved away before he answered. "Hey, gorgeous."

His great-aunt Louise snorted. "Don't pull that flirty playboy stuff with me, Matthew McPherson, especially when you've fallen down on the job. You told me that you would introduce that reclusive brother of yours to your harem of women, and here you are in Sin City without Patrick."

"Hold on, Wheezie," Matthew said. "I invited Patrick, and he turned me down."

"So use some of that charm of yours and change his mind. Or does that only work on women?"

"Pretty much."

Another snort had him smiling. "Well, I guess it's too late to worry about it now. You're there getting plenty, and he's here getting none. But when you get back, I expect you to make more of an effort. Patrick is next in line to find his perfect match, and he won't find her amid all those construction workers he hangs out with. I'm not getting any younger, and I refuse to leave this world until all of Big Al's kids are happily married."

Which explained why Matthew wasn't making more of an effort to get his brother to the altar. Besides keeping his feisty aunt around, he wasn't about to become her next target and be manipulated into spending his life with just one woman. It would be like spending his life with just one van Gogh. But he couldn't deny Wheezie, either. Despite being the worst kind of matchmaker, she was the funniest and most endearing relative he had.

"Okay, I'll do my best to fix Patrick up when I get back," he said. "But I can't make any promises. Paddy seems quite content with his bachelor's life."

"No man is content without a woman," Wheezie said. "They just need to find the right one to prove it to them. Now try not to break too many hearts in Vegas, and I'll see you when you get back. Happy New Year, handsome."

"Same to you, gorgeous."

Matthew was still grinning when he hung up and took his seat back at the table where the guys were placing their orders with the waitress. A waitress who, after bringing their drinks, slipped Matthew a cocktail napkin with her number on it. The gesture gave Mitch a perfect mark for his pent-up anger.

"You are so full of it, McPherson," he said. "And that napkin is a perfect example. Here you are spouting off all kinds of shit about collecting information and charming women, when it all boils down to one thing: physical attraction. You haven't said one word to that waitress, besides the name of that damned Scottish ale you drink, and she still gave you her number. Which means that everything you've just told us only works for guys like you, guys with more looks and money than they know what to do with."

Matthew shook his head. "You're wrong. Women don't care about physical looks as much as personality. Make them laugh and feel good about themselves, and they're yours."

"I don't know," Tubs said. "I make girls laugh like crazy, and I still can't get as many as you do, Mattie."

"I must concur." Stan tipped his glass at Matthew. "Women do seem to love your looks. In fact, I think you could out-and-out ask and that woman at the bar would let you pet her sweet puppies."

Mitch pulled out his wallet and tossed some money onto the table. "Let's bet on it, shall we?"

Matthew stared down at the hundred-dollar bill. "You're betting a hundred bucks that I can walk up to the woman and ask to feel her breasts and she'll let me?" He sat back in the chair. "Sorry, but that's not my style."

"Because you know I'm right." Mitch took the hundred back and slipped it in his wallet. "Women care about looks as much as the rest of us."

Matthew never went in for petty bets, but he really wanted to prove Mitch wrong. Not only to save face with his buddies, but also because just the thought that he had wasted his time and energy all these years on being charming and witty when brutal honesty would've gotten him in the same number of bedrooms was horrifying. It was also doubtful and ridiculous. But no one could ever accuse Matthew McPherson of not looking at things from all the angles.

Or of backing down from a challenge.

"Fine," he said. "But I refuse to be the only one proving my theory." He nodded at the bar. "While I'm getting slapped by the short one, you need to approach the tall brunette in the white dress and try talking to her about something other than her great body parts. If you score and I get slapped, I win. And if you get the shaft and I get a feel, you win. And if it's one or the other, we call it a draw."

"Deal." Mitch shook Matthew's hand.

While Stan and Tubs took sides and joined in on the wager, Matthew looked at the woman in question. The fondling had long since stopped, and she was now chatting it up with some guy who couldn't seem to take his eyes off her breasts. She wasn't even close to being Matthew's usual choice. She was too short on hair and legs. But there was something about her that was cute and . . . he watched as she went to take a sip of her drink and poked herself in the chin with the stirring straw . . . awkward. And maybe that was exactly what he needed to help him win the bet: A cute, smart, awkward woman who was not used to Vegas nightclubs or being treated rudely. A woman he would never have to see again when the experiment fell flat.

And it would fall flat.

Matthew smiled. He'd make sure of it.

ELLIE WAS HAVING FUN.

The three Cape Cods probably had a lot to do with it. Or the celebratory atmosphere. But some of it had to do with finally being able to let Riley go. For months, she had held on to the hope that he would get over his commitment issues and come back. Now she knew that would never happen. And as angry as she was by his cheating, she was thankful that he had broken up with her before they'd gotten married—and before children were involved.

While Sidney flirted with some guy who looked like he'd needed a fake ID to get in, Ellie got up from her bar stool and headed for the dance floor. Having never been much of a dancer, it took her a while to find the rhythm of the Bruno Mars song. She bounced and jiggled for three straight songs before the music stopped and the DJ's voice blasted through the speakers, starting the countdown for the New Year. Surprised that it was already midnight, she tried to make her way back to the bar to celebrate with Sidney. But as the countdown continued, even more people flooded the floor, leaving no room to take a breath, let alone move.

With nothing else to do, Ellie counted down with everyone else. With each shouted number, she released the pain of the previous year and pinned her hopes on the coming one. After a loud chorus of "Happy New Year," she watched as couples kissed amid the colorful balloons and confetti that fell from the ceiling. Depression was about to set in when a man appeared out of nowhere. Ellie batted a blue balloon out of her face. No, not man. Men, even nice-looking ones, had at least one or two flaws. But from what Ellie could tell, this man didn't have a one.

From the top of his thick, wavy black hair to the tips of his polished brown leather shoes, he was pure perfection. His light green button-down shirt tapered just enough to showcase nice shoulders, a muscled chest, and flat stomach, while his designer jeans defined long legs and lean, muscular thighs. Topping off the well-proportioned body was a face that would make a modeling agent weep: Strong chin with a tiny cleft. Firm lips with just enough plump. And a nice-size nose that complemented high cheekbones and thickly lashed eyes.

Eyes that appeared to be staring directly at her.

Although she figured it had to be a trick of the flashing strobe lights. Greek gods did not go for average women who couldn't dance. Fortunately, Ellie had never gone for Greek gods, either. She had discovered a long time ago that the prettier the face, the more arrogant and obnoxious the man. So instead of bowing down and worshipping at his feet like most women, Ellie waited for him to move on.

Except he didn't move on. He just stood there looking at her as if he wanted to say something.

While her Cape Cod–soaked brain tried to figure it all out, the music started back up, and a wild dancer bumped her from behind. She stumbled on her heels and would've disappeared into the sea of balloons and confetti if the Greek god hadn't caught her. He lifted her clear off her feet and pulled her against a body as hard as it looked.

Suddenly, sexual attraction became something more than just a definition in a textbook. Like iron filings to a magnet, every cell in her body shifted toward the man. Her heart thumped like crazy, her breath paused, and the pit of her stomach felt as if she had just reached the top peak of the highest roller coaster.

For a moment, his eyes seemed to beg her forgiveness before he leaned closer and whispered something in her ear. At the touch of his warm lips, chill bumps spread through her, and liquid heat pooled in the crotch of her panties. She had this thing about her ears. Something Riley hit on a few times but never really figured out. If he had, it was doubtful she would still be a virgin. And with the way she felt at the moment, she might not be one by the time she got off the dance floor. Especially when the man released her and her body did a slow slide down soft denim and hard male. The sensations that assailed her brought her within seconds of orgasm.

And if anyone knew about orgasms, Ellie did. She hadn't had sex, but she'd had orgasms.

A lot.

And alone.

Embarrassed by her reaction, she took a step back. His eyes remained on her face as if waiting for something. Probably a reply to whatever he'd whispered in her ear. The logical answer would be no. But for some reason— Riley's infidelity or the sexual desire that flooded her body—Ellie wasn't thinking logically.

Slowly, her head bobbed up and down.

A frown tipped the corners of his mouth. He looked puzzled, then after a few seconds, resigned. Without another word, he took her hand and led her off the dance floor. And she followed. Somehow her body had gone on autopilot and wasn't about to let her logical brain get in the way of what it had been denied for thirty years. And wasn't this exactly what she'd wanted? To be someone different? Someone who could immerse herself in the wicked wiles of Las Vegas? Well, what could be more wicked than leaving a bar with a hot stranger? A hot stranger who had chosen her. Not Sexy Sidney. Or the gorgeous Amazons. Or Valerie Sawyer. But her—Virginal Ellie Simpson.

Once they reached the entrance, one of the bouncers directed them to an elevator located in a corner. An elevator far away from the set of elevators she had arrived on. The bouncer held the door and discreetly accepted the tip her escort offered him.

The doors slid closed, and suddenly, Ellie came face-to-face with her own reflection in the highly polished gold. It was like a cold slap in the face. For as much as she wanted to be someone else, it was the same Ellie Simpson who stared back at her. The same Ellie who made the hotel bed every morning and hung up all the towels. The same Ellie who kept water, a PowerBar, and blankets in the backseat of her Honda Civic in case she got stuck in a fluke blizzard. The same Ellie who, despite Riley's betrayal, couldn't have sex with a man she didn't know.

And no amount of Cape Cods or heartbreak would change that.

Or even a perfect god of a guy.

She dropped her gaze and cleared her throat. "I'm sorry, but—"

The elevator came to a jerky stop, and she glanced over and forgot what she was about to say.

While the bright lights highlighted her flat hair and mascara-smudged eyes, they made him appear even more of a god. A god in vivid color. His skin was a smooth, even brown that no tanning product could duplicate. His lips a subtle, tempting rose that held a trace of moisture as if his tongue had just swept over them. His hair expertly cut waves of black velvet that begged for a woman's caress. All set off by a pair of piercing green eyes. A green so vibrant and intense it reminded her of the eighteenth hole at her father's golf course after a light spring shower. Those eyes stared straight through her as his finger slid away from the bright red stop button on the wall of the elevator.

"Did you just stop—?"

The rest of what she was going to say ended up muffled beneath firm lips as she was guided back against the wall and lifted to her toes. Unlike Riley's gentle hunt and pecks, this man went straight to the good stuff. And the good stuff was the best she'd ever had.

She tried to remember what she was going to tell him, but his mouth wiped away all thoughts from her mind like a damp paper towel on a dry-erase board. He devoured her hungrily, leaving no room for breath or refusal. Not that she wanted to refuse him. At least, not yet. Once he ended the kiss, she would put a stop to things. But for now, she was quite happy doing exactly what she was doing. She liked how his lips molded to hers and how his long fingers flexed at her waist with each sexy flick of his tongue. But she especially liked the way his body held her in place, the hard press of his chest, stomach, and thighs papering her against the wall.

Unfortunately, all good things must come to an end.

Ellie tensed as one of his hands released her waist and crept toward her breasts. It was inevitable. No boy had ever kissed her without wanting to feel her up. And once they were allowed access to her breasts, attention to all other parts of her body ceased in their sheer enthusiasm for such a plentiful bounty.

Except this man didn't seem that enthusiastic. In fact, his hand stopped a good two inches from her breast. With a nip of her bottom lip, he ended the kiss and nibbled a heated path to her ear. It was only after his tongue and lips had turned her into a quivering mass of incoherent female that she felt a light caress on her breast. So light that she barely felt it through the material of her dress and bra. But she did feel the brush of his warm fingertips when they reached the top of her dress and came in contact with naked skin. He painted a slow heated path over the top of one breast to her cleavage, where he dipped inside the crevice before caressing the top of her other breast. And with each back-and-forth stroke, he pushed the bodice of her dress lower and lower. And made her heart rate higher and higher. When he finally exposed one breast, Ellie was ready for the groping to begin. Instead, he gently cradled it in his hand, his thumb lightly strumming the nipple.

"I'll be damned." His words vibrated through her earlobe and clear down to her cramped toes. His breath rushed out as his hips flexed against her. She might not understand what his words meant, but she understood what the hard bulge in his jeans did. And after an entire lifetime of denying her sexuality, she suddenly embraced it.

With a deep, satisfied moan, she buried her fingers in his thick, wavy hair, pulling his mouth back to hers. This time, she was the one to devour him, swirling her tongue along the edges of his perfect, even teeth, exploring the warm recesses of his mouth. His hand slipped from her breast to pull her closer, leaving her with an ache she couldn't ignore. Without a thought to how wanton it looked, she fondled her breast and caressed her nipple. He pulled back from the kiss and watched through those incredible long lashes.

"Sweet Jesus," he groaned before he pushed her hand out of the way and lowered his head.

The first touch of his mouth on her breast had Ellie almost jumping out of her heels. Then those perfect lips moved, and everything inside her melted. She started to slide down the wall of the elevator, but he caught her, hooking her leg around his waist before the delicious torture started again. The rhythmic flick of his tongue and the hot, wet pull of his lips turned her breast into an orb of tingling sensation that radiated out to every nerve in her body. Especially the ones between her legs. Before she knew what was happening, she stood on the brink. And she couldn't do anything to stop it. All she could do was hold on and catch the wave.

It washed over her in a swell that had her moaning out her release. It was the longest, most wonderful orgasm she had ever experienced. When it was over, all she wanted to do was snuggle up to the warm body next to her and sleep.

His deep voice interrupted.

"Did you just…?"

Ellie tucked her face in his neck and smiled.

Yep, she sure had.

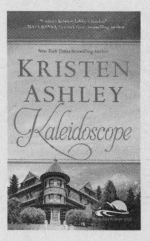
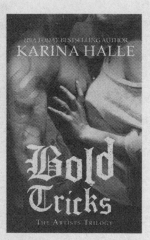

Fall in Love with Forever Romance

DECADENT
by Adrianne Lee

Fans of Robyn Carr and Sherry Woods will enjoy the newest book set at Big Sky Pie! Fresh off a divorce, Roxy isn't looking for another relationship, but there's something about her buttoned-up contractor that she can't resist. What that man clearly needs is something decadent— like her...

THE LAST COWBOY
IN TEXAS
by Katie Lane

Country music princess Starlet Brubaker has a sweet tooth for moon pies and cowboys: both are yummy—and you can never have just one. Beckett Cates may not be her usual type, but he may be the one to put Starlet's boy-crazy days behind her... Fans of Linda Lael Miller and Diana Palmer will love it, darlin'!

Fall in Love with Forever Romance

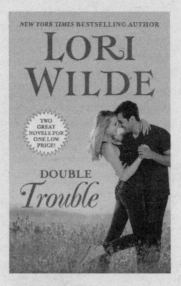

DOUBLE TROUBLE
by Lori Wilde

Get two books for the price of one in this special collection from *New York Times* bestselling author Lori Wilde, featuring twin sisters Maddie and Cassie Cooper from *Charmed and Dangerous* and *Mission: Irresistible*, and their adventures in finding their own happily ever afters.